DOUBLE-

"Then I guess   Luke
suggested. "What if Oliver is right   make
sure we're not compatible?"

Bernie raised her chin. "You specifically said you
weren't interested in me that way."

"I don't think I did. I said it was a surprise." He
walked toward her. "One kiss is hardly enough to go on,
is it?"

"A kiss you regret and have apologized for on multiple
occasions," Bernie reminded him as he came even closer.
"And you're not yourself right now. Are you sure you're
making good decisions?"

He smiled at her. "You sound jumpy."

"I'm . . ." She looked up into his blue eyes and forgot
how words worked.

"We're both intelligent people, so how about we try
this kissing thing again?" Luke murmured, his fingers
coming up to caress her jawline. "It won't take long to
see whether that first one was a fluke." As if sensing her
protest, he continued. "What's wrong with an experiment?"

She gulped in some air and managed to nod as he
leaned in even closer. She'd never been good at making
instant decisions, and her common sense battled against
her desire to be kissed by the object of her dreams.

"Mmm . . ." Luke murmured as he dropped a series of
light kisses on her lips. "You always smell like coffee and
caramel."

He teased her lower lip until she opened her mouth
and let him inside, and then it was easy to stop thinking
and just experience the toe-curling reality of being thoroughly kissed by Luke Nilsen. . . .

Books by Kate Pearce

The House of Pleasure Series
SIMPLY SEXUAL
SIMPLY SINFUL
SIMPLY SHAMELESS
SIMPLY WICKED
SIMPLY INSATIABLE
SIMPLY FORBIDDEN
SIMPLY CARNAL
SIMPLY VORACIOUS
SIMPLY SCANDALOUS
SIMPLY PLEASURE
(e-novella)
SIMPLY IRRESISTIBLE
(e-novella)

The Sinners Club Series
THE SINNERS CLUB
TEMPTING A SINNER
MASTERING A SINNER
THE FIRST SINNERS
(e-novella)

Single Titles
RAW DESIRE

The Millers of Morgan Valley
THE SECOND CHANCE
RANCHER
THE RANCHER'S
REDEMPTION
THE REBELLIOUS
RANCHER
THE RANCHER MEETS
HIS MATCH
SWEET TALKING RANCHER
ROMANCING THE RANCHER

Three Cowboys
THREE COWBOYS
AND A BABY
THREE COWBOYS
AND A PUPPY

Anthologies
SOME LIKE IT ROUGH
LORDS OF PASSION
HAPPY IS THE BRIDE
A SEASON TO CELEBRATE
MARRYING MY COWBOY
CHRISTMAS KISSES WITH
MY COWBOY
LONE WOLF

The Morgan Brothers Ranch
THE RELUCTANT COWBOY
THE MAVERICK COWBOY
THE LAST GOOD COWBOY
THE BAD BOY COWBOY
THE BILLIONAIRE
BULL RIDER
THE RANCHER

Published by Kensington Publishing Corp.

Three Cowboys *and a* Puppy

KATE PEARCE

ZEBRA BOOKS
Kensington Publishing Corp.
www.kensingtonbooks.com

First Printing: November 2023
ISBN-13: 978-1-4201-5496-2
ISBN-13: 978-1-4201-5497-9 (eBook)

10 9 8 7 6 5 4 3 2

Printed in the United States of America

*Many thanks to Sian Kaley and Jerri Drennen
for beta reading the book for me and to Meg Scales
for everything ranch-related.
I couldn't do it without you!*

CHAPTER ONE

Nilsen Ranch near Quincy, California

Bailey Harding was something all right. . . . Luke looked across the dinner table at the laughing face of his best friend's sister. Smart, funny, beautiful, and with a great sense of humor . . .

Max elbowed him in the ribs. "You keep staring at Noah's sister like that and he's going to be all up in your face," he murmured.

"He's too busy smiling at Jen to notice what I'm doing," Luke replied.

"Nah, your tongue's hanging out of your mouth. Even your mom's noticed."

Luke instinctively glanced over at his mom, who winked at him.

"Dammit." Luke returned his attention to his food.

"Let's be honest here, boss. You can smile at Bailey all you like, but you're not in her league, and you never will be." Max never knew when to shut up. "She's recently come out of a long-term relationship and she's not going to want to jump back into dating any time soon."

That was unfortunately true. Luke had noticed times when Bailey's smile disappeared and that stricken look in her brown eyes returned. He wasn't sure whether he wanted to punch the guy who'd made her feel that way or shake his hand. Bailey had been staying at the ranch for three weeks and showed no signs of returning to San Diego anytime soon. Apparently, most of her work as a paralegal and her studies for law school could be handled remotely.

Which, if she chose to stay on the ranch permanently—with him—would make life very easy. Luke drank his water. The problem was that Max was right. What did he have to offer a successful, independent woman who lived and worked in a thriving city by the ocean? He glanced around the kitchen. An old house that needed a lot of work, a ranch that required all his attention, and a man who'd been to war and never really gotten over it.

Jen, Noah's girlfriend, and soon-to-be on call midwife at his mom's medical practice, waved at him.

"I'm going into town after lunch. Didn't you say you had to meet up with Bernie?"

"Yeah, something about the charity puppy auction, I think she said, but you never know with Bernie. It could be anything."

"She's a busy woman," Jen agreed. "What with the coffee shop, the online baking thing, *and* the humane society, I don't know when she sleeps. We can go together if you like and save some gas."

"Sure." Luke nodded.

"Would it be okay if I came with you?" Bailey asked. "I have to mail something from the post office." Bailey glanced between Luke and Jen. "If I won't be intruding?"

"Not at all," Luke replied promptly. "The more the merrier."

"Bernie has the best coffee and pastries in the valley," Jen said. "And I really like her. She was the first person I met when I came up to the ranch." She grinned at Noah. "She gave me directions to here, a flask of hot coffee, and made me promise to let her know I arrived safely."

Luke smiled. "Sounds like Bernie. She was always the mothering type, even in kindergarten."

Bailey looked over at Luke. "I guess you and your family know everyone around here, right?"

"Well, Mom does. Being a doctor means she's in everyone's business." Luke smiled at his mom. "But I went to school with a whole bunch of kids who've never left the area."

"Whereas San Diego is a much more transient place—what with the military and people chasing their Californian dream," Bailey said. "It's hard to get to know people. I'm glad I had my sisters around while Noah was overseas."

Max picked up his plate. "I don't have time to go to town. There's work to do in the barn."

"I'll bring you back one of Bernie's doughnuts!" Jen called out to him as he put his glass in the dishwasher.

"Talk to me when you bring back a dozen." Max said, and departed.

Noah set down his fork with a sigh. "I guess I should be getting out there, too." He kissed the top of Jen's head. "I'll keep an ear out for Sky and get him up from his nap if you're not back."

"Thank you." Jen smiled blissfully after Noah as he went out. "He really is the best guy."

"You got a good one there," Luke agreed.

Bailey nodded. "My brother's amazing." She pointed at Jen. "But you're good for him. I've never seen him smile this much in his life."

"Yeah, it's quite unnerving, isn't it?" Luke agreed, which made Bailey laugh.

She did like him, Luke thought, but whether she saw him as anything other than her brother's best friend was debatable and probably unlikely, seeing as he had no idea how to change her opinion of him. What he needed was a new strategy. . . .

He pushed back his chair and rose to his feet. "Give me fifteen minutes to get the kitchen cleaned up, and I'll be ready to go."

Bernie handed over the chai latte to the stressed-looking woman with the crying toddler and smiled down at the little girl.

"Do you want some milk, sweetheart?"

"I want CAKE!" the tiny tyrant said forcefully. "NOW."

Bernie looked at the woman. "I can give her a cake pop for free if it gives you time to enjoy your latte."

"That would be so kind of you," the woman said. "We've got another seventy miles to drive before we get to our next stop, and I'm not sure I'll make it without some caffeine." She yawned and then slapped the hand that wasn't holding on to her daughter over her mouth. "Sorry."

"Are you sure you should be driving?" Bernie couldn't help but ask. "There is a hotel right across the street if you need to take an earlier break. The roads out of the forests aren't the easiest to drive on, even at this time of year."

"Really?" The woman glanced wistfully out of the plate-glass window at the well-lit Victorian house opposite. "Is it a nice place?"

"The best. But I am biased because my cousin Lucy runs it." Bernie smiled. "I can call her and see if she has space for you. Maybe even just for a nap before you get going again?"

The toddler glared up at her. "Cake, Momma!"

Bernie crouched in front of the little girl. "You can have your cake if you sit right here." She patted the seat of the nearest empty booth. "What's your favorite kind?"

"Pink!"

"I have just the thing." Bernie hoisted the kid onto the seat. "Sit tight and I'll get it for you."

The mom slid in next to her daughter, effectively blocking her in as Bernie quickly found the cake pop and brought it and the mom's drink over to the booth.

"Here you go."

"Thanks." The woman yawned again. "Do you think you could ask your cousin whether she has a room for us? I'd rather make it back in one piece than risk driving on unfamiliar roads with a screaming toddler in the back. I can call my husband and let him know so he doesn't worry."

"I'll text her right now," Bernie assured her.

Fifteen minutes later the toddler and her mother were on their way across the street to Lucy's place and Bernie was wiping cake crumbs and frosting off every single surface of the booth. The bell jangled, and she looked up to see Jen and Luke coming into the coffee shop.

"Hey, you." Luke smiled, and her heart did its usual jumpy thing. "Jen wanted coffee, and I guess we need to talk about the humane society fundraiser?"

"And cake." Jen grinned at her. "And doughnuts to take back, of course."

"It's been a slow day, so I still have a little of everything left," Bernie said. "I've already sent out the online orders."

"What time are they picked up?" Jen asked as they followed her up to the counter.

"Ten."

Luke chuckled. "In the morning? You hate mornings."

"I used to. Now, I get up at four and start baking," Bernie said. "I've been doing it for over a year."

She was slightly hurt Luke hadn't inquired about her new business venture before Jen brought it up, but he did have a lot on his plate.

Luke pulled a face. "Gah, I'm sorry, Ber. I did know that. I'm not sure where my head is this afternoon." He punched her gently on the arm. "You're killing it with your sixteen-hour days."

Bernie made the coffee for Jen and Luke, an herbal tea for herself. If she kept sucking down caffeine all day she couldn't sleep, and according to everyone, she wasn't doing enough of that already.

"I'll keep an eye on things if you want to talk to Luke," Jen offered.

"I'd appreciate that," Bernie said. "Mary's due in an hour, after she's finished her online classes, but until then it's all me."

Bernie took Jen's and Luke's drinks and sat in the booth closest to the counter. He looked his usual self— fair hair cut military short, tight beard, eyes blue as the California sky, and a warm smile to match. Outwardly, he hadn't changed much since she'd first been paired up with him as her buddy for a field trip in kindergarten, when they'd discovered a mutual admiration for frogs.

But there was a wariness behind the easy smile, a tension that his years in the military had activated and now he was never without. He was a lot less jumpy and drawn than he'd been when he'd first come home, but she had a sense that the old Luke, the one she'd given her heart to at the age of ten, no longer existed. He kept things from her with a smile and a joke, and she didn't know how to break through his reserve.

"So, what's the plan?" he asked.

"Well, I thought we'd stick with the original auction idea for the prequalified dog owners, but that we should also try something new."

"Which would be what?"

"We take photos of locals with their pets, and people can bid on having a coffee date with them here at the shop."

"Who would want to do that?" Luke looked slightly bemused.

"Lots of people. It's a way to make new friends with fellow pet lovers and might even lead to some hookups." Bernie beamed at him. "Come on, Luke, it's a great idea! Can't you just see Max with Blinky and you with Winky?"

Luke sat back. "Hell, I'm not doing that."

"Why not? There are lots of women who'd love to have coffee with you."

"Then why don't they just ask me? I mean, aren't we all supposed to be equal these days?"

"Hi Bernie!" Bernie looked up to see Bailey Harding coming through the door. She looked fantastic as usual, her dark hair held back from her face with a blue scarf and her makeup perfectly applied to her already stunning face. "What's Luke fussing about now?"

Luke scooched over to make room for Bailey in the booth.

"I'm trying to persuade him to be in the dog auction with Winky," Bernie said.

"As someone people can bid on to have a coffee with their pet," Luke hastily added. "Not to adopt."

"I'd adopt you." Bailey winked at him. "You're cute."

Luke smiled. "Thanks for the vote of confidence, but I'm still not sure I want to do it."

"But it sounds like a great idea!" Bailey returned her attention to Bernie. "Like a low-key singles site but with pets, coffee, and no pressure."

"Exactly." Bernie nodded. "Luke doesn't think anyone would be interested."

Bailey raised her eyebrows. "Has he *seen* the volunteer fire department out here washing their fire trucks? And those awesome women who run the trail rides about a mile down the road? They are all super-hot. I'd bid on any of them."

"We don't know if they have pets," Luke countered.

"Maybe they could borrow a pet for the shoot from the humane society?" Bailey looked at Bernie. "I mean, who wouldn't want to adopt a dog or a puppy being lovingly cradled in a half-naked firefighter's arms?"

Luke held up his hands. "Fine, I'm obviously outnumbered, but I'm not taking my shirt off for anyone."

"Why not?" Bailey poked him in the ribs. "I've seen you coming out of the bathroom with just a towel wrapped around your waist, and you look damn fine to me." She rose to her feet. "I'm going to get some coffee and make sure Jen isn't eating all the doughnuts. Anyone want a refill?"

Bernie nodded, her attention on Luke, who was blushing like a rose. He wasn't even looking at her, he was staring after Bailey. A sense of disquiet niggled at her.

"Everything okay?" she asked as he continued to look past her with a dopey smile on his face.

"Yeah! Sure." He took a sip of coffee. "Bailey's great, isn't she?"

"She is." Bernie paused. "I guess she'll be heading back to San Diego soon, right?"

"She hasn't said anything about leaving yet." Luke set his mug back down. "I get the impression that she's taking some time to work out what she wants to do next."

"She just split up with her long-term boyfriend so she's probably dealing with that fallout," Bernie said as Luke's gaze went past her again and focused on Bailey. "That must be tough."

"Yeah," Luke said. "I guess."

Bernie cleared her throat, and Luke's gaze snapped back to her.

"Sorry." He half smiled.

"Is there something wrong?" Bernie asked cautiously. "You seem distracted."

"I'm just wishing I could be more, you know?"

"More what?"

He shrugged. "Interesting, I guess."

"I think you're very interesting."

"You have to say that because we're BFFs." He reached over and lightly punched her on the shoulder. "But we both know I'm kind of dull."

It was Bernie's turn to sit back. "Why would you think that?"

His gaze slid away from her again. "I guess it's when you see yourself through someone else's eyes."

"Are you talking about Bailey, here?" Bernie asked slowly.

Luke stood up and grabbed her hand. "Come outside a minute."

Bernie followed him out onto the covered porch that wrapped around the building. It was warm enough not to need a coat, but hardly sunny. There was very little traffic on Main Street, making it unfortunately easy to hear what Luke wanted to say. She folded her arms over her chest as he paced the porch and then came back to her, his hands in the front pockets of his jeans.

"I really like her."

"Bailey?"

Luke nodded. "She's incredibly talented, great looking, and has purpose in her life."

"And she'll be going back to San Diego soon." Bernie tried to speak evenly as her heart sank to her boots.

"She doesn't seem keen to do that right now," Luke countered. "And, if she wanted to stay here, we could make it work."

"And that's what you want?"

"Yeah, and that's where you come in." Luke held her gaze.

"Like how, exactly?" Bernie didn't dare look away.

"You know me better than anyone—faults and all, right?"

Bernie nodded as a sensation of dread overcame her.

"Then I want you to help me become a better version of me—someone Bailey will admire and want to be with."

Bernie opened and closed her mouth like a fish on a hook until Luke frowned.

"Are you okay?"

"I'm fine." She took a steadying breath. "The thing is, Luke. I like you just the way you are, so why would I want to change you?"

Apparently oblivious to the faint wobble in her voice, Luke carried on talking.

"Because you're my best friend? I don't have anyone else I can ask, Ber, and I trust you." He grinned. "I'll even take my shirt off for that damn auction if it'll seal the deal."

Bernie just stared at him until he nodded.

"Okay, I get that it's a lot to ask and that you need to think about it. Shall we go back in?"

He gave her a friendly hug, turned on his heel, and went back into the coffee shop, leaving Bernie frozen in shock.

"Oblivious, stupid ass," she muttered as she kicked the doorframe. "You want me to do what, Luke Nilsen? Change you into the kind of man another woman gets to take home and live happily ever after with forever?"

The door opened again, and she hastily stepped out of the way as Bailey emerged with Luke behind her.

"Hey, thanks so much for the coffee." Bailey held up her drink. "I got it to go. Luke's going to show me where the post office is." Her smile faltered. "I decided to mail the jewelry Will gave me back, and it needs to be signed for."

"It's always good to see you, Bailey," Bernie said, deliberately not looking at Luke. "Come back if you need a refill for the journey up to the ranch."

Luke winked at her as he followed Bailey down the steps and pointed out the post office, which was clearly visible from the coffee shop. Bernie went inside, where the familiar scent of coffee, vanilla, and cinnamon for once failed to comfort her.

Jen was packing up her doughnut haul and setting the boxes on the counter.

"I've got at least two dozen. I've already paid for them, and—" she paused. "What's up? You look like someone kicked your favorite puppy."

"Nothing. . . ." Bernie automatically smiled as she came behind the counter to stand next to Jen. "Did you sell anything while I was out talking to Luke?"

"Bernie . . ." Jen said softly. "We're friends, right? You can tell me anything."

Bernie wiped down the already immaculate countertop and considered what to say. "Luke's being . . . weird."

"Totally." Jen chuckled. "He's got the hots for Bailey."

"You knew?" Bernie blinked at Jen.

"Hard to miss when he's literally hanging on her every word like a teenager. Noah's not happy about it. He loves Luke like a brother, but that doesn't mean he thinks anyone is good enough for his sister." Jen regarded Bernie carefully. "You're fond of Luke, aren't you?"

"Yes, well, we've been best friends since I was five and he was my fourth-grade buddy." Bernie tried to sound casual but wasn't sure she succeeded.

"But it's more than that, isn't it?"

"Obviously not for Luke." Bernie pulled a face. "I guess I'm the stupid one, thinking he'd eventually notice I was the best thing in his life." She rinsed out the cloth in the sink. "And now he wants *me* to help change him into the kind of man Bailey might want."

"Like, Luke seriously said that?" Jen asked. "To *you*?"

"I'm his best friend," Bernie said miserably. "He trusts me."

Jen frowned. "He's also an idiot. Bailey's last boyfriend was a city-born lawyer."

"But as that didn't work out, Luke obviously thinks she wants something different," Bernie pointed out, trying to be fair. "Maybe someone like him. He's college educated, was an officer in the marines, and he runs his own ranch."

"Nothing wrong with any of that, but I just can't see Bailey . . ." Jen trailed off, her gaze settling somewhere in the middle distance. "Can I get back to you on this?"

"Sure! I mean it's definitely not your problem, so don't feel like you have to do anything," Bernie assured her. "I'm fairly certain that when Bailey goes back to San Diego, Luke will change his mind."

"If she goes back."

Bernie considered that nightmare scenario.

"But even if she leaves, that doesn't solve the problem," Jen said thoughtfully. "He needs to step up regardless."

"I don't follow."

"For *you*. Maybe while Luke's busy thinking you're turning him into the man for Bailey, you're really making him into the man *you* deserve."

"I can't do that," Bernie objected. "I like him just how he is."

"Maybe that's part of the problem and why he takes you for granted," Jen said slowly. "So while you're busy with Luke, I'll help you."

"Do what exactly?" Bernie asked, confused.

Jen smiled. "Work out whether Luke really is the guy for you or if *you're* the one who needs to shake things up a bit and find someone new!"

CHAPTER TWO

"Is that you, love?" Bernie's mom, Linda, called out as she came down the stairs. "I've left your dinner warming in the oven."

"Thanks, Mom!" Bernie said as she took off her work shoes and put on her fluffy slippers. Her feet always ached from standing behind the counter all day. She went into the large, cozy kitchen attached to the family room and looked around. "Where is everyone?"

"I finally cracked and murdered them all," said her mom, who had the same red hair as Bernie. "They're all upstairs watching the sports ball on the big TV in my bedroom."

A roar came wafting down the stairs and Bernie smiled. "Sounds like we're winning whatever it is."

She sat at the tiled kitchen counter, moving a pile of schoolbooks and random magazines to one side to make a space for her mom to set her dinner in front of her.

"Thanks so much for keeping this for me."

"It wasn't easy. Bill ate enough for three and still complained he was hungry."

"Teenagers," Bernie said as she gulped down the spaghetti in cheese sauce. "I think they have hollow legs."

"Mike's nearly as bad, and he's my age." Linda set a glass of water beside Bernie's plate. "But working a ranch does use up a lot of calories, and there's not an inch of fat on the man."

Bernie's stepdad Mike had ranching in his blood just like Luke Nilsen's family. He was a big man who didn't say much but showed his love for his wife and family in many less-obvious ways. He'd married Linda when Bernie was three and had always treated her like his own. She loved him and her two half brothers and sister dearly.

Linda leaned back against the countertop opposite Bernie and drank her coffee.

"We're worried about you, love."

"Why's that?" Bernie managed to ask between forkfuls of pasta and drinking half her glass of water. "I'm fine."

"You're doing too much," her mom said. "You hardly have time to sleep, and now with the animal shelter auction coming up, things will get even worse."

"I've got lots of help for that. In fact, I was just talking to Luke about it earlier."

"Luke's probably got enough to do up on that ranch to have much time to spare for you," Linda said as she refilled Bernie's glass of water. "If you're going to continue to do so much, you need permanent, paid help."

"I have Mary," Bernie pointed out. Her half sister was currently watching the café, while Bernie took her dinner break.

"Who is still in school and can only work part time right now."

"I also have Casey and Pen who help out, too," Bernie said. "I like everything I'm doing right now, Mom, and I don't want to stop."

Linda sighed. "Sometimes you remind me so much of your father. He never knew when to stop, either."

"I will try and find more help," Bernie said. "It's just hard to find it around here. Lucy struggles to get staff at the B&B as well."

"I know. The twins love it when they can go to town and earn some money." Linda chuckled. "Lucy says they make great bussers and wood choppers."

"Hopefully, not at the same time." Bernie finished the pasta and put down her fork. "Thanks for the food."

"You're welcome, love." Linda started making a fresh pot of coffee as Bernie rinsed her bowl and put it in the dishwasher. "I got MJ to feed the pets, so you don't have to go out and do that."

Bernie walked over to her mom and hugged her. "You are so good to me."

"I know." Linda hugged her back. "MJ said that he thought Pandora was close to having her puppies."

"She's certainly due," Bernie said. "I wonder what they'll look like."

Pandora, the poodle, had come to them from a kill shelter in northern California, already pregnant and probably kicked out by her owner for that reason. She was a pretty but timid dog who hated loud noises and wasn't very keen on men. Luckily, every animal on the planet took to MJ, so he had gained her trust quite easily.

"Who knows?" Linda handed Bernie her coffee. "But it will be nice to have more puppies for the auction. As soon as they're ready I'll get their pictures up on the website for you. What did Luke think of your other idea?"

"He hated it." Bernie sighed. "But luckily Bailey, who's staying up at the ranch, persuaded him to change his mind."

"Noah's sister?" Her mom knew everything that went on in the valley. "The one who's studying to be a lawyer?"

"That's the one. She's really nice." Bernie sipped her coffee. "Luke likes her a lot."

"Does he now." Linda met Bernie's gaze. "And does she like him back?"

"I have no idea." Bernie smiled. "Nothing to do with me."

"Bernie, love . . . you've had your eye on Luke Nilsen since you were five."

She tried not to wince at the sympathy in her mom's voice. "That doesn't mean he feels the same way about me, and he obviously doesn't, because he wants me to help him get it on with Bailey."

"No." Her mom's face looked exactly like Jen's had. "What a complete knucklehead. Men can be so . . . dim sometimes. I mean look at your father—he gave up a wife and child just to chase some foolish obsession with coding software."

"His loss, Mom." Bernie had never met her father and had no real interest in learning anything about him.

"He . . . contacted me recently."

Bernie set her mug down on the countertop. "Who did?"

"Brian. Your father."

"I hope you told him to take a flying leap."

"Almost my exact words." Linda smiled at her. "I blocked his email after that."

"Well done." Bernie checked the time. "I've got about twenty minutes before I need to get back, close up shop, and drive Mary and myself home." She rinsed out her mug. "Plenty of time to visit Pandora and see how she's doing."

"Or you could just put your feet up," her mom suggested.

"I can do that when I'm a millionaire running twenty-five bakeries, Mom." Bernie went back toward the mudroom to put on her boots.

She didn't wait to hear her mom's reply, knowing she wouldn't like it—and what was there to say anyway? She wanted to be successful, and she was prepared to work hard to get there.

The walk down to the second barn, which housed the humane society pets and a few of Bernie's own rescues, wasn't far, but it gave her plenty of time to think. Had she crammed her life full of work to avoid the fact that Luke was never going to love her the way she loved him?

Even worse, had she created all her businesses at home to avoid having to leave, and centered them around her certainty that Luke would want her to stay and work alongside him? She suspected at some level she had, but that was too embarrassing to admit to herself, let alone anyone else.

She was a mass of contradictions, and it wasn't surprising that someone like Luke, who planned everything out in minute detail, wasn't interested in her. . . . Sure, he liked her being his friend because they were so different, but as a life partner? Maybe not so much. He was calm and measured with his approach to new things, whereas she jumped in headfirst and started swimming. He was good at people managing while she tended to go by instinct and was sometimes too honest for her own good.

As she approached the barn a chorus of yelps and excited barks rose to greet her, and she had to smile. Two of the feral barn cats strolled out to stare at her. One of them even deigned to wrap himself around her legs and purr. She checked water bowls and food containers, but MJ had done his usual excellent job and put everything back in its right place as well. He wanted to be a vet, and Bernie thought he'd be awesome at it.

She walked past the spacious pens where various animals were either recuperating, resting, or waiting to be adopted, and unlatched the last one.

"Hey Pandora!" Bernie called out. "How's it going?"

There was no sign of the small white poodle until Bernie crouched on the straw-covered floor and checked the bedding under the shelf at the back of the pen. From what she could see, Pandora was too busy having her pups to worry about chatting with Bernie. Bernie watched for a few minutes to make sure everything seemed to be proceeding normally and then sent a text to her mom and to Janice, the local vet, to let them know what was going on.

Five minutes later, there was a tap on the door and her brother MJ, who was five minutes younger than his identical twin, Billy, appeared.

"Mom sent me to keep an eye on Pandora while you go and lock up."

"Awesome." Bernie stood and dusted herself off. "She's doing great. I see three puppies right now." She checked that MJ had his phone. "You know what to do if she has any problems, right?"

"Yeah, yeah, call Dad and Janice." MJ settled down with his back against the wall and started tapping away on his cell. "But I think she's going to be fine."

Bernie didn't doubt his quiet confidence. He had a sixth sense for animals, and they'd all grown to rely on his insights.

She ruffled his thick, red hair as she went past, and he reacted like she'd poisoned him.

"Ew. Keep away from me, woman."

"My pleasure."

Bernie checked that she had the keys to her truck, washed her hands, and went back out into the cooling breeze coming off the forests that surrounded the ranch. There had been some huge fires over the past few years, but so far nothing had come close, and they were all truly thankful. Bernie had an emergency plan in case the worst happened and she had to evacuate the pets and people on the ranch, but she hoped she never had to put it into practice.

Her cell buzzed as she got into her truck and displayed a text from Luke. For the first time in years, Bernie didn't rush to open it and reply. Luke could wait while she attended to her own business. If he truly wanted her help, perhaps it was time he realized there were plenty of other calls on her. In fact, she was expecting one from Jen about her plans to make Bernie a new woman.

Not that she was sure that would work . . . but she had to try something.

Luke glanced down at his phone and frowned. It wasn't like Bernie not to respond to his texts straight away. Had he overstepped, asking her to help him out with Bailey? Maybe she didn't know how to tell him he was chasing an impossible dream.

"What's up?" Max rarely missed a thing. "Bailey ignoring you?"

"You're not funny." Luke put his cell away and returned to his task of mucking out the stalls. "I was texting Bernie."

"She's a busy woman these days," Max said as he hefted another load of sodden straw into the wheelbarrow. "She makes the best damn doughnuts in the county."

"I'm supposed to be helping her with the pet auction."

"She's doing that as well?" Max raised his eyebrows. "She probably sleeps even less than I do."

"As you said, she's busy." Luke shut the stall door. "But she's always had a soft spot for animals, and nothing either of us could say would make her give that up."

"I don't know about that," Max spoke over his shoulder as he took the wheelbarrow out. "She listens to you."

Luke went on to the next stall and filled up the water bucket. It was warm enough to turn the horses out during the day, and there was grass for them to graze on, which meant they were spending less on hay. There was always the danger of a late frost, but having grown up on the ranch, Luke had a fair idea of the weather patterns and had family records going back three generations, to when his Scandinavian ancestors had first come to California.

He checked his phone again, but Bernie still hadn't replied. He tapped her number, and it went straight to voicemail.

"Hey, it's Luke. Give me a call when you get a chance, okay?"

He finished his tasks and went to help Max. "Did I mention that Bernie wants you to pose half naked with Winky or Blinky for her new auction idea?"

"Yeah?" Max looked up and flexed his biceps. "I'd be down for that."

Considering Max's pitch-black hair, intense blue eyes, and super-fit physique, Luke wasn't surprised he was on board with the idea.

"She's got this weird idea that people would want to

bid on a local coffee date with a pet and its owner kind of thing."

"It's a good way to meet someone." Max closed the feedstore door. "In a nonthreatening way."

"So I'm the only one who thinks it's odd, then?" Luke asked as they walked back to the house together.

"Why don't you like the idea? You're the most social of the three of us and a big hit with the ladies."

"Maybe that's why." Luke grimaced.

"If Bailey's still around it might make her see you with new eyes—as a good catch rather than her brother's best friend."

Luke considered that option. "I guess."

"See?" Max rolled his eyes. "Now you're all for it."

"Bailey already told me she thought it was a great idea, and Bernie's going ahead with it anyway."

"Good for her." Max opened the door into the mudroom and let Luke go by him. "I'm all about helping the pets." He paused. "And meeting some new women. You should try it sometime."

Luke toed off his work boots. "I guess."

"You've given up chasing Bailey?" Max undid his jacket. "Great."

"I didn't say that." Luke lowered his voice in case there was anyone in the kitchen. "The trouble is that I've known everyone here my whole life. Bailey offers a new perspective on everything."

"You're planning on living in San Diego then?"

"Maybe." Luke shrugged.

"And leave this place to run itself?" Max's tone was skeptical.

"It's still Mom's ranch, Max. You and Noah can handle it for her perfectly well." Luke went through to the kitchen. "Why are you looking at me like that?"

"Because I can't imagine you anywhere but here, and if you don't mind me saying so, you've barely traveled five miles down the road since we got back."

"I've got time," Luke said. "I'm only turning thirty-five this year."

"You're getting old, bro, and you've already been out in the world," Max reminded Luke as he followed through into the kitchen.

"Only the violent parts." Luke poured them both some coffee. "I'd like to view it in a different, more peaceful way now."

Max leaned back against the countertop and sipped from his mug. "You don't need a woman to make that happen. You've got the time and the funds to go off by yourself."

Luke snorted. "Hardly."

"We'd cope."

"I know you would, but money is really tight right now."

Luke was not going to tell Max why the thought of leaving the safety of the ranch sometimes gave him nightmares. He was supposed to be the sane, level-headed, officer-class one, not the screwup. That was usually Max's job. If he could persuade Bailey to stay here, he'd at least have a chance to find out if she was the woman for him. . . .

"Luke."

"What?"

"You're thinking too hard." Max tapped his skull. "That's my department. Why don't you just ask Bailey out on a date and take it from there?"

"Because Noah would kill me?"

Max frowned. "It's nothing to do with him. He's not her keeper."

"I'll think about it." Luke took out his phone. There was still no response from Bernie, and he could really do with some advice right now. "Where's Jen?"

"She's out. Noah's on Sky duty until your mom gets back in half an hour. We're supposed to be getting dinner on."

Luke glanced at the clock. He didn't have time to chase Bernie down. "You might have mentioned that earlier. It's already past six."

"I was thinking a mountain of pasta, pesto from the refrigerator, and salad, but if you want something more elaborate . . ." Max walked into the pantry, his voice fading.

"Sounds great to me." Luke grabbed a pan. "I'll put the water on to boil."

CHAPTER THREE

Bernie had just walked into the house with Mary when Jen's truck pulled up in the yard. She took off her shoes and went back to the door.

"Hey!" Jen waved as she walked across the yard. "I hope I'm not too early?"

"No, come on in."

Jen grinned as she came through into the mudroom and took off her boots. "Sorry, can't shake the military habit of being obnoxiously on time for everything."

She'd worked on the USN hospital ships as a mid-wife and been based in San Diego until she'd met Noah and fallen in love. Bernie had been the first person in Quincy to meet Jen and help her find her way up to the ranch.

"Noah's looking out for Sky, and he said to take my time and enjoy myself."

"He's a good man," Bernie said.

"Yeah." Jen's smile turned goofy. "I kind of like him a lot." She walked into the family room. "Where is every-one?"

"Probably doing homework or playing awful games

online," Bernie said. "Mom and Dad installed two comfy chairs and a big TV in their bedroom, so they hardly come down here now."

Her phone buzzed, and she checked it. "Oh! Mom's over at the barn. Pandora's finished having her puppies, and she's doing great with them."

"Can we see them?" Jen asked, her expression hopeful. "I love babies."

"Unlike human mothers, it's probably best to leave Pandora alone for a day or two to see how she copes," Bernie said. "But I'll definitely let you know when you can take a peek." She moved over to the counter. "Can I get you some coffee and a snack?"

"Just coffee for me." Jen followed her. "I don't need anything sweet. I had two doughnuts for dessert. Mind you, Max had four and Noah had three."

Bernie indicated the couch in front of the stone fireplace. "Shall we sit here? We can see anyone who drives up."

"Always a good plan when you're plotting something." Jen sat down and took her mug from Bernie. "Have you heard any more from Luke about his man makeover?"

"He texted me, called, and left a message, but I haven't replied to him yet." Bernie curled her legs underneath her on the couch. "To be quite honest, I don't know what to say."

"That explains why he kept looking at his phone during dinner this evening," Jen commented.

"He's probably used to me replying immediately." Bernie made a face. "I guess I've made it easy for him to take me for granted, haven't I?"

"You've been a good friend, if that's what you mean," Jen countered. "This isn't about you, Bernie. It's Luke who's failing to see what's staring him right in the face."

"All he sees is Bailey right now." Bernie sipped her coffee. "He's totally besotted."

"Which, according to Noah, isn't like him at all," Jen said slowly. "Max thinks there's something else going on beneath the surface, and he knows Luke almost as well as you do."

"Like what?"

"Luke always seems to be the calm, sensible one, but Max says that's the problem."

Bernie nodded. "Luke hasn't been the same since he came back from active duty. He tries to pretend he hasn't changed, but there's something off. And he won't talk to me about it."

"Or Noah," Jen added.

"I've tried not to push too hard because he doesn't have to share everything with me, but I have felt . . . shut out," Bernie admitted. "I hoped he could talk to Noah, Max, and his mom about those things, but from what you're saying, maybe he doesn't do that, either." She frowned. "But what any of that has to do with his fixation on Bailey, I'm not sure."

"What we need to do is stop him thinking about Bailey, who I'm pretty certain is still in love with her old boyfriend, and get him to focus on you." Jen considered Bernie. "Maybe you *should* push more. Try to get past those boundaries he's erected around himself."

"And risk losing his friendship? I really don't want to do that, Jen. I'd rather . . ."

Bernie refused to think about what she'd rather do.

"Stay invisible and help him to find someone else? Really?"

"I don't want that, either," Bernie muttered.

"Then perhaps the way to proceed with Luke is to persuade him to get some counseling, or to open up to you so that he's ready for a new challenge?" Jen pursed her lips. "That might be a good strategy. And while you're doing that, we'll be working on getting your life running just the way you want it so that you can free up some time for dating."

"Dating?" Bernie blinked at Jen. "Like whom, exactly?"

"There must be some guys out here who are worth a second look," Jen said. "What about the hotties at the firehouse?"

Bernie met Jen's gaze. "Here's the thing—I grew up with most of these guys. I was literally that weird red-headed stepchild at school who didn't fit in with anyone and never has."

"But you're not in high school anymore. You run a successful business, you're nice, and you're cute as hell!" Jen set her mug down. "One of the things you have to do, Bernie, is stop thinking of yourself in the past and *be* the amazing person you've become."

"That's really easy to make into a meme and not so easy to do," Bernie objected.

"Because up until now you haven't *wanted* to do anything to change because you've been waiting on Luke to make up his mind, but that needs to stop."

"Wow, you're mean." Bernie pretended to pout. "Like making me face up to the truth and everything."

"It's part of my charm." Jen grinned. "Ask Noah." She paused. "I want you to step outside your comfort zone and at least go on a few dates."

"But I don't have time," Bernie said, trying to defend her life choices. "I have two businesses to run, and the humane society takes up a lot of my time."

"Then we'll get you some help." Jen wasn't giving up. Bernie could only imagine what she was like supporting a mother in labor. "And if you're worried about finding the time to meet people, you can start with coffee at your place and use your lunch or break time."

"I suppose I could do that." Bernie agreed.

"Great!" Jen held out her hand. "Now give me your phone and let's get you set up on some dating apps. I have hours before I need to go home, and I'm determined to get you a date before I leave!"

Bernie clutched her phone to her chest. "Should I just call Luke back first?"

"No!" Jen snapped her fingers. "Remember the purpose of this? We're de-Luking you."

"Fine." Bernie sighed and surrendered her cell. "I'll get some more coffee."

Half an hour later, her sister Mary came down the stairs. She was like her father in demeanor and had the same brown hair, soft hazel eyes. "Hey Jen, how are you?"

"I'm good thanks!" Jen looked up from Bernie's phone. "How's school?"

"Boring. But I'm almost done." Mary got a glass of water and came back to the family room. "I think I want to go into nursing or computers."

"Yeah? I've certainly enjoyed my career so far." Jen smiled at the younger girl. "Have you decided on a specialty yet?"

"Not quite." Mary sat on the arm of the couch. "Is that Bernie's phone?"

"I'm just helping her figure something out," Jen said. "I'm almost done."

"Oh! I forgot." Mary got her phone out of her pocket and started talking. "Hey, Luke? Are you still there? I found Bernie. The reason she's not answering her phone is because Jen has it."

"Well, put her on, then."

Bernie cringed as Mary handed the phone over. Luke was on speakerphone and Bernie gazed pleadingly at Jen, who shrugged.

"Hey!" she said brightly. "What's up?"

"Is everything okay?" Luke asked.

"Everything's great, thanks." Bernie pressed her lips together to stop herself from babbling.

"I've been trying to contact you all day."

"Really? I hadn't noticed. Sorry about that," Bernie added. "Is something wrong?"

"I hope not." Luke paused. "Are you mad at me because of what I said about Bailey?"

"Why on earth would I be mad?" Bernie asked, wondering for a moment whether he'd finally figured things out and she was about to get her just reward.

"Well, maybe mad isn't the right word. I guess you probably didn't know how to tell me I'm never going to be good enough for Bailey."

Bernie gripped the phone so hard she was surprised she didn't break the glass. She forced a laugh. "That's funny because I really haven't thought about you all day because I've been so busy."

There was a pause. "Okay."

Jen, who was very obviously listening in, gave Bernie a thumbs-up.

It was Luke's turn to laugh. "I guess I shouldn't assume

I'm the most important person on the planet all the time. I'm sorry, Ber. You have a lot more than my stupid problems to think about."

"I didn't say your problems were stupid." Bernie took a deep breath. "If you like Bailey that much you should just ask her out. You don't need my help to do that."

"Max said the same thing."

"Then do it. What's the worst that could happen?" Bernie asked.

"She could say no."

"But at least you'd know where you stand," Bernie said. "It's not like you to be shy, Luke."

"True. I suppose it's because she's so special."

Bernie briefly closed her eyes. At least Luke couldn't see her face because she was fairly certain she looked feral right now.

"I just don't want to screw it up, you know?" Luke continued, unaware of his peril. "And she's living in my house, which makes things extra awkward."

Bernie made a massive effort to pretend it was anyone but Luke on the other end of the phone. "I can't help with that, but if you really like her then you should ask her out on a date."

Luke went quiet for so long that Bernie thought she'd lost the connection.

"How about we do it this way?" Luke asked. "I ask her to come out with me, but bring her over to your place, like as a casual friend, but could be a date kind of thing."

Jen flopped back on the couch, her hand over her mouth as she tried to stop giggling. Bernie glared at her.

"Sounds doable," Bernie said.

"You could see how she is with me, and if you think

she likes me, I could take her out for lunch or dinner on a real date."

"Sure!"

"Awesome. Then I'll get back to you with some dates and we can take it from there. Thanks, Ber. You're the best."

Luke ended the call and Bernie silently handed back the phone to her open-mouthed sister.

"I always thought Luke was smart, but he's really dumb, isn't he?" Mary said, shaking her head. "I mean who *does* that?"

Bernie sighed. "Please don't tell anyone about this, Mary."

Her sister shuddered. "Like, I wouldn't embarrass my worst enemy by sharing that conversation."

"Thanks."

"Doesn't Luke know how you feel about him?" her sister asked.

"Obviously not." Bernie held her sister's indignant gaze. "And no one, including you, is going to mention it to him, right?"

Mary headed for the stairs. "I won't say a thing. If he's really that dense he doesn't deserve you."

Jen sat up and pointed at the retreating Mary. "There goes the voice of reason."

"She's just like Dad," Bernie said glumly. "Annoyingly accurate in her assumptions but with a teenage tendency to repeat them out loud. How can Luke be so unaware?"

"Because it's easy for people to take those around them for granted," Jen replied. "And you've been making Luke's life easier since you were five."

Bernie's phone buzzed and Jen looked down at it.

"Success! There are five guys wanting to connect with you right now." She patted the couch seat beside her. "Now, come over here and let's go through them and pick you a date."

Luke heard Jen come back into the house and sauntered into the kitchen like he hadn't been lying in wait for her return at all.

"Hey." He made his way to the sink. "Do you want some hot chocolate? I was just about to make some."

"Sure, why not?" She removed her jacket and went to hang it in the mudroom. "Is Sky in bed?"

"Yeah, he went around seven, and Noah turned in about nine." Luke heated up some milk in a pan the way his mom had taught him. "Max and Mom are watching some reality show in the family room, and I've just finished with the feed accounts and needed a break."

Jen got the hot chocolate out of the pantry and took out some mugs.

"How was Bernie?" Luke asked. "Noah said you were over there."

"She's great." Jen offered him a spoon. "Busy as ever, of course."

"Yeah, so I gathered." Luke stirred the milk. "Do you think she's overdoing it?"

"I think she could do with some help to free up her time, yes." Jen leaned back against the counter, her gaze on her striped socks. "She needs to do something other than work."

"I agree. She barely has time to talk to me these days, and I'm one of her oldest friends." Luke smiled like it wasn't bugging him at all. "And when I ask if she's okay, she says everything's fine."

"Sounds just like you," Jen said.

"Maybe that's why we're friends. We both tend to keep our feelings to ourselves." He took the milk off just before it boiled and poured it over the hot chocolate powder. "Did she ask you to go there for any specific reason?"

"Why would you think that?" Jen widened her eyes at him.

"I just wondered if she was mad at me. I asked for her help with something, and I guess I feel bad for bothering her in the first place."

"She didn't mention you at all." Jen accepted her mug of hot chocolate. "Thanks. She wanted my advice about what to wear on her date."

"Bernie's got a boyfriend?" Luke tried not to sound as surprised as he felt.

"It's too soon to say that, but she is meeting this guy later in the week." Jen smiled sunnily back at him. "We were just plotting strategy, you know—how to make sure he's on the level, having a buddy close by in case things go wrong. That might be why she's a bit distracted right now."

"Who's the lucky guy?"

"You'll have to ask Bernie." Jen sipped her cocoa. "This is really good."

"She didn't say anything about this to me."

"I guess she thought you had other things on your mind." Jen shrugged.

Luke grimaced. "I have been distracted recently, dealing with the aftermath of the snowpocalypse, but Bernie knows that."

"She obviously wasn't mad at you because she barely mentioned your name," Jen pointed out.

"And she didn't mention Bailey at all?"

"No. Why would she?" Jen held his gaze. "As I said, she was more interested in her date and the new puppies in the barn." She looked past him to the door.

"Hey, Bailey."

"Hi." Bailey came in. She was wearing her pajamas and a thick robe, and her hair was around her shoulders. She looked worn out. Luke wished he had the right to walk over and enfold her in his arms. "I smelled hot chocolate."

Luke held up his mug. "I can make you some if you'd like."

"That would be so nice of you." Bailey smiled at him and then at Jen. "I'm finding it hard to sleep right now. I keep wondering what Will's up to and wanting to text him to find out."

"He's probably asleep," Luke said as he set the milk onto heat. "It's late in New York."

Bailey smiled. "I doubt it. He's usually still up working. That new job of his is a killer. Even if I'd moved with him, I wouldn't be seeing him much."

"That's tough," Jen agreed. "But when you start something new, you generally have to put in the hours."

"I know all about that." Bailey handed Luke a mug from the cupboard. "I've got a ton of work to complete for my law degree classes before the end of the semester while still working full time as a paralegal." She sighed. "I should probably go home. God knows what my sisters are getting up to without my supervision."

Neither Jen nor Luke replied, probably for very different reasons. Luke spooned in the cocoa powder, added the milk, and stirred the contents vigorously.

"Here you go."

"Thanks, Luke. You're such a sweetheart."

"Mom puts cinnamon on hers if you want some," Luke suggested.

"It's good just as is." She smiled up at him. "It'll definitely help me sleep."

"Any chance you can take some time off at the end of the week and come out with me?" Luke asked.

"I think I can manage that," Bailey said. "Where are we going?"

Luke shrugged like it was no big deal. "I have to stop by Bernie's place and then maybe afterward we can get lunch or dinner?"

"Sounds like a plan. I'll check my work schedule and firm up on that date, okay?" She turned toward the door. "'Night, Jen, 'night Luke. See you in the morning."

Luke waited until she'd disappeared before he raised his fist and punched the air. He turned to find Jen giving him the eye.

"What?"

"Was that your way of asking her out on a date? Because I don't think that's what *she* thinks she's doing."

"Bernie will tell me whether she thinks it's on or not. I trust her."

"Lucky old Bernie." Jen placed her mug in the dishwasher and smiled at Luke. "'Night, Luke. And good luck."

She walked out leaving Luke feeling like he'd missed something. He quickly got over that and focused on the fact that he'd have Bailey to himself for a few hours and could make his feelings for her clear. Or clearer. At least then he'd know whether he stood a chance. And whatever Jen thought, he knew Bernie would be on board with what he wanted to do.

He finished his cocoa and rinsed the cup. While he was at Bernie's place, he'd make sure to ask about her potential new boyfriend. That, after all, was what best friends did for each other, and he wanted her to be as happy as he hoped to be. The trouble was, he couldn't think of a single guy in the valley whom Bernie hadn't known since she'd started school. If it was someone new, Luke would do a thorough background check on the guy before he let Bernie get carried away. She deserved the best, just like he did.

CHAPTER FOUR

Bernie rushed into the back of the café and checked her appearance in the small mirror on the door. Nothing had changed in the past hour. She was still redheaded, pale-skinned, and freckly, but her makeup looked good, as did her lip color. Oliver, the guy Jen had helped her choose for her first definitely not-Luke date was due at the coffee shop at twelve.

Even as she considered adding another layer of mascara, the café doorbell jangled, and she went out to find an unfamiliar man at the counter. He had a backpack over one shoulder, a nice ski jacket, and a patterned shirt tucked into jeans. His hair was black, and he had kind, hazel eyes and a nice mouth.

"Hi!" he said with a smile. "Are you Bernie?" He held out his hand. "I'm Oliver. It's great to meet you." He looked around. "This is a nice place. I wish I'd known it existed earlier. I've missed good coffee."

Bernie smiled back at him. Anyone who praised her shop was off to a good start. "Luckily for you, excellent coffee is my specialty. I roast my own beans once a week."

"Yeah? That's so cool. I moved here from Seattle, so I'm missing the good stuff."

"Then I'll get you a mug." Bernie moved along the counter. "How do you like your coffee?"

"Just black as it comes," Oliver said. "Will your boss be okay with you joining me?"

"I am the boss, so yes." Bernie filled a mug with freshly brewed black coffee. "My friend's due any minute now to take over for half an hour so we can chat."

"Cool."

Bernie looked up as the shop door opened, expecting Jen, and found Bailey waving at her instead.

"Hey! Sky was sniffly this morning, so I offered to come in Jen's place." Bailey walked up to the counter. "I've worked in plenty of coffee bars, so you can trust me." She winked at Bernie. "Go and enjoy yourself."

Bernie made herself a gingerbread latte and joined Oliver at the table. So far he seemed remarkably normal.

"So, what brought you to live out here?" Bernie asked.

"Work." Oliver sipped his coffee and briefly closed his eyes. "This is heaven. Thank you. I'm employed by the Parks and Wildlife Commission to monitor trees and plants threatened with extinction in Northern California."

"Wow, that's an important job," Bernie said.

"It has its moments, but it can be downright depressing sometimes. Between Mother Nature, people, and industry I always feel like I'm in a fight."

"I bet," Bernie said. "Where are you based?"

"About five miles away in a log cabin in the middle of the forest." He grinned. "Slightly different from down-town Seattle." He looked out of the window. "I'm glad to find this little oasis, especially with this kind of coffee."

"I bake cakes and pastries as well," Bernie said. "Are you hungry?"

"Always."

"Then I'll get you some things to try." Bernie rose and walked back to the counter where Bailey gave her a thumbs-up and whispered, "He looks nice!"

"So far so good," Bernie murmured. "He likes my coffee."

She took the loaded plate back to the booth and set it between them. Oliver shook his head.

"You bake as well as make great coffee? Why are you still single?"

"Just picky, I guess." Bernie shrugged and then stiffened as Luke came into the shop and headed straight for her. "Hey. Did you come for Bailey?"

"Hey." Luke briefly acknowledged her and then turned to Oliver. "Hi, nice to meet you, I'm Luke."

"Hi." Oliver shook Luke's proffered hand, his expression slightly puzzled.

Bernie tugged hard on Luke's jacket. "Bailey can get you some coffee, Luke. I'm kind of busy here right now."

"Oh, sorry!" Luke straightened up. "You know me, Ber. Always looking out for your interests. Didn't mean to interrupt a business thing."

"It's not business, which is why I want you to go away," Bernie said sweetly. "I'm on a date."

Luke grimaced. "Sorry, my bad. I'll talk to you later, okay? We need to firm up on the pet auction thing. Nice to meet you."

Bernie sat down and stared at her companion. "Luke's my oldest friend. Sometimes he's a complete ass."

"I suppose he's just got your back. I can understand that." Oliver placed one of the doughnuts on his plate. "I can't wait to taste this. It reminds me of the malasadas my grandma used to fry up in her kitchen."

He bit into the fried dough and groaned as the sweet lemon curd inside hit his tongue. "Man, this is awesome!" He grinned at Bernie. "Whatever happens between us, you can be sure I'll be a regular customer at the coffee shop."

"Good to know." Bernie smiled back. "Now, tell me more about what you do."

Luke sat at the counter and tried to listen to Bailey and keep an eye on what Bernie and her dude were talking about.

"Let her be, Luke." Bailey set a cup of coffee in front of him. "She's fine. He's a nice guy, and he's making her laugh."

"Seems weird that he'd suddenly appear out of nowhere like that," Luke commented. "I mean, who is he? I've never seen him around before."

"People do move here, doofus. Look at me."

"You're staying?" Luke asked. Was it time to ask for some kind of commitment from her—at least to the town? "You could start your own law office right here on Main Street."

"If I were qualified, I'd consider it, but I've a long way to go." Bailey topped up her own drink. "I think he said he worked for the forestry commission or something."

"He's probably a lumberjack, which means he'll be off at the end of the season."

"You don't know that." Bailey was looking at him strangely. "And Bernie's a grown woman. She can make her own decisions."

"Her last couple of boyfriends were complete losers,"

Luke commented. "I was the one who had to mop up her tears and tell her they weren't worth crying over."

"And maybe you'll have to do that again, but you don't get to tell her not to keep trying to find Mr. Right." Bailey sighed. "At least, that's what everyone keeps saying to me."

"It's tough when you break up with someone," Luke agreed. "All that shared history . . ."

"All that love." Bailey blew out a breath. "I still keep wondering if I made the right decision."

"Noah thought you did."

"Yeah, but he's my brother. He'll always agree with me." Bailey busied herself rearranging the mugs. "Maybe I just need to talk to Will one more time."

Even as Luke's heart sank, Bernie's laughter floated over to him, and he turned to look at her and her friend. They were having a great time. What right did he have to interfere with Bailey's and Bernie's choices? They weren't under his command, and he had no authority over them. He was just a rancher.

"I think you should do what feels right for you," Luke said to Bailey.

"Thanks, Luke." She smiled at him. "I really appreciate your support."

"Bye, Oliver." Bernie walked him out to his truck, which was parked directly outside the door. "It was really great meeting you."

"Yeah, I enjoyed it." He paused. "Would you consider going out to dinner with me?"

She looked up at him. He was kind, respectful, hadn't

monopolized the conversation, and deserved a second date.

"Yes, I'd like that very much." She indicated his phone. "You've got my number, so call me."

"I'll do that." He put his backpack in the truck. "I'd better get back to work. Those squirrels are a menace."

She laughed and he bent to kiss her cheek. "Bye, Bernie. Have a great rest of your day."

"You do the same."

She was still smiling as she waved him off and walked back up the step into the coffee shop, where she immediately bumped into Luke.

"Sorry, I didn't see you there. Sun's in my eyes."

"Sure, it is." He took hold of her elbow and maneuvered her around the corner where there was some privacy and shade. "Well?"

"Well, what?" She looked up at him.

"I'm just asking how it went."

She met his blue-eyed gaze and tried to remember all the things Jen had told her not to do or say. "That's none of your business, is it?"

He had the nerve to frown. "We're friends."

"Exactly." She eased her elbow free of his grasp. "And friends respect each other's boundaries."

"I don't want you to get hurt again."

"I don't think that's going to happen, Luke. Oliver's a really sweet guy."

"You know that after thirty minutes when he's on his best behavior and on your turf?"

A faint sense of annoyance pierced her good mood.

"I didn't ask you to turn up and keep an eye on me, so maybe you should stop talking and butt out?"

"There's no need to get salty with me, Bernie. I'm just trying to—"

"Interfere? Tell me what to do? I thought you wanted me to help you with *your* love life, not to blunder into mine!"

"I do!"

He still wouldn't get out of her way. She placed her hand on his chest and tried to push him back, but he wouldn't move an inch. She shoved again, harder, and he rocked back on his heels.

"Luke . . ." She looked up into his eyes and couldn't look away. Under her palm his heart rate picked up like a runaway train. "What the hell—?"

His mouth crashed into hers and for a shocked second, she did nothing before her instincts kicked in and she kissed him back. He set his hands on her shoulders and set her away from him.

"*Shit!* I don't know what happened, Bernie. I—"

She wiped her mouth, glared at him, and pushed past, unable to deal with anything now.

"I must get back to the shop. It's lunch hour and it gets busy. I'll send Bailey out to you."

"Bernie . . ."

She went back inside, not sure whether she needed to cry or throw something.

"You okay?" Bailey asked. "Did Oliver turn out to be a jerk?"

"No, he was really cool." Bernie found a smile somewhere and looked around the café, which was filling up. "Thanks so much for helping me out. I can take over from here, and Casey's due in ten minutes. Anything I should know before you leave?"

* * *

Luke kept quiet on the way back to the ranch. Bailey obviously preferred to stare out of the window, and he . . . had a lot to think about. Why the hell had he kissed Bernie? When she'd tried to get by him, something inside him had flared out of control, and he hated that. He was the least temperamental person he knew, and he prided himself on his ability to remain calm, so how had one exasperated friend made him go off like that?

The fact that she'd kissed him back, and for an instant, he'd wanted to wrap her in his arms and keep going, was no excuse. She was his best friend, and she deserved better.

"Bernie seemed to like that guy," Bailey suddenly said.

"Yeah?" Luke kept his gaze on the road even though he could drive it in his sleep. "Good for her."

"I think she's pretty impressive."

Luke nodded as he reached over his head to punch in the code for the top gate of the ranch. After a couple of instances of folks dropping by unexpectedly the year before, Luke had found the money to automate the gate and put in a small camera. There was no way Jen's ex was getting in to cause havoc again without warning.

"I think I'm going to call Will this weekend," Bailey said.

"Sounds like a plan."

"But I can come with you to Bernie's on Friday. She says they have new puppies."

"Yeah? Perfect timing for the auction because at eight weeks they can technically leave their mother."

Luke slowed down on the bumpy track that meandered through the tall redwood trees that surrounded the ranch. The snow had gone, and the scent of pine and rotting vegetation perfumed the air. He loved the place with all his soul. It was in his bones. Sometimes the thought of ever leaving it again gave him nightmares.

"Bernie said the puppies are very small, so the father probably wasn't much bigger than Pandora."

"It's always interesting trying to figure out the DNA," Luke said. "Bernie and I never agree."

Bailey chuckled. "Seems to be your default behavior with her."

Luke considered that as he parked the truck in front of the house and Bailey took off her seatbelt. He and Bernie were besties. When had that friction crept into their relationship, and how bad had he just made things by kissing her?

"You'd better make sure Bernie will be there on Friday," Bailey said as she opened the passenger door. "She might be out with her new guy."

"I'll do that." Luke went to cut the engine and then changed his mind. "Hey, Bailey? I just realized I forgot something in town. Can you tell Mom I'll be back in an hour?"

"Sure! Thanks for the ride." She blew him a kiss and shut the door.

Luke waved as he pulled forward and started back down the track. He couldn't leave things as they were with Bernie. Whatever was going on between them he needed to fix it fast because right now, not having her as his friend was not an option he could bear to contemplate.

Mary, who had an unexpected half day off school, came into the back of the café where Bernie had just finished setting the overnight doughs to rise. The rest of her staff, who started at four in the morning, left between two and four in the afternoon, leaving her and whatever help she could get to manage the café until six, when she closed.

"Hey. Doofus is here."

"Which particular doofus?" Bernie set the bowls in the industrial-size refrigerator that dominated the small space. She'd bought it secondhand when the bakery one town over had gone out of business. Her stepdad had hauled it in the bed of his truck back to the coffee shop. "There are so many in this town."

"Luke."

Bernie paused as her stomach knotted up. "He was just here an hour ago. Did he forget something?"

"He didn't say. He just wanted to know if you had a minute to talk to him. I said I'd ask."

For a moment, Bernie looked longingly at the back door and then remembered Luke knew where she lived.

"Tell him I'll meet him out back when I've finished what I'm doing."

"You have finished," Mary pointed out.

"But Luke doesn't know that, and I do have to clean up."

"Okay. I'll go and tell him." She took a tray of cookies with her. "We're running out."

"Make him coffee if he wants some!" Bernie called out and was answered with a wave.

Bernie took her time loading the dishwasher and the deep sink before she got herself a glass of water and sauntered out onto the patio behind the store, where she took her breaks if it was warm enough. Luke was standing facing away from her, his hands in his pockets, his Stetson low over his face.

"Hey."

He turned around, his expression unusually sober. "Hey. I felt like we needed to clear the air."

She set her glass down on the table and folded her arms over her chest. "Well, I have a business to run, so can you keep this short?"

For once, she didn't need to think about how Jen would want her to respond because she was still ticked off with his behavior.

He grimaced. "I don't know why I acted like that. I've been trying to think it through. I suppose at some level it was a real dick move in response to seeing you with that guy."

"As in?" Bernie wasn't going to make it easy for him.

"I don't know." He met her gaze, his expression frustrated. "Because I sure as hell don't have any romantic feelings for you or anything. Maybe it was because I haven't been more successful with Bailey."

"Okay." Bernie took in a long, slow breath. "So, what you're implying here, Luke, is that you kissed me because you can't have Bailey?"

In any other scenario the dawning horror on his face might've made her smile, but not this time.

"Hell—*no*! That's not—"

"Thanks so much for clearing that up. Now, can I get back to work?"

Luke took a step toward her. "Look, I'm obviously making things worse."

"You don't say."

"You know that's not what I meant." He removed his hat and shoved a hand through his blond hair. "I don't know what I'm doing here, Bernie. I don't know why I'm obsessed with Bailey, and I don't like being at odds with you."

"Then maybe you should get some help with figuring

that out," Bernie said steadily. "And I mean not from me, but from a professional."

He recoiled as if she'd slapped him. "I don't need a shrink. I'm the sane one in the family."

"You sure don't sound like it." Bernie met his gaze. "And you haven't been yourself since you came back from that last tour in Afghanistan."

"Why are you bringing all this up now?" Luke asked.

"This Bailey thing—maybe it's all tied up with that?"

He turned, picked up his Stetson, and rammed it down on his head. "I didn't come here for a lecture on my mental health, Ber."

"Then why did you come?" she asked.

"To apologize!"

"Except you haven't actually done that have you?" Bernie pointed out. "You basically told me what happened was due to circumstances beyond your control that might or might not be related to your obsession with Bailey, and then attempted to justify yourself. That's not an apology, Luke. That's a bunch of bullshit."

He opened his mouth, then stopped and just stared at her.

Bernie smiled. "Bailey sent me a text earlier to say she's coming with you on Friday. Hopefully by then you'll have worked out what you want or stopped being so stubborn and gotten professional help." She turned away. "Bye, Luke. Have a great rest of your day."

"Bernie . . ."

"What?"

"I really am sorry."

She purposely didn't slam the door when she went back in and was glad to find herself alone. She wrapped her arms around her waist and stared unseeingly out of the small window. So much for trying to help her best friend. She'd told him the truth, and he didn't want to hear any of it. Maybe she'd gotten things all wrong, but she didn't think so. At least one thing was absolutely clear:

Luke Nilsen was never ever going to be her man, and right now she wasn't sure she'd ever want him to be.

CHAPTER FIVE

Luke checked his phone, but there was nothing from Bernie telling him she'd changed her mind and not to come. He'd sent her a text earlier making sure she was still okay with him bringing Bailey over, and she'd replied with a thumbs-up. Friday mornings had always been her day to get the accounts and ordering done while her staff took care of the café, so she was usually home for at least a couple of hours.

He hadn't slept well since their last encounter, and he still felt bad about everything he'd said and done. He didn't know what was wrong with him or how to fix it, and that wasn't something he was used to. He'd always excelled at anything he'd tried, and failing wasn't in his mindset. Even worse, whenever he *had* felt the need to talk through something Bernie had always been his go-to person.

"What time are you heading out?" Noah asked as they rode back to the barn after checking the state of the fields closest to the boundary line.

"Around eleven." Luke leaned down to shut the gate after Noah, his horse, and the dogs went through. "Bailey's hoping to see the new puppies, and I have to firm up a few details for the pet auction with Bernie."

"Bailey said Bernie's got a new man."

"I guess. He seemed okay."

"I suppose you met him when you took Bailey into town the other day." Noah clicked to his horse. "Where's he from?"

"How the hell would I know?"

Noah turned to look at him. "Because you're usually an overprotective jerk where your friends are concerned?"

"Bernie wouldn't appreciate that from me right now."

"So I hear."

Luke waited, but Noah, who wasn't known as a chatty type, remained infuriatingly silent.

"What's Jen been telling you?"

"None of your business." Noah shrugged. "And even if it was, my loyalty is always going to be with her now."

"Thanks for nothing." Luke let his gaze sweep over the field where the cattle grazed peacefully against the backdrop of the dense pine forest.

"And this isn't about Jen anyway."

Luke sighed. *Now* Noah wanted to talk. . . .

"You're not yourself right now, Luke. Max and I are worried about you."

"Funny," Luke said. "When most of my energy goes toward getting you two out of scrapes."

Noah reined in his horse and turned to face Luke. "You don't need to do that anymore, boss."

Luke's attempt to laugh sounded lame even to his own ears. "I can't seem to stop myself."

"I get that." Noah nodded. "It's hard not to revert to military behaviors. I have a bit of it myself."

"A bit? You're like a goddamn tank when you want something."

Noah cracked a smile. "I'll take that as a compliment, but it can be a liability, too. I almost lost Jen because my plans were too rigid to include her."

"You worked it out."

"Eventually, with a lot of help from my friends. And that's what I'm trying to do here, boss. Help you because you're struggling."

Luke attempted to deny this and instead looked away. Noah was saying almost exactly what Bernie had tried to tell him the other day.

"There's no shame in asking for help."

"Since when?" Luke turned back to look at his friend. "You know that's not true. No one wants to look weak or out of control."

"I didn't say you were either of those things." Noah wasn't letting him off the hook easily. "I said we all need help sometimes. I'm seeing a counselor; we both agree Max should be doing that too. So how about you?"

"I'm fine, thanks." Luke gathered his reins. "And I don't have time to sit around chatting when we've both got things to do, okay?"

"I hear you loud and clear, you stubborn ass." Noah offered him a salute. "Let me know when you change your mind, and I'll be here for you."

They continued the rest of the journey in silence as Luke wrestled with about a thousand different things he wanted to say, but what was the point? In his own way, Noah had offered his help, and it was down to Luke as to whether he wanted to accept that offer. Because things were not fine, even he knew that. It was as if the life he'd so carefully rebuilt after coming home was showing some cracks, and papering over them wasn't working anymore.

And now he had to face Bernie, who was mad at him, while trying to get Noah's sister to relocate to a tiny, isolated town just so she could go out with him. If that didn't tell him things were out of whack, nothing would.

Bernie hadn't told anyone about what had happened between her and Luke. She might have been able to explain the fight, but the kiss and her response to it were inexplicable. She'd tried to convince herself that Luke must have felt the spark between them too. But he'd been the one to draw back, and he'd suggested later that she'd just been a Bailey substitute, which had hurt more than she'd anticipated.

After a couple of restless nights, where she'd alternated between dreams of making love with Luke and images of dropping a safe on his head, she'd decided to do everything she could to help him with Bailey. At two in the morning her reasoning had seemed sound, but facing Bailey and Luke in the brightness of a sunny California morning was harder than she'd thought it would be.

"Hey!" She directed her attention at Bailey. "I hear you want to see the puppies?"

"Only if it's okay." Bailey grinned at her. "I don't want to upset them or their mother."

"Pandora is a very good mom, so she's not going to let you anywhere near them," Bernie said. "But she's also a terrible show-off, so she does like to bring them out to be seen occasionally." Bernie took out her phone. "I have a camera in her stall, so if she's up we can check her out. There are lots of other things to see in the barn if you want a tour?"

"I'd love one, but only if you have the time." Bailey looked up at Luke. "I'm sure this guy knows his way around this place and could show me."

"I could do that if you're busy, Ber," Luke said.

"Fine by me." Bernie nodded, which meant she didn't have to look directly at Luke. "I'll send you a text if Pandora's up and about and come down to introduce you."

She looked at Bailey's tennis shoes. "It rained overnight so you might want to borrow a pair of boots. We have a whole mudroom full of them."

"That's a great idea." Bailey chuckled. "You'd think after a month at Luke's place, I would've gotten used to horse shit, but I guess I'm still a city girl at heart."

Bernie couldn't help but glance at Luke as Bailey followed her inside and then wished she hadn't. He looked stressed, and every instinct she had made her want to rush over and make things better for him. But what had that gotten her in the past? A man who saw her as his friend and, even worse, a sister, and that wasn't what she wanted at all.

"Everything okay up at your place, Luke?" she asked as they watched Bailey try on boots.

"Yup."

"Good." Bernie nodded. That was all she could manage right now.

Luke stared down at his boots as Bernie asked herself if things had ever been this strained between them before. Even their disastrous double date, when their partners had ended up going off together, hadn't been as awkward as this. Something about his attitude was like a burr stuck under her saddle. She couldn't seem to let it go, and neither could he.

"Anything I need to do auction-wise, right now?" Luke asked.

"Not really. I was just going to have a go at writing the text and updating the website." Bernie grimaced. "And I probably need to bribe one of my siblings for that."

"I could help you." Bailey looked up from checking out the row of boots. "I'm great at that stuff. How about you come on the tour with us now, and I can sit down with you afterward and take a look?"

Bernie knew she probably should say no, but the thought of getting the task completed and off her back was too tantalizing to resist.

"I think Luke wanted to leave as soon as possible?" Bernie tried to be respectful of her friend's desires.

"I'm good if you two want to chat," Luke said. "There's no rush."

"Then that would be awesome, Bailey. Thank you."

So much for her idea of handing Luke over to Bailey tied with a red ribbon. If Luke wanted more time with Bailey, he'd have to make it happen himself, or have the balls to ask Bernie directly to go away.

She went out into the sunshine, Luke and Bailey behind her, and started toward the barn. If Luke truly wanted to know whether Bailey was into him, Bernie would tell it to him straight.

Luke studied the back of Bernie's head as he followed her to the barn where the humane society held most of its animals. She was obviously still mad at him, and he wasn't in the mood to apologize again, even though he knew she was in the right. Between Noah, Bernie, and his mom's pointed comments the evening before, he was sick and tired of being judged.

He was the one who held the ranch together, letting his mom carry on her work as the local doctor. From the moment he'd separated from the service, he'd hit the ground running, restructuring the debt, changing the farming and ranching methods, dragging the ranch into the twenty-first century . . . and everyone had been fine about that.

"Luke?" Bailey touched his arm. "Are you and Bernie fighting?"

"What makes you think that?"

She rolled her eyes. "Because two of the nicest, sweetest people I've ever met are barely speaking to each other, and the tension's so thick I could cut it with a knife."

"We've been friends since we were kids." He shrugged. "Sometimes we fight."

But not like this. Luke wasn't going to say that part out loud. This was something different. Usually one of them caved and made things right. What was worse was that he wasn't even sure what they were fighting about.

Bernie turned to wait for them at the barn door, and Luke took the opportunity to really look at her. Her red hair was braided down her back and glinted copper in the sunlight. She'd never been one to wear much makeup, but today she had bright-red lipstick on along with her usual mascara that she said darkened her sandy eyelashes. Her smile was bright, but not convincing to someone who'd known her for years.

She looked over at him and didn't look away, her

brown-eyed gaze serious, and for a second, he remembered what it had been like to kiss her. . . .

"Where would you like to start?" Bernie addressed Bailey. "Are you a cat, dog, or bird person?"

"All of the above, but I do have a special love for kitties." Bailey glanced up at Luke. "They suit my apartment lifestyle better and don't require walks."

Luke grinned. "I love cats and they usually like me—except Bernie's cat hates me."

"It's true," Bernie confirmed. "Cleopatra can't bear the sight of him." She gestured at the barn. "We have barn cats, truly feral cats who almost never come inside, and reluctantly willing-to-be domesticated cats we put up for adoption."

Bernie went to the left side of the barn and into a walled-off section—a wall Luke had helped Mike build during one of his military leaves. "Some folks come to us for their barn cats as well."

"What about the feral ones?" Bailey asked.

"Sometimes they agree to be domesticated a little, but a lot of them prefer not to get close to humans. We let them make their own decisions." Bernie walked into a room lined with large cages. "We open up on weekends to the public, have all the animals online, and when we have the opportunity, we take them to local pet stores and meetups. We always insist on meeting the person the cat will live with before we decide to let them go."

"That's great." Bailey was already distracted by the cats and kittens and was walking along the rows cooing at the various occupants. "God, I want them all."

Bernie beamed at Luke before quickly turning back to Bailey.

"If you decide to stick around, I'd be delighted to help you out."

"We already have a kitty at home." Bailey sounded regretful. "And I miss her so much." She petted a small tabby cat through the bars. "But thanks for letting me get my cat fix on."

"Enjoy." Bernie eased past Luke, making sure not to brush against him. "Take your time while I go and check Pandora and her puppies."

Luke waited until Bernie was out of earshot before he spoke again.

"I wish you would stay here."

Bailey looked back and smiled. "Aw, that's so sweet of you, Luke."

"I mean it."

She took a deep breath. "You're such a nice guy, but I'm not your person, Luke. I'm not even sure who I am right now, and pretending anything else would be wrong and hurtful."

"I guess you're still hung up on Will."

"It's not even just that. I need to work out what I want before I jump into any new relationships." She walked back toward him, her expression wry. "Or back into an old one. Will and I have been together since we were eighteen, and I've never had to think for myself or be by myself since then. And I need to do that—to find me. Does that make any sense?"

"So, there's still hope?" Luke asked.

She punched him playfully on the arm. "There's always hope, but I can't see myself as a small-town girl, Luke. It's just not my thing."

"I guess I could move."

"I can't see you anywhere but here, since you fit so perfectly." She smiled at him. "This place is in your DNA."

He smiled down at her. "Friends, then?"

"Friends." She cupped his chin and kissed him lightly on the lips. "Forever."

Bernie froze in the doorway as Bailey leaned in and kissed Luke right on the mouth. She couldn't hear what they were talking about, but their body language and smiles told her everything she needed to know. She retreated into the central area of the barn and took several deep breaths. She should be pleased for Luke who always got what he wanted, but man it hurt. . . .

All she could do now was focus on plan A, make herself get over him, and find new purpose in her life. She'd been a fool to hang around waiting for him to notice her and love her. Lots of people had tried to tell her that over the years, but she'd believed in that love so much.

And Bailey would be good for him. She was smart, funny, and got things done, and maybe that was what Luke needed right now.

One of the barn cats rubbed against her legs and she bent down to pet him. When she straightened up, Luke and Bailey were coming toward her.

She smiled brightly. "Pandora's up and about if you want to sneak a peek at the puppies."

"I'd love to." Bailey looked way more relaxed than she had earlier, and who could blame her? She'd got Luke by her side and her future looked great. "Maybe it will help me forget about all those adorable, adoptable cats."

Bernie led the way into the canine part of the facility, which was relatively quiet, as most of the dogs were outside in the play area. She quietly opened the top section of the stall where they'd put Pandora and her puppies.

"Hey, little momma!"

Pandora, who was used to her voice, looked up and whuffed gently. She lay on her side on the straw, and six little puppies were lined up getting their milk on.

"Man, they're both small *and* ugly," Luke murmured from the other side of Bailey.

"They're beautiful!" Bailey elbowed him in the ribs. "Any idea who the father was, Bernie?"

"Not yet, although the size of the puppies indicates he wasn't that big."

"I'm sure Pandora was pleased about that," Luke murmured.

Bernie kept her attention on the puppies as Luke's shoulder pressed against her own. He smelled like lemons and leather, which made her want to bury her face in the curve of his neck. She might have decided he was off-limits, but her body and her emotions hadn't got the memo.

"Smaller dogs always do well in the auction," Bernie said. "Although we're lucky around here that a lot of the ranchers have the space for the bigger breeds, too."

"I can't wait to see what they look like at eight weeks," Bailey said. "You'll have to send me some pics, Bernie."

"You can come and visit anytime," Bernie offered.

"Not from San Diego." Bailey smiled. "And I really have to get back there very soon."

So Luke was going to try a long-distance relationship. That was interesting. He'd always been a good correspondent when he'd been away with the military and had always replied promptly to her long, chatty letters and messages. Bernie tried not to cringe as she thought about

all the stuff she'd told him, but it was too late to take any
of her youthful confidences back.

"We'd better leave her be." Bernie blew Pandora a kiss.
"Do you want to see the birds, or have you two somewhere else to be?" She finally looked right at Luke. "I
think you said you were planning on taking Bailey out
for lunch, right?"

"I was, but—" Luke hesitated and glanced over at
Bailey, who nodded encouragingly. "I guess I still am."

"Nice!" Bernie started walking. "Then let's make this
quick, and you can be off."

"Not until I've helped with the website," Bailey reminded her.

"Oh, you don't have to worry about that," Bernie said.
"I mean . . ."

Bailey mock frowned. "I'm doing it. We've got oodles
of time haven't we, Luke?"

"Totally." Luke turned to Bernie. "Is Mike around? He
wanted to show me his new bull calf."

"He's probably over at the main barn," Bernie said.

"Then I'll go over and see if I can find him while you
two deal with the website." He nodded at Bailey. "Text
me when you're ready to go, okay?"

Bernie watched him walk away, her thoughts all over
the place. He'd had other girlfriends in the past, but he'd
never seemed as invested in any of them as he was in
Bailey. She couldn't blame him for that when Bailey was
so adorable.

"Hey." Bailey waved at her. "Are you okay?"

"Yeah! Sorry, my mind was wandering." Bernie led
the way into the house. "Too many things to do and not
enough hours in the day."

"Well, maybe I can help you with one thing." Bailey

sat down at Bernie's cluttered desk. "Now, what exactly do you need to do?"

Bernie pulled up a chair beside the desk and opened one of her folders. "I have all the details here, so most of it is getting the new landing page for the auction up and functioning on the existing website. Once that's done, I can add the pets and the additional pictures for the coffee-with-your-pet thing as and when they become available."

"I get it. You have the original website, so you can upload new stuff when necessary." Bailey started typing and clicking things. "Do you have new graphics for this year's auction?"

"Not really. Luke usually helps. . . ." She paused. "And I've been too busy."

"You do a lot. Jen thinks you could do with full-time help with the animal shelter."

"So does everyone else. I know they're right, but finding someone out here isn't easy."

"I should imagine."

"And I can't pay them much to start with."

"If I were you," Bailey's ability to talk and get things done was admirable, "I'd find a business partner for your online baking business—someone who'd be willing to put in the hours for a long-term return."

"That might be a possibility." Bernie nodded. "Despite appearances, I'm not a total control freak. I know I could expand that part of the business if I had more help and resources."

"You could also talk to the local catering college and see if any of their students can work for you as part of their training. Some of them might live out this way and be grateful they don't have to travel too far for work experience." Bailey turned the screen toward Bernie.

"How about something like that for the pet auction home page?"

"It's awesome." Bernie smiled properly for the first time that day. "I can't believe you did that so fast."

Bailey winked at her. "You're not the only person who can multitask. Now, let's just focus in on the details and you'll be good to go."

CHAPTER SIX

"It will be fun! I promise you." Luke took Bailey's hand and towed her up the steps into the town's only B&B. Bailey was leaving the ranch at the end of the week. He'd booked them spots for the Italian cooking class Lucy Smith ran at the historic hotel every month so that her visit would end on a high note.

"But I can't cook!" Bailey was laughing as she followed him.

"Doesn't matter." Luke held the door open for her. "Lucy's guest chefs are great at breaking everything down into easily understandable bites, and you'll get to eat what you cook."

"I like the eating part," Bailey said.

They walked into the large kitchen at the rear of the house where Lucy, the chef, and two other couples were already gathered around the large central island.

"Hey, Luke!" Lucy waved. "Hey, Bailey! You're just in time."

It hadn't taken Luke more than a second to notice that Bernie was also there with the guy he'd met at the coffee shop. Deep in conversation with her companion, she didn't seem to have noticed him. She had her hair on the top of her head in a messy bun and wore a sweater in a greenish-yellow color that looked great on her. He wasn't used to seeing her wear makeup, but she looked radiant.

She was laughing as she turned her head to look at the new arrivals and immediately stopped when she saw it was him.

"Hey." Luke waved at her.

"Hey." She smiled, but she didn't exactly look thrilled to see him. "Great idea to bring Bailey to Lucy's class."

Bailey groaned. "I hate cooking."

"Not the way Giancarlo teaches it," Bernie reassured Bailey, who took the seat next to her. "He's amazing."

"Hey." Luke nodded at Bernie's boyfriend. "How's it going?"

"Luke, right?" The guy offered his hand. "I'm Oliver."

"Yeah, Bernie's told me all about you."

That wasn't true because Bernie wasn't really talking to him right now, but he wanted to make sure Oliver knew she had backup.

"All good, I hope." Oliver smiled. "She said you'd been friends forever."

"That's right." Luke looked over at Bernie who was clearly ignoring him. "I've always been there for her."

Giancarlo clapped his hands. He was about Luke's age with black, curly hair, soft brown eyes, and the kind of foreign accent that made the ladies sigh.

"Tonight, we will be making black squid ink pasta with a garlic, lemon and caper sauce, and everyone's favorite dessert—tiramisu."

Bailey raised her hand. "Can I just watch and eat?"

"It's much more fun if you cook it yourself," Giancarlo reassured her. "I'll help you." He smiled at everyone. "We'll start with the pasta and then set up the various parts of the tiramisu so that everything is ready to eat at the appropriate time."

He went around the table and handed everyone a bowl full of flour. "Have you all washed your hands?" Everyone nodded. "Then, the first thing I want you to do is dump this on the work surface and make a hole in the center." He grinned. "We're going to get messy."

Fifteen minutes later everyone was up to their elbows in flour and eggs, and Luke and Oliver were discussing the best way to operate a hand-cranked pasta machine. Bernie glanced over to see Oliver laughing at something Luke said. She should have been pleased they were getting on so well, but she was beginning to feel a little left out.

Bailey nudged her. "Good to see the guys bonding over pasta. I know Luke's been fretting about Oliver."

"That's just the kind of person he is," Bernie said. "Although, I don't need to tell you. You're the one who's dating him."

"We're not dating," Bailey said as she patted her pasta into shape.

"I thought—"

"I'm not in a good place to have a relationship with anyone right now, and that's what I told Luke."

"Oh." Bernie didn't know what to say. "Like . . . really?"

"I'm not over Will yet." Bailey paused. "I need to sort myself out before I screw up anyone else's life."

"You wouldn't do that. You're a good person."

Bailey winced. "Sometimes you still hurt people whether you mean to or not, and Luke's also a good person."

"We can agree on that." Bernie nodded.

Bailey lowered her voice. "I already told Noah this, but I don't think Luke is sleeping well. Sally's worried about him."

Bernie's gaze flew to Luke just as he looked up, and their eyes locked until she looked away. She hadn't really talked to him over the last couple of weeks. She'd decided that despite her best efforts, she couldn't deal with him dating Bailey and to focus on her relationship with Oliver, who was a darling.

"Will you try and get him to tell you what's going on after I've left?" Bailey asked. "If he's willing to confide in anyone, it'll probably be you."

Bernie was no longer sure about that. "When are you leaving?"

"At the end of the week." Bailey sighed. "I have a load of work to catch up on, and I need to be home to do it."

"We'll miss you," Bernie said. Whatever had happened between Luke and Bailey, she had truly come to like Noah's sister. "Any chance you can make it back for the puppy auction?"

"I'll see how things go. I'd love to be here for that." Bailey grinned. "I might even bring my sisters. They haven't seen Noah for a while."

Giancarlo raised his voice over the happy chatter in the kitchen.

"Now, we're all going to run our pasta through the machine and hang it out to dry while we focus on the tiramisu. Once that's assembled, we'll start on the sauce."

After half an hour of wrangling pasta through the machine, even Luke's arm muscles were sore, but he had to admire the drying racks filled with grayish-black strips of black ink fettucine. Giancarlo said the pasta would do best if left overnight but that it would work well enough to be eaten now.

Luke glanced over at Bernie, who was chatting to Bailey and Oliver, her infectious grin flashing out as she demonstrated something with her hands that made them both laugh. He missed that. He missed *her*. Oliver was a nice guy, but whether he was right for Bernie was still up for debate. Luke hadn't expected to like him but had found it hard not to, which was just the kind of territorial behavior Bernie would hate because he didn't have a claim on her. In fact, he'd told her straight out that he didn't like her that way.

Which was weird because he couldn't stop thinking about their kiss. . . .

"What's up?" Bailey had come up behind him. "Not liking the pasta making after all?"

"I'm loving it. How about you?"

"Well, having a hottie like Giancarlo helping me get things right is certainly helping." She smiled. "If he was in my kitchen every day, I'd be a lot keener on being there, too."

Giancarlo gathered them around the stove.

"The first thing we're going to do is put the big pans on to boil the water for your pasta. Fresh pasta cooks fast so you need to have your sauce ready to go the instant the pasta's been drained so you can toss them together." He indicated his pan. "This is a light sauce, more of a selection of flavors than a coating mechanism. We want the taste of the pasta to shine through."

Three huge pans of water were set to boil on the back burners of Lucy's industrial-size stove and Giancarlo started chopping garlic and basil at a speed Luke could only aspire to. Giancarlo placed his pasta in one of the pans of boiling water, and Lucy started timing it.

"Each couple can work together—one on the pasta and the other on the sauce." Giancarlo splashed olive oil into the hot pan, which immediately started sizzling, and added the chopped garlic. "You want the garlic cooked, but not burned." He expertly tossed the garlic. "When you're happy with it, add your lemon juice, the zest, the capers, seasonings, and basil right at the end, and voila!"

Lucy drained the pasta into a metal bowl and Giancarlo added the sauce and gently combined them. The aroma made Luke's mouth water.

"Buon appetito!" Giancarlo slid the pasta into two bowls, added a sprig of basil, and grinned at Lucy. "Your dinner awaits!"

"Oh my god," Bailey breathed. "That looks so good! Can we go next?"

"Go ahead." Luke bowed. "Do you want to manage the sauce or the pasta?"

"I'll do the pasta," Bailey said. "Less to screw up."

Giancarlo turned his attention to helping Bailey, leaving Luke to fend for himself. He set the frying pan on the range and turned on the gas, only for it to click and not ignite.

"Dammit," Luke muttered and bent closer to look. "Missed the spot."

As he tried again a lick of flame shot out, caught some of the oil on the side of the pan, and flared up in his face.

"Shit!" Luke recoiled as a whole other world of burning and screaming opened up in front of him and he tried not to breathe in the smell of burning flesh.

He backed up and bumped into Bailey.

"Luke, are you okay? Did you burn yourself?"

"Maybe . . ." Vaguely aware of the concerned faces

around him and the buzz of questions. "Just need to run my hand under the cold water."

Ignoring the sink, he went out of the back door, the warmth of the air hitting him hard after the air-conditioned kitchen. He forced himself to slow down and sank onto the back steps, his shoulders heaving and his breath coming in short gasps.

He didn't hear the door open behind him and the touch on his shoulder made him jump.

Bernie sat beside him and set her hand on his knee.

"It's okay."

He wasn't capable of forming a sentence, let alone a reassuring one.

She didn't say anything for a long while as he tried to fight the past and get a grip on the present.

"If it helps," Bernie said softly. "My therapist says to focus on the things around you . . .the scent of Lucy's roses as you walk up the path, the birds settling down in their nests for the night, that kind of thing."

Luke slowly inhaled Bernie's favorite lavender soap and felt the press of her thigh against his, the touch of her hand on his knee, and the past faded back to where it was supposed to be.

"I'm okay." He managed to get out the words.

"That's good. Let's sit here for a moment." She paused. "It's kind of nice to be here with you right now."

He nodded, and even though he was still shaking, he brought his hand up to cover hers.

The sun was disappearing behind the towering pine forest, glaring red and black as if reluctant to leave. The wind picked up, sending gusts of colder air down Main Street that never let you forget the inevitable return of the snow. Beside him, Bernie shivered, and he instinctively put his arm around her.

"How's your hand?" Bernie asked.

He turned to look at it. "Seared a few hairs off my wrist but that's about it."

"Good." She sighed and leaned slightly into him, and he gathered her closer.

He vaguely remembered some counselor or other telling them all to live in the moment, and now he got what it meant. If he could stay like this with his arm around Bernie for the rest of time, he'd be okay.

"Hey, guys?" Lucy's tentative voice brought him even more firmly into the here and now. "Everything okay?"

Luke turned to look at her. "We're just coming." He disengaged from Bernie and got to his feet. "I feel like a fool having to go back in there."

Bernie looked up at him. "I don't think anyone except Bailey and I noticed what happened. Everyone else was too focused on their cooking."

"Yeah, right." He reached out and cupped her cheek. "Thank you."

A slight blush crept up from her neck to her face. "You're welcome."

"You won't tell anyone about what happened, will you?"

She met his gaze, her brown eyes serious. "Only if you do something about how you're feeling."

"I'm fine." He didn't look away. "Everyone who's been in combat gets flashbacks sometimes."

She didn't look convinced, and he didn't have the energy to get into it with her.

"Shall we go in? I'm dying to try that pasta."

"Sure." She bit her lip and turned to the door. "I hope Oliver managed to get it all done."

He stood there for a moment after she went in,

breathing deeply and preparing himself to respond to any questions with his usual calm humor. It was getting harder and harder to pretend there was nothing bothering him, but he wasn't going to break down in the middle of a pasta-making class when he was trying to give Bailey a great send-off. There were plenty of quiet places on the ranch where he could have a complete meltdown and no one would ever know.

He straightened his spine, plastered a smile on his face, and went back in where the tantalizing smells of garlic and lemon made his mouth water. Bailey waved at him from her seat at the central island.

"I did it! It tastes fantastic!"

Oliver grinned. "With a little help from Chef, but she did time and drain both pots of pasta perfectly."

"Don't tell him that part." Bailey waved her fork at Oliver. "I want him to be amazed by my new skills."

"It looks great." Luke took the stool beside Bailey, which meant that Bernie was right opposite him. "I'm already impressed."

"Wait until you taste it." Bailey elbowed him in the side. "I'm thinking about bribing Giancarlo to marry me and come back to San Diego."

Giancarlo chuckled. "I am very happily married already, but I appreciate the offer." He turned to Luke. "Is your hand, okay?"

"Yeah, I just caught my shirt cuff." Luke shrugged. "Flame caught late and jumped out at me."

"It happens," Giancarlo said. "I once singed off both my eyebrows when I leaned in too close to a frying pan."

Everyone laughed and Luke concentrated on his pasta and the glass of chianti someone had poured for him. It wasn't hard to stay in the moment when the food was this good. He made himself slow down and savor every mouthful. Bernie was talking quietly to Oliver, and for the first time he wondered whether she had any explaining to do. Would Oliver have wondered why his girlfriend disappeared outside with another man for quite some time? He didn't seem bothered, but you never knew what people were capable of when they got jealous. Or maybe Bernie was just explaining that her lame-ass friend needed to have his hand held sometimes because he couldn't cope.

The tiramisu was just as good as the pasta, and the combination of coffee, sugar, and whatever alcohol was in it helped boost Luke's energy levels. He sipped his coffee, made small talk, and almost convinced himself that nothing had happened—except there was a look in Bernie's eyes every time she glanced his way that spoke of her continuing concern.

At the end of the class, they got to take home the rest of the tiramisu along with copies of the recipes they'd cooked and Giancarlo's website address. Luke was just relieved he'd gotten through the rest of the evening without embarrassing himself, and that Bailey hadn't said a thing about it.

He went to say goodbye to Giancarlo and Lucy and waited for Bailey who was chatting with Oliver and Bernie. The kitchen still smelled great, and he'd remember the meal for a long time—and not just because he'd freaked out like a newb.

"Hey, do you think we could take Bernie home?" Bailey came up beside him. "Oliver has to get back to work."

"Sure!" Luke said. "I'll go and clean off the back seat because I suspect it's covered in dog hair and drool."

* * *

Bernie kissed Oliver and smiled up at him.

"Thanks for a great evening."

"I'm just sorry I have to leave before I can take you home."

"It's all good," Bernie reassured him. "Work comes first."

"Unfortunately." Oliver paused. "Was Luke okay?"

Bernie considered what to say, and Oliver put his hand on her shoulder.

"Hey, we trust each other, right? I promise I won't blab whatever you tell me."

"It's not you." Bernie hastened to reassure him. "I'm just trying to think what to say. Luke's a retired marine. Sometimes he gets . . . flashbacks."

"Ah." Oliver's expression sobered. "My Dad's army. I get what you're saying."

"He's fine most of the time."

"So was my dad, but he couldn't stand fireworks or loud bangs." Oliver grimaced. "I guess something triggered Luke. It was good of you to look out for him."

"We've been friends for a long time. It's hard not to care for him."

"I don't expect you to justify your friendships, Bernie. Luke's still your bestie." He kissed her forehead. "I'd better go. It was fun tonight. We should do it again."

"I'd like that," Bernie agreed. He was such a good person.

Oliver blew her a kiss. "I'll call you, okay?"

"Okay."

Bernie's smile faded as he went out the front door, and she turned to go to the back of the house, where she assumed Luke had parked his truck. She didn't really want to go with Luke and Bailey, but it was that or stay the night at Lucy's. She knew her cousin would find her a room, but she'd also want to know all the gossip about what was up with Luke, and Bernie didn't feel like sharing. She already felt bad about saying anything to Oliver.

"Bye, Lucy!" Bernie picked up her cardigan and purse from her chair and smiled at her cousin, who was deep in conversation with Giancarlo. "Thanks for a great evening!"

"You're not staying to help me clean up?" Lucy asked.

"Sorry, have to go."

"Remember, we have those catering students coming tomorrow at ten for their interviews!" Lucy called out as Bernie made a run for it. "You could stay over and—"

Bernie slammed the door and went down the steps. The rear door of Luke's truck was already open, and he and Bailey were in the front seats.

"Thanks for the ride," Bernie said, then climbed in the back, moving a halter and a couple of leather straps out of the way.

"Not a problem," Luke said as he maneuvered the large truck down the narrow drive. "We're practically neighbors."

"I had such a great time this evening," Bailey said as she patted Luke's knee. "I doubt I'll attempt the home-made pasta again, but I might have a go at the sauce and the tiramisu."

"Giancarlo explained everything really well," Bernie agreed.

"He's so dreamy." Bailey sighed. "Those intense brown eyes, that accent, that hair!"

"Lucy's got him booked for the rest of the year."

"Good for her."

"I think he's making gnocchi next time."

"My favorite!" Bailey groaned. "I almost wish I lived here."

"Luke and Noah would probably like that," Bernie said.

"I wouldn't complain," Luke said as they turned onto the county road. "It's been fun having you around."

"I'll be back," Bailey growled in her best Terminator voice. "But I miss San Diego and the twins more than I thought possible."

"Come for the auction," Bernie reminded her.

"I'll try." Bailey turned around to grin at Bernie. "Any idea what Pandora's puppies are breed-wise?"

"Still too hard to tell, although they aren't going to be big."

"Send me pictures, so that I can update the website." Bailey's cell buzzed and she took it out of her pocket. "Darn it." She turned to Luke. "Can you take me back first? There's a document I need to resend as soon as possible."

"Sure," Luke said.

When they arrived at the Nilsens, Bernie got out of the truck to hug Bailey and wish her a safe trip home, and then reluctantly climbed into the front seat beside Luke.

He didn't say anything as he turned the truck around and set off up the gravel driveway back to the gate at the top of the property. Bernie concentrated her attention on the road and the gradually encroaching darkness.

"I guess we should talk about what happened," Luke said.

"There's no need."

He glanced over at her and smiled. "There was a time when you used to pester me until I'd tell you anything."

Bernie shrugged. "Maybe we're not kids anymore and I've learned to respect your boundaries."

There was a long pause before he answered her.

"I kind of liked it when you did."

"Well, now you have Max and Noah to talk to instead." Bernie crossed her arms over her chest. She hated this—hated not being able to help him with all her heart, but what would she get in return? Another shot of foolish hope and another slap in the face.

Luke frowned. "It's not the same as talking to you."

He turned into the entrance to Bernie's ranch and tapped in the security code at the gate, allowing the truck to pass through to the drive. To Bernie's surprise, he immediately pulled over and parked beneath the pine trees.

Bernie reluctantly turned to look at him. "I don't know what you want me to say anymore, Luke."

"And that's what sucks." He held her gaze. "Did I destroy our friendship when I kissed you?"

"We're still friends," Bernie protested.

"Not like we were before. We told each other everything, and if I screwed that up by kissing you, then I'm sorrier than I've ever been in my life." He took a quick breath. "I'm not myself. I do stupid stuff and not having you to talk to about any of it isn't helping."

Bernie just looked at him.

"What?"

"I don't know where to start." She shook her head. "I mean, can we be honest here?"

"Absolutely," Luke said, the intensity in his gaze overwhelming her.

"This has nothing to do with that kiss. You stopped telling me 'everything' when you came out of the marines. You stopped talking to anyone."

A crease appeared between his brows. "Because I had a ranch to save. You know that."

"You certainly had a lot on your plate, but you also stepped away from everyone." Bernie tried not to make it all about her. "I'm not the only person in your life who feels that way."

"I'm not talking about everyone else. I'm talking about you and me. Now that Bailey's leaving—"

Bernie raised her finger. "Hold up. Are you about to say that you'll have more time for me or something even worse?"

"Why does it matter?"

"Because I'm not your backup plan, Luke." Bernie only realized how upset she was when her voice started shaking. "I'm not boring old convenient Bernie whom you'll be nice to when there's no one better around."

"That's not what I meant—"

Bernie glared at him. "Will you please take me home, or do I have to get out and walk?"

"You're not being reasonable," Luke said. "And it's just because of that kiss—which was a colossal mistake."

"Good night, Luke." Bernie undid her seatbelt, opened the door, and got out of the truck.

She hadn't gone more than ten feet before he called out from behind her.

"Come on, Bernie, this is stupid."

She kept walking, and he kept talking.

"We're better than this." He easily caught up with her, grabbed hold of her hand, and turned her to face him. "Bernie . . ." he paused, and the horror on his face might have been almost amusing in other circumstances. "Don't fricking *cry*."

Luke instinctively reached out to cup Bernie's chin,

and she jerked away from his touch. He stepped back and held up his hands.

"I'm sorry. I just . . ."

She took a tissue out of her pocket and blew her nose. "Will you just go away?"

"If I've made you cry, I need to fix things."

"You can't fix everything." She sounded defeated, and it made his heart ache. "And I think right now you should be focusing on yourself."

"Do you think I can do that when I've hurt my best friend in the world?" He tried to explain again. "I know I'm not getting things right, and as soon as I get some time, I promise I'll go see someone and talk all this shit out."

"That's . . . good." She nodded. "I just want you to be happy, Luke." She half turned away. "I think I can walk from here, so you can go."

"I'm not going anywhere." He took a step toward her. "We can both get back in the truck or I'll walk with you."

Her shoulders slumped. "Can you just . . . *stop*? I can't deal with you right now."

Luke started talking fast, to stop her going anywhere. "If this is about Bailey, you're right, I had some stupid dream that I could make things work with her, and they were all on me. She never gave me the slightest encouragement."

Bernie just looked at him.

"And I know you told me to ask her out and see what happened, and I did that." He paused, searching her face. "I *listened* to you."

She still didn't say anything.

"And I was glad we had that conversation because

when Bailey turned me down, I wasn't surprised, and I didn't really mind."

"Okay."

"That's all you've got?" Luke asked. "You asked me to be honest and I'm really trying here. Maybe I'd appreciate some feedback."

"I'm glad you sorted things out with Bailey." Her voice was flat, and she still wouldn't look at him.

He shoved a hand through his hair. "I'd much rather sort things out with you. Hell, we live next door to each other. I can't keep doing this for the next fifty years."

She smiled. "Maybe I'll move away."

"Not because of me."

"Not everything has to be about you, Luke." She met his gaze. "I don't want to fight with you."

"That's not how it feels from my side. It's like you're angry with me all the time and I don't know what the hell I'm supposed to have done."

She bit her lip. "You know what you just said about having unrealistic dreams about Bailey and that she never gave you any encouragement?"

"Yeah," Luke said cautiously.

"Well, pretend that's me talking about you."

It took him a few moments to work through what she meant, and then a lightbulb went off in his head.

"You." He pointed at his chest. "Have feelings for me?"

Bernie raised her eyebrows.

"That's . . . nuts."

"Thank you." She turned her back on him. "And that's exactly why I decided it had to stop."

CHAPTER SEVEN

When Bernie woke up the next morning her first thought was of Luke's expression when she'd finally told him the truth. She groaned and rolled over until her face was buried in the pillow. He hadn't exactly looked horrified—more like someone had dropped a bale of hay on his head, but that wasn't much better.

She tried to think of the positives. Everything was out in the open now. She could pursue her romantic relationship with Oliver and go back to just being Luke's friend. She reached out a hand, grabbed her phone, and turned onto her back as she started texting Jen.

> I might have blown it with Luke last night. I kind of told him how I felt.

She waited for a few moments as the bubbles in the corner of the screen ebbed and flowed as Jen composed her reply.

> That def wasn't part of the plan. How did he take it?

> Like he had no idea what I was talking about.

Bernie winced at the memory.

And then what?

I walked away.

And he didn't follow up? That's not like Luke.

I did tell him I'd stopped now so he had nothing
to worry about.

This time the pause was so long that Bernie had time
to get up, use the bathroom, and turn on the shower
before Jen got back to her.

Sorry, I had to change Sky's diaper. It's good
that you told Luke you're over him.

That's what I'm hoping—that we can just be
friends now. Did he look okay this morning?

Looked fine to me, but Sally said she'd found him
sleeping on the couch when she got up to feed
the dogs.

Bernie frowned at the screen. That wasn't good, but
knowing Luke it might not have had anything to do
with her and everything to do with what had happened
at Lucy's.

Did he say anything about the class we took
last night?

Only that both he and Bailey enjoyed it. Why?

Just wondering.

Even though Jen was a trusted friend and a medical professional, Bernie didn't think it was right to share what had gone down with Luke without his permission.

> Bailey's leaving around noon. Are you going to come by and wave her off?

> I don't think I should be near Luke right now and I did say my goodbyes last night.

Jen sent a thumbs-up. One of the best things about Jen was that unlike Luke, she knew when to push and when to step back. Something Bernie really appreciated at the moment. She started texting again.

> I have a meeting at 10 at Lucy's with some catering students who might want to work at our businesses.

> Awesome! Gotta go. Sky wants to go to the barn and see the horses and his Nono.

Nono was Sky's name for Noah, who had taken to the duties of fatherhood like a pro when Jen's ex had dumped the baby at the ranch and scuttled off before Jen could get there.

Bernie set her phone down and got into the shower. The thought of getting some extra help with the food side of her business was exciting. She'd push Luke to the back of her mind for the rest of the morning and worry about him later.

Max glanced over at Luke as they checked the fence that ran alongside the county road at the top of the ranch.

It was late afternoon and they'd been out for hours fixing things.

"Missing Bailey already?"

Luke smiled. "I think we'll all miss her."

"I assume she turned you down as a potential mate?"

"Yeah."

"Not much of a surprise. She's way out of your league."

"Thanks." Luke got down to bend a strand of barbed wire back that had curled inward toward the pasture.

"She's a city girl, and you're not happy in crowded places," Max continued. "She's ambitious and she's still hung up on her old boyfriend, and you're a homeboy scared of commitment."

"I said I get it." Luke mounted his horse. "No need to labor the point."

"What gets me is why you even thought you stood a chance."

Luke pressed his lips together hard and mounted his horse as Max's laughter rang out from behind him. "Can we talk about something else?"

"Sure!" Max said, a hint of humor in his tone. "What's with you sleeping on the couch? That's usually my job."

Luke turned in the saddle to look at his friend. "Did you just wake up wanting to needle me today? Because I'm not feeling the love."

Max's amused expression disappeared. "You're not sleeping well, you're way more jumpy than usual, and you seem to have lost your sense of humor. And that's not all on Bailey."

"I never said it was." Luke reined in his horse and swung around to face Max. "I know I'm screwing up right now."

"So what are you going to do about it?"

"How the hell you have the nerve to talk about any of this when you're the one who desperately needs some therapy is beyond me."

Max raised an eyebrow. "Nice attempt to deflect, bro. Let's just say that Noah's away with his sister, Sally and Jen are busy at the clinic, Sky's too young to make much sense, so that leaves me to try and work out what's going on with you right now."

"By attacking me?"

"If you see this as an attack then . . ." Max shrugged. "You're definitely screwed up."

Luke stared at Max for a long time. "I'm going to get some help."

"Good, because if you aren't doing okay, where does that leave the rest of us? We're used to you being the sane one."

"Maybe that's the problem," Luke said. "I guess you can only pretend everything's okay for a while before things come back to bite you in the ass."

"Yeah, that's for sure. What does Bernie think about this?"

Luke frowned. "What's that got to do with anything?"

"She's your BFF. You tell her everything." Max studied Luke's face. "Don't tell me you messed that up as well."

"It's . . . complicated."

"You might as well tell me because, as I said, I'm the only one around to listen to you right now." Max hesitated. "And I really do want to help. I mean, you've saved my ass a lot."

Luke considered his friend. Max wasn't the most reliable of people, and he had a habit of dropping explosive stuff into conversations just to see what happened next.

"If I tell you anything, you have to keep it to yourself."

Max rolled his eyes. "You know I can't promise that."

"At least you're being honest. Maybe I'll wait and talk to Jen." Luke clicked to his horse and started moving again.

"Jen's best friends with Bernie. She's a higher security risk and much more likely to be a leaker than me," Max said. "And I think I know what's going on anyway, so you might as well spill."

Luke kept quiet, his gaze on the terrain ahead.

Max kept talking. "Okay, so you going after Bailey upset things, right? Because Bernie's always had a thing for you."

Luke stopped his horse again and waited for Max to reach his side.

"What makes you think that?"

"You're a terrible liar." Max shook his head. "It's obvious to anyone with eyes. Did Bernie finally say something to you?"

"What if she did?"

"Well, obviously the real question here is, how did you respond to her?" Max studied Luke's face. "Were you shocked?"

"Wouldn't you be shocked if someone who'd been your best friend for years suddenly said they had feelings for you?"

"Hell no, because at some level, I think I'd already know that."

Luke didn't like the way Max was looking at him. "I didn't."

"I bet the thought that Bernie was there for you just in case you needed her was always in the back of your mind."

"Bullshit," Luke snapped as Max unconsciously echoed what Bernie had said to him the previous evening.

"Bernie's my friend. If she suddenly decided I was something more, that's on her."

"Okay, so now that she knows you have no romantic interest in her, what do you think she'll do?"

"Hopefully, go back to being my friend." Luke answered. "If things were reversed, I'd do that."

"You sure?" Max clicked to his horse and moved off. "Can't have the great Luke Nilsen being inconvenienced, can we? Can't have Bernie not getting with the plan and pretend nothing happened."

"That's not fair," Luke hollered, but Max eased into a lope and was soon out of earshot. Luke finished his thought. "Why wouldn't Bernie want things to go back to how they were?"

He made no effort to rush off after Max and kept his horse at a walk as he turned down the drive toward the house and barn. Except what if Bernie didn't see it that way? What if she wasn't willing to be his friend anymore?

The thought of not having her around was like a punch in the gut. Luke stared out over the pine forest. For the thousandth time he regretted kissing Bernie for all the wrong reasons and not the right ones. Had that one stupid kiss encouraged her to think he liked her?

"Dammit," Luke muttered. "I screw up everything good in my life."

He reached into his pocket for his phone and checked his calls and messages. There was nothing from Bernie. There hadn't been anything for days. On impulse, he called her and was surprised when she picked up.

"Hey!" She sounded flustered. "I'm in the middle of something. Can I call you back?"

"Why did you pick up the phone if you couldn't talk?" Luke asked.

There was a longish pause and then a sigh.

"I guess I kind of panicked because I really don't know what to say to you right now."

"Maybe we could meet up?" Luke suggested. "Talk things through?"

"I'm not sure that's a good idea, Luke."

"Why not?" God, it was good to hear her voice even if she didn't sound her usual self.

"Because I've got a lot going on right now and I need to concentrate on me and my future."

"Which doesn't include me?"

She went quiet again. "I know this might be hard for you to comprehend, but this isn't about you. I need some space."

"I get that, but—"

"I don't think you do. I've spent most of my life accommodating you and your needs and I have to stop."

"I never asked you to do that," Luke countered.

"You're right, you didn't, so that's totally on me. Which means I'm the one who has to fix it." She paused again. "Can you just try and understand that I need to do this in order to move forward with anything?"

"First you're saying that this isn't about me, and then you're suggesting that I've been such a major influence on your life that you need space to get over me."

She gave a gurgle of laughter. "Yeah, I suppose I am."

"You know that doesn't make any sense, right?" Luke asked. "I mean, logically—"

"Look, I really do have to go. Oliver's just arrived, and we're going out. Can I call you this evening when I get back?"

Before he could reply, she ended the call, leaving him more confused than ever. He tucked the phone back into his jacket pocket and set off for the house. He needed to see her, and if that meant heading over to her house after she'd finished whatever she was doing with Oliver, then that was what he'd do. Some things were too important to let go, and Bernie's friendship was one of them.

Bernie ended the call and turned to smile at Oliver, who was approaching the counter. He had his backpack slung over the shoulder of his puffy, green ski jacket and wore his best hiking boots, black jeans, and a sweater.

"Hey you." He grinned at her. "Ready to go?"

"Yes, definitely." She pointed toward the kitchen. "I just need to let Anton know I'm leaving and grab the picnic things."

"No rush."

She fled into the kitchen where her assistant raised an eyebrow. He was a tall, elderly Black guy who had worked in some of the best restaurants in the world and had somehow ended up at her place, where she treated him with the respect and love he deserved. She had no idea how long he intended to stay, but she hoped it would be forever.

"What's got you so hot and bothered?"

"Just life." Bernie took the stack of containers she'd prepared earlier that morning out of the refrigerator, added her water flask, napkins, and disposable silverware.

"Where are you off to?"

"A hike in the forest. I'll be back in about three hours."

Anton waggled his eyebrows. "*If* you come back. How well do you know this guy?"

"Well enough. I hope."

"I'll send out a search party if you're not back by six."

"Thanks." Bernie gathered her supplies and put them in her backpack. "I've left a note with our intended route on the counter, just in case."

"Smart girl." Anton went back to his pastry. "Have fun."

She walked back to Oliver, who was studying the community noticeboard at the back of the shop.

"I'm all set."

"Do you have a rainproof jacket?"

"In my backpack." Bernie patted her bag. "And a hat."

"I guess you've done this before." Oliver held the door open for her to go through.

"Not with someone who knows the forest quite like you do."

"I must admit it's one of my favorite things to do— share the place I love with someone," Oliver confessed. "But feel free to tell me if I start getting too boring."

"I doubt that would happen." Bernie jumped into his jeep. "I love learning new stuff, and I really needed a break this week."

Oliver gave her a sidelong glance as he started the engine. "Any particular reason why?"

"Just general life stuff. Too much to do and not enough time to do it in."

"You can tell me that stuff, you know," Oliver said as he drove out toward the national park boundary. "I'm a good listener."

Bernie sighed and settled back against the seat. "The thing is—I know what the problems are, and I even know how to solve them, but I just can't make myself give anything up to make my life easier."

"You do juggle a lot of things," Oliver agreed. "But if

you don't give one hundred percent then you wouldn't be true to who you are."

"I guess I'm quite ambitious," Bernie admitted. "Mom says I get that from my real dad."

"Yeah?" Oliver slowed down to take a sharp turn.

"My mom was married to a techie who ran off to fulfill his dreams in Silicon Valley, leaving her with a baby and very little financial support."

"That sucks."

"I dunno. She met Mike, who is the best of men, and I got to have some adorable half-siblings. I don't remember my dad, and I certainly don't miss him."

"My parents stayed together for us kids, but they don't really like each other. I almost wish they'd divorced because they've spent the remaining years reminding us of what they sacrificed to give us a secure home and using us as emotional hostages."

"Ugh. Sounds awful."

"That's why I don't go home very often." Oliver turned off the road into a small parking lot next to a barred gate. "We can get through here. I have the access codes."

"Nice."

After Oliver shut off the engine, Bernie took a deep breath and faced him.

"I should probably wait until after the hike so that you don't abandon me in the forest, but there's something I need to say."

Oliver's amused gaze settled on her face. "Let me guess: We should just stay friends and not date?"

Bernie nodded. "I really like you, and I enjoy our conversations so much, but I'm not in the right place to have a deep and meaningful relationship with anyone right now."

"Okay." Oliver paused. "Does this also have something to do with how you feel about Luke?"

Bernie just stared at him until he started to laugh.

"You must know Luke has a thing for you? I mean it's so obvious he can't deal with you going out with someone else," Oliver continued. "Not that he's been awful to me or anything, he's always really nice, but I see the way he looks at you when he doesn't think you'll notice."

"And I think you've got it the wrong way around." Bernie finally recovered her ability to speak. "I'm the one who needs to get over Luke."

"Whatever." Oliver grinned. "The pair of you need your heads knocked together. It's like you missed an opportunity to go out with each other when you were younger and get it out of your systems so it's just 'there,' hanging between you like a tantalizing thought."

"I've never thought of it like that."

Oliver shrugged. "Then you're welcome."

"You're not mad?"

"Why would I be? I really like you, too, Bernie, but I had something to tell you today as well."

"You might as well get it off your chest," Bernie said. "It seems to be that kind of day."

"Okay." Oliver held her gaze. "I'm off on a course for the next four weeks in Yosemite. I was going to say that maybe we should see it as a cooling-off period and that we could reassess the status of our relationship when I got back." He cleared his throat. "One of the reasons I moved here was because my long-term relationship broke up and I couldn't stand being in the city without her. Even though I really like you a lot, I don't think I'm in a good position to start a serious relationship yet, either."

Bernie sighed. "Now I wish I'd let you go first because

that sounds way more reasonable and responsible than
my lame excuses."

"How about you take this as an opportunity to sort things
out with Luke and get back to me?" Oliver suggested.

They smiled at each other, and Bernie leaned in to kiss
his cheek. "You're a really good person, Oliver."

"I know." He kissed her back. "And so are you."

Bernie was still thinking about how much she'd enjoyed her hike with Oliver when she pulled into the drive
of her home later that evening. Despite their earlier conversation they'd remained at ease with each other, and
she truly believed they stood a chance of staying friends.
He'd told her all about Annie, his ex, who sounded
lovely. On her return to the café, she'd had a text from
Bailey with some suggested updates to the charity auction
website that she was dying to try out. Despite everything,
it had been a successful and relaxing day. She reminded
herself that dealing with two businesses, the humane
society, the auction, *and* a romantic relationship would be
too much for anyone.

Her smile wavered when she walked into the kitchen
to find Luke perched on a stool at the kitchen counter,
chatting away to her mom as if nothing had changed.
Could she go back to just being his friend or had that
kiss changed something inside her that could never be
forgotten?

"Hey!" He smiled at her. "I came to see the puppies.
Bailey's demanding pictures for the auction site."

Linda came out of the kitchen to give Bernie a kiss
and a hug. "I said he'd have to wait until you came back

to decide whether that was okay, so I fed him some pie to keep him sweet while he waited."

"It was really good pie," Luke said.

"I'm sure it was." Bernie set her backpack against one of the kitchen cupboards. "What happened to your hand?"

Luke held up his two bandaged fingers. "I tried to say hello to Cleopatra. She still doesn't like me."

"Did you tickle her tummy?"

"Yeah, and then she grabbed hold of my arm with all four paws and clung on like a face hugger until I yelped. And then she tried to bite me."

Linda patted Luke's shoulder. "It was only a graze. She didn't really sink her teeth in."

"Lucky old me." Luke cast an amused glance over at Bernie's calico cat who was glaring at him from the couch in the family room. "She still hates me."

"She's just very protective," Bernie said.

She wasn't sure how she was behaving so normally when everything inside her was reacting so fiercely to Luke's presence. She wished she could stop feeling like that, but her body wasn't on board with her thoughts. He just looked so . . . wholesome and wonderful sitting there, his face alive with rueful laughter, his lack of resentment over Cleo's treatment of him so typically Luke that she wanted to smile back at him. She reminded herself that twenty plus years of seeing him as "the one" wouldn't be overcome in a few weeks.

"I can take you down to the barn before the light fades if you like," Bernie offered.

"What about your dinner?" her mom asked.

"I ate so much on the hike that I'm not really hungry," Bernie said. "I'll get something later if I need it, okay?"

"Sure. There's soup warming on the range and pie in

the pantry." Linda turned to Luke. "Don't keep her out there all night. She needs her sleep."

Luke picked up his Stetson and got off the stool. "This shouldn't take long. Thanks for the pie and the great conversation, Mrs. Murphy."

Bernie turned back to the door and waited for Luke to join her outside. They started walking, the lights from the house fading as they approached the line of trees heading down the hillside. There was a faint smell of pine and a hint of rain in the air.

"It's going to get dark soon." Luke looked up at the sky.

"Are you scared?" Bernie asked.

"Yeah, actually." He half smiled. "I always wonder what's coming at me out of the trees. Force of habit."

"Sorry." Bernie winced.

"No need to apologize. It's definitely a me problem."

"The barn is well lit. I take pictures of the animals for the humane society website all the time in there." Bernie kept her tone light and agreeable. "The puppies are starting to look like individuals, so you should get some good shots."

"Bailey will be thrilled."

Bernie stepped into the barn and snapped on the lights, catching the glare of several of the feral cats' eyes as they fled the space. She refilled the water and food bowls, Luke working companionably alongside her as if they did it every night.

"Let's go and see Pandora." Bernie led the way to Pandora's stall. "We might move her up to the house when the puppies get a bit older so we can keep a better eye on their development, but it can get a bit crowded up there."

"Sounds good." Luke took out his phone. "If the pictures

turn out okay, I can forward them to you for the auction website."

"Thanks."

Bernie reminded herself that she could do this—be polite and warm without getting into anything else. Luke would probably be grateful she'd returned to normal.

She unlatched the door and went in, and Luke followed.

"Hey, sweetie!" Bernie crouched in the straw as Pandora came over to greet her while the puppies crawled over each other in a never-ending scrum. "How are the kids doing?"

Beside her, Luke chuckled. "Momma looks like she needs a break, and I don't blame her." He kneeled beside Bernie and got out his phone. "Okay, I'm not sure if I'll be able to get them individually at this point, but I bet Bailey will work out which one is which."

His thigh brushed hers and in her rush to move away, she almost toppled into the straw. Luke caught hold of her elbow and held her steady.

"You okay?"

"Fine, thanks." Bernie eased free of his grasp and stumbled to her feet. "I'll get out of your way."

"You're good where you are."

Bernie didn't say anything as she went to lean against the far wall. Luke took some shots of Pandora and attempted to disentangle the puppies, which was like separating spaghetti. Bernie chuckled.

He glanced over at her, his eyes warm. "Nice to see you smiling."

She shrugged and immediately felt self-conscious. "I forgot to check on the birds. I'll meet you outside."

"It's okay, I'm almost done, and . . ."

She left, carefully closing the door behind her, and

released a breath. It was stupid to be so acutely aware of him, but she couldn't seem to stop. She took her time checking the bird feeders, refilled the water bottles, and went back into the center of the barn, where she found Luke leaning against one of the tables as he contemplated his boots.

"Hey," she called out to him. "Did you get some good pictures?"

He raised his head to look at her, his expression difficult to read. "Yup."

She gestured at the door. "Then shall we go back up to the house? I'm sure Mom has more pie if you want another piece."

"Could we stay here a minute and talk instead?"

Bernie went still. "If you want me to apologize for what I said—"

"I don't." He met her gaze. "I always want you to be honest with me."

"Okay."

"You're the only person I've ever been able to rely on completely, and if that's how you feel, then that's how you feel." He hesitated. "The real question is how we move on from here."

"I don't know if I can pretend nothing happened and just go on as before," Bernie said slowly. "I wish I could, but it's awkward."

"I get that." Luke nodded.

"Oliver said we should've made out at school, realized we weren't meant to be more than friends, and gotten over it earlier."

"You told Oliver?" Luke cleared his throat. "I mean, I guess you would, seeing as he's your boyfriend."

"Actually, we're on a break. He's on a training course

in Yosemite for a month and yeah, we talked about a lot of things."

"But you're on a break?" Luke asked, his gaze narrowed on her.

"Yes, Oliver thought I should . . ." it was Bernie's turn to pause ". . . take the time to sort things out with you. Not that there's anything we need to sort out."

She met his gaze and neither of them looked away.

"Then I guess we should try something new?" Luke suggested. "What if Oliver is right and we should make sure we're not compatible?"

Bernie raised her chin. "You specifically said you weren't interested in me that way."

"I don't think I did. I said it was a surprise." He walked toward her. "One kiss is hardly enough to go on, is it?"

"A kiss you regret and have apologized for on multiple occasions," Bernie reminded him as he came even closer. "And you're not yourself right now. Are you sure you're making good decisions?"

He smiled at her. "You sound jumpy."

"I'm . . ." She looked up into his blue eyes and forgot how words worked.

"We're both intelligent people, so how about we try this kissing thing again?" Luke murmured, his fingers coming up to caress her jawline. "It won't take long to see whether that first one was a fluke." As if sensing her protest, he continued. "What's wrong with an experiment?"

"What if one of us hates it and the other doesn't?"

"Then we'll keep trying until we reach a consensus." He rubbed his nose against hers. "Come on, Bernie. We can do this."

She gulped in some air and managed to nod as he leaned in even closer. She'd never been good at making instant decisions, and her common sense battled against her desire to be kissed by the object of her dreams.

"Mmm . . ." Luke murmured as he dropped a series of light kisses on her lips. "You always smell like coffee and caramel."

He teased her lower lip until she opened her mouth and let him inside, and then it was easy to stop thinking and just experience the toe-curling reality of being thoroughly kissed by Luke Nilsen. He was meticulous, she'd give him that, acutely aware of what she responded to and how to coax her response. She went on tiptoe and slid one hand behind his neck to anchor herself against the sweet onslaught.

His arm came around her waist, drawing her tight against him. She was only aware that he was backing her against the wall when she hit it. He adjusted the angle of his head and kissed her again. Her body reacted with such enthusiasm that she couldn't imagine ever letting him go. His thigh pushed between hers and she pressed shamelessly against the hard intrusion.

His hand edged under her shirt, his fingers shockingly warm against her skin, and she moaned into his mouth.

"Bernie? Where are you? Mom says it's time to come in."

Bernie froze, her body plastered against Luke's, her brain not fully functioning, her heart thumping in unison with his in the sudden silence. She tore her mouth away and whispered.

"It's Mary."

Luke's groan echoed exactly how she was feeling.

"She won't go away."

"Okay, just . . ." He disentangled his hand from her shirt. "Give me a minute."

"I'll go talk to her," Bernie whispered. "Then I'll come back."

She redid some of the buttons on her shirt that had somehow come undone and smoothed her hair before strolling toward the entrance of the barn as if she didn't have a care in the world.

Mary was stroking one of the feral cats, who instantly ran away when Bernie appeared. Bernie smiled at her.

"Hey, Luke's just getting a few pictures of Pandora and the puppies. He'll be out in a minute."

Mary raised an eyebrow. "Weird, because that's the first place I looked and neither of you were in there."

"We needed better light to see the pictures he'd already taken, and now he's gone back to take some more." Bernie hated lying, but Mary was a great believer in speaking the truth, and Bernie couldn't handle that right now.

"Why is your face all red?" Mary asked.

"I bent down to fill the water bowls and stood up too fast," Bernie said.

"It's not that." Mary was examining her closely. "You look . . . different. Sort of puffier, like you've been crying, but also happy."

Bernie half turned toward where she hoped Luke was still hiding. She had to get Mary out of there and let her friend take care of himself.

"Luke?" she called out. "Take your time. I'll meet you back at the house, okay?"

Luke got Bernie's message loud and clear and stayed where he was until the sisters' voices faded. He needed a few minutes to get his unruly body under control.

Holy crap . . .

He briefly closed his eyes and leaned against the wall, vibrating from the kiss he'd shared with his BFF. Things hadn't gone to plan at all. If Mary hadn't turned up, he wasn't sure he would have stopped until he'd been buried deep inside Bernie. He'd had his fair share of girlfriends, but none of them had made him feel like this.

Was it because his whole life felt out of whack, or was there something more fundamental going on—that Bernie was just the right woman for him? Luke felt like a fool for even second-guessing himself, but he'd always been a meticulous planner and his current state of indecision was unsettling. But man . . . that *kiss*—like she belonged with him and completed him and somehow filled in all his spaces.

He blew out his breath and turned toward the barn entrance, suddenly aware that he was on his own. Beyond the barn the sky was now a dense black with a few emerging stars and the thinnest moon possible.

He hadn't been kidding about his fear of the dark and here he was, in a relatively unfamiliar place, facing a trek back to a house he couldn't see through the trees. His fingers brushed his belt seeking the weapons he needed to defend himself in hostile territories and found nothing but his own paranoia.

He took a hesitant step through the open door until he was almost outside, keeping one hand on the frame to orient himself. The only sounds were the familiar ones he'd grown up with: packs of hyenas calling to each other in the forest, owls hooting, squirrels scrambling up and down the redwoods, their claws rattling the rough bark.

Nothing to worry about—except he couldn't seem to move his feet.

"Okay, hotshot, take some deep breaths. You've done

this hundreds of times, it's no big deal," Luke said out loud. "You just need to start walking."

He uncurled his fingers from the doorframe and made himself walk across the graveled parking lot toward the avenue of trees that led up to the house. He was doing okay until the forest closed around him and he was suddenly short of breath, his head whipping back and forth between the black pools of nothingness that might conceal anything.

"Luke?"

His gaze fastened on a light coming down the path toward him, and he hastily cleared his throat.

"Hey, I was just coming."

Bernie appeared on the trail above him, her cell phone in her hand, the bright white light making him shield his eyes. How could he have forgotten that he had his own phone and light source?

"Sorry I had to rush off, but you know Mary." Bernie reached him and took his hand as if it were the most natural thing in the world. He had to stop himself from gripping it like a lifeline. "It dawned on me that you might not be familiar with the route back to the house in the dark."

She started back up the slope, and he followed her like a lamb as his fears receded against the certainty of her voice and company.

"I don't think I've been out here this late for a while," Luke agreed as the comforting presence of the house emerged through the trees.

"I keep asking Dad to put some lights on the path, and he keeps saying he'll do it, but he's so busy it gets put back." Bernie chuckled. "I guess I should stop asking and do it myself."

"Hey." Just before they left the shelter of the trees, Luke drew her to a stop. "Thank you."

"For what?" She looked up at him, the warmth in her brown eyes a balm to his soul.

He smoothed a loose auburn hair away from her cheek. "The kiss?"

Even in the darkness, he saw her blush. "Oh, that."

"Didn't work for you?"

"You know it did. If Mary hadn't turned up—"

He spoke over her. "I would've backed you into one of those empty stalls and had my wicked way with you."

"Really?" She smiled up at him like it was a surprise.

"Really." He gently kissed her forehead. "Let's sleep on it and compare notes in the morning, okay?"

She nodded and started walking again, and he followed her into the circle of light surrounding the house. Her family was visible through the large windows in the room that looked out over the forest.

"I won't come in," Luke said.

"Okay." She kissed his cheek. "I'll speak to you tomorrow, and don't forget to send me those pictures."

He waited until she went into the house and then turned toward his truck. His heartbeat had returned to normal, and he was smiling again—all thanks to Bernie, who had come back to make sure he was okay and not made a big deal out of it at all.

CHAPTER EIGHT

"Will you think about it?" Bernie asked Anton, who was working alongside her in the kitchen at the coffee shop.

It was five in the morning, and they'd been at work for an hour already. Having not slept much after kissing Luke, Bernie was running on coffee fumes and hope. He'd said he'd enjoyed kissing her, but what if he changed his mind after a night's sleep? And why had she agreed to such a stupid experiment anyway? She was just opening herself up to being hurt all over again.

"I mean you're brilliant at what you do, and if you wanted to be my partner as we expand the business, then . . ."

"Been there, done that." Anton kept working, shaping the croissants as he answered her. "Got the bankruptcy papers to prove it."

"Well, dammit." Bernie was making the chocolate version of the croissants, which took a little more time. "Okay, so do you know anyone who might want to be my partner in this business?"

Anton finished the tray, set it to rise, and started on another.

"I do know a guy who might suit you, but I'll have to talk to him first."

"That would be great." Bernie opened another industrial-size bag of chocolate chips and grabbed a couple for herself. "I'd really like to develop the on-the-go and delivery options for the bakery, but with everything else, I can't do it alone."

"You could give up the pets."

Bernie hid a smile. She was aware of Anton's feelings about animals and the countryside in general. "I'd rather give up the coffee shop."

He shook his head. "I've never understood why people keep pets. They tie you down."

"Maybe some people like that."

"I had a cat once. When Fee Fee LaBelle died it damn near broke my heart. I couldn't go through that again."

"You had a cat?" Bernie paused to stare at Anton.

"Yeah." He winked. "Don't look at me like that."

"I thought you hated animals, not that you were too afraid to love one again. That gives me hope." Bernie dusted her board with flour. "You should come out to the humane society and find a new cat."

"Not happening," Anton said. "I'm not sure how long I'm going to stick around, and pets need a stable home."

"That's true. And by the way, if you are thinking about leaving, give me a few weeks' notice, won't you?"

"Sure." He pointed at the oven. "Bread rolls and the brioche should be ready to come out now."

Just as he spoke, the timer went off, and Bernie walked over to the industrial-size oven. Some of the doughs were left to rise overnight so they could go straight in the next morning while they were prepping the rest. The aroma of perfectly cooked brioche wafted over her as she emptied the ovens and reset the temperature for the first batch of croissants.

Anton had moved on to morning rolls and muffins.

"You like baking, don't you?" he asked as Bernie washed her hands.

"I love it."

"Then be careful what you wish for. Sometimes you end up so busy running things and trying to keep the money straight that you never get to do the thing you love."

"You sound like you're speaking from experience."

"As I said. I went into partnership with a two-star Michelin chef, and we still couldn't make it work. Then the chef left me with all the bills and waltzed off to a new job without a backward glance."

He stacked the last tray of croissants on top of the others. "This guy I'm thinking of hasn't had things easy the last couple of years. This would be a chance for him to turn things around."

"Is he a good person?" Bernie asked.

Anton held her gaze. "The best."

"Then I can't wait to meet him." Bernie consulted the list on the refrigerator door and took a deep breath. "I'd better get on with the rest of the muffins."

Luke stared at his accountant and tried to form the right words into a sentence. He'd hitched a ride into the next-biggest town with Noah to pick up some ranching supplies and meet the woman who helped balance the books—or in this case, not balance them. Patty and her family had been working with his for three generations and specialized in agricultural properties. He never made a financial ranching decision without checking in with her first.

"I mean, I knew that the storm took out a lot of my stock, but . . ." He paused. "It's really that bad?"

Patty nodded, the sympathy in her eyes genuine because she came from a ranching family and knew exactly what he was going through.

"There are a lot of government support programs you can apply for both statewide and through the USDA." She glanced at her screen. "I've already started working on the best options for you."

"I don't want to make things worse," Luke said.

"You won't. There are also programs run through the NRCS that will help optimize the land and support wildlife and local flora. I know you're super keen on that." Patty's printer came to life and started churning out pages that she handed to Luke. "There are some good options here. Talk to Sally and get back to me."

"Will do." Luke gathered the pages together and folded them in half. "Are we okay to pay our bills this quarter?"

"Yes, you can manage that, but the next payments might be more of a struggle if you can't think of a way to increase revenue. I'm in close contact with Joel, your financial officer at the bank, and we'll coordinate with you to make sure you're getting the best deals out there."

"I appreciate that." Luke tried not to let his anxiety show.

"We'll get through this," Patty said bracingly. "We always do."

"Thanks." Luke groaned. "It's like all the last years of effort have been wiped out and I have to start again with a whole new plan."

"I'm sorry, Luke," Patty said. "I'm not sure if it helps, but you're not the only one of my clients currently struggling after that terrible winter."

"My dad always said that misery loves company." Luke rose to his feet and Patty did the same. "I'd better get back and help Noah with those supplies."

"Better make sure he doesn't spend too much money on them," Patty joked.

Luke found a smile somewhere. "I'll keep in touch and get back to you about what we need to do."

"The sooner you do, the easier things will be." Patty came around her desk to pat his shoulder. "And give Sally my love, won't you?"

Luke left the office, his smile fading as he went down the street toward the feed-and-grain store on the corner. Noah's truck was backed up by the loading bay, but there was no sign of him. Luke went into the store and found his friend interrogating one of the employees, who didn't seem to be enjoying the experience.

"I'll check out back, sir." The young guy dodged around Luke and scuttled off toward the rear of the store.

"Why did you scare him?" Luke asked.

"I wasn't trying to." Noah raised an eyebrow. "I just wanted to know why something wasn't on the shelves where it should have been." He paused. "You okay?"

"Just talked to Patty."

"Not good, eh?"

"Nope," Luke said. "So don't throw our money around."

"I never do." Noah looked vaguely insulted. "I keep better spreadsheets than you."

"True," Luke acknowledged. "I need to talk to Mom, and then we can all sit down and discuss what's going on, okay?"

"Fair enough." Noah consulted his cell phone. "Do

you want to go through my list and make sure we need everything?"

"Nah, I trust you."

Noah gave him a searching look and then nodded. "Okay. I'm almost done here. Anything else we need in town before we head back home?"

"A beer would be nice, but I'm not sure I could stop at one," Luke turned toward the front of the store. "I'll wait for you at the counter."

Luke waited until everyone had finished their dinner and Jen had put Sky to bed before opening his laptop.

"I spoke to Patty today."

"How is she?" Sally asked. "I haven't seen her in ages."

"She's doing good and sent her love." Luke tapped away on his keyboard, brought up the spreadsheet of the ranch finances, and turned the screen so that everyone could just about see it. There was silence while everyone read the information and then looked at Luke.

Jen was the first to speak. "I'm not great at math, but that doesn't look good."

"It isn't." Noah, who was the ranch spreadsheet king agreed. "In fact, if we don't get our finances in order, we're in trouble."

"Correct," Luke said. "Patty has a couple of ideas for us to consider." He passed around the pages she'd printed out for him. "But I wanted to hear from you guys as well."

Sally put on her reading glasses and sighed as she passed the papers over to Noah. "I'm so sorry, Luke. You've worked so hard to get the ranch back onto an even footing, and that darned winter ruined it all."

"Can't win against Mother Nature," Luke reminded her.

"I know, but she can be very cruel," Sally said. "I could go back full time if that would help."

"I don't want you to have to do that, Mom," Luke said.

"But it would add to our total income." Sally looked around the table. "And help pay more of the household bills."

"I think you should do what you think is right, Sally, but I suspect the problems go far deeper than that." Noah looked around the table. "We need a massive financial overhaul and reinvestment strategy to make the ranch profitable again. I think Patty's right to talk about looking for alternative sources of income and government subsidies."

"But won't that make things worse in the long run?" Jen asked. "I mean, isn't that just kicking the can down the road?"

"I guess it is," Luke said slowly. "But if it's that or lose the ranch, I know what I'm going to pick."

Silence fell around the table until Max stood up and looked at Luke.

"I know this sounds corny, but if anyone can bring this ship around it's you, boss. I trust you to make the right call."

Luke met Max's gaze. "I appreciate that."

Max nodded. "I'll be in the barn if anyone needs me."

Luke watched Max go. It probably wasn't the right time to tell his buddy that he felt like a complete failure and wished someone else could take the weight of decision-making from him for a year or so. He was so damn tired of everything coming down to him . . .

"Hey." Noah cleared his throat. "We've got this. If you

want me to take a look at some financial options let me know."

"Be my guest." Luke rubbed his hand over his chin and realized he hadn't shaved for days and basically had a beard. "The quicker we work out a way to become solvent, the better we'll all sleep at night."

"You're not sleeping at night at all," Sally commented. "I wish—"

It was Luke's turn to get up. "I promised Bernie I'd help with the auction stuff tonight. Are you guys okay to finish up here and in the barn?"

"Sure." Noah had a concerned look in his eyes that Luke didn't want to deal with at the moment. "Go ahead. We've got this. I'll be working on my spreadsheet if you need to talk."

"Thanks."

Luke took his glass over to the sink and left the kitchen, aware that Sally, Jen, and Noah were all trying not to look at him, which meant they'd be discussing him after he left. Not that he could do anything about that, and he was acting weird.

He thought about riding over to Bernie's place, but Max was in the barn, and he didn't want to talk to him, either. It was also getting dark, and being lost amongst the redwoods and having another panic attack wasn't high on his to-do list. He got into his truck and headed out along the familiar road to the top gate, from which a five-minute drive along the county road would bring him to Mike's ranch.

It only occurred to him after he bypassed the main house and drove down to the second barn that he'd forgotten to let Bernie know he was coming. He took out his phone and sent her a text.

Hey, are you around?

I'm in the pet barn-where are you? Bernie texted back.

Right outside. ☺

Seconds later, she appeared at the open door, her smile a welcome dose of sunshine. She wore tattered overalls with a plaid shirt underneath and her hair was braided and hanging down her back. He got out of his truck and went over to her.

"You look like Jessie from *Toy Story*."

She rolled her eyes. "Like I've never heard that before." She angled her head as he came toward her. "What's wrong?"

"Where would you like me to start?"

Her smile faltered. "If you've changed your mind—I'd like to start there."

"About us?" He bent to kiss her cheek. "Absolutely not. How would you feel about running away with me?"

"Like right now?"

Luke pretended to look around. "Sure, why not?"

She set her hand on his shoulder, her thumb brushing the skin above his collar. "Are you sure you're okay? Why don't you come into my office and we can talk this through?"

"You have an office?" Luke followed her toward the barn.

"Well, it's more like a storage area, but I have a desk, a phone, and an internet connection. "She glanced back at him as she walked. "And a door I can close."

"Sounds like heaven."

She went into a small space at the farthest corner of the barn and turned to face him, her arms spread wide.

"Welcome."

There was still a distinct smell of animal feed and fertilizer, but the rest of the space definitely resembled an office, with an old-fashioned oak desk, two sturdy chairs, and a filing cabinet with rusting corners. A small window—covered in spiderwebs—on the outside wall let in the light.

Luke took out his handkerchief and advanced toward the window. "I know you can't bear to de-home spiders, but these webs are ancient and uninhabited, so I'm cleaning them off for you."

"Thanks." Bernie sat in one of the chairs. "This furniture came from Mike's dad's old office up at the main house. It was stored out here, so I repurposed it."

"It's good, solid stuff," Luke took the other chair, which creaked when he sat down. "Why waste it?" He looked around. "Shame you don't have a refrigerator."

She grinned at him. "Do you want a beer? I keep some in the main-barn refrigerator with the vet-prescribed medications."

"Not right now, but that's good to know." He took a deep breath and looked at her. "I guess getting drunk or running away won't solve anything right now."

"As far as I know, those things don't usually solve anything. How about you talk to me instead?" Bernie held his gaze.

"Ranch debt, dead cattle, bad weather, high-interest loans, you name it, I'm dealing with it right now." Luke sighed. "And I know that's what I signed up for when I took on this place, but sometimes it feels like I take one step forward and three back."

"Dad's feeling the pinch, too," Bernie said. "I overheard him talking to Mom last night, and he sounded worried."

"The winter screwed us all," Luke agreed. "Worst one

on record, and before that we had the fires and drought to contend with."

"It sucks." Bernie reached out and took his hand. "I'm so sorry, Luke."

"And I don't feel I can complain because they're all depending on me to make things right." He grimaced. "Except here I am complaining to you."

"Because you know I'm neutral." Bernie nodded.

"Neutral? I was hoping you'd be on my side."

She squeezed his fingers. "I *am* on your side. I guess everyone assumes you have all the answers because you're so good at being the calm person in charge."

"I used to be that guy." Luke released a breath. "I feel like I'm on the verge of letting everyone down."

"You're not." She frowned. "You're doing the best you can in difficult circumstances."

"Thanks for the support." He brought her hand to his mouth and kissed her knuckles. "My champion."

"I've always been that, Luke." She met his gaze, her brown eyes steady. "You're my best friend."

"And all I do right now is take and take," Luke said. "I haven't even asked how things are going with your life."

She chuckled. "Please don't beat yourself over that as well. I'm fine."

"I'm glad one of us is."

She raised her eyebrows. "You're having a temporary meltdown. You'll be back to your usual bossy self in no time."

"Temporary, eh?" He pulled her gently toward him until she ended up in his lap. "I think I need some more up-close-and-personal persuasion."

She cupped his stubbled chin. "I am not an antidote for your problems, Luke Nilsen. If that's what this is all about, then—"

He cut her off with a searing kiss that had her kissing him back. Eventually, he eased back to study her.

"I'm being more honest with you than with anyone else in my life right now. That's all I can give you. Is it enough? Because if it isn't, I need to know."

Was it enough? Bernie studied Luke's face and the resolution in his eyes. It was hard to separate her old instincts to comfort and protect him from her desire to be honest about what she wanted now. And she wanted him. Just sitting on his lap and being kissed was giving her life. . . . And maybe, just like Luke, with everything going on in her life, she deserved something entirely for herself.

"I think we both need this," Bernie said slowly. "And I think we should go for it."

"Until we find out if it will stick or it blows up in our faces?"

"Or we might just enjoy it and then decide we're done," Bernie reminded him. "If we're careful, we can go back to being friends."

"I'd like that." Luke tucked a wayward hair behind her ear. "I can't imagine not having you to talk to."

"I also think we should try and keep it quiet."

His smile was a welcome relief from the seriousness of their conversation. "Like you don't think your family will work it out in a nanosecond?"

"They might speculate, but if we keep our mouths shut, they won't be able to confirm their suspicions."

"Max and Noah will make up their own minds without any assistance from me and my mom. . . ." Luke paused. "Dammit. She'll want to know everything."

They both contemplated trying to deceive their mothers.

"Then we'll proceed on a need-to-know basis," Luke said firmly.

"Okay." Bernie cupped his chin. "Could you kiss me again?"

Luke obliged her, and within seconds she was threading her fingers through his hair and pressing against his chest with a desperate need that was almost embarrassing.

"Hey." Luke eased back a little, his voice hoarse. "What's the chances of us being interrupted right now?"

"Not high," Bernie said. "Everyone's either watching the game or doing homework."

"And does this door have a lock on it?"

"It doesn't, but I have been known to move the filing cabinet in front of the door to keep everyone out."

"Perfect." Luke set her gently on her feet and moved the cabinet in front of the closed door with a speed and efficiency she could only admire. "Now, where were we?"

Bernie eyed him hopefully. "About to get busy?"

He patted the desk. "How about you hop up on here?"

Bernie eyed the old piece of furniture suspiciously. "Is it strong enough?"

"We're about to find out." Luke crooked his finger at her, his smile a mixture of pure devilry and lust that made her pulse pick up. "But don't worry. I'll catch you if you fall."

Bernie moved past him and gingerly sat on the edge of the desk. "It seems okay."

"Good." Luke put his hands at her waist and eased her back until her knees hit the edge of the desk and he could stand between her spread thighs. "That's better."

Bernie instinctively put her hands on his shoulders and looked up into his face. "I feel kind of . . . exposed."

"Yeah?" He leaned in and kissed her with a thoroughness

that thrilled her to her core. "Then I've got a lot of work to do, because all you should be thinking about is how many times I'm going to make you come."

She shivered as he continued to kiss her, his fingers working on the straps of her overalls until they fell to her waist, the metal clips hitting the desk with a soft clang. He slid his hand down over her shirt and cupped her butt, pushing the overalls all the way off to pool on the floor.

"That's better."

"What about you?" Bernie asked as she surreptitiously eased off her socks.

"All in good time." He undid the top two buttons of her shirt and pulled it over her head. His breath caught at the sight of her cotton sports bra, which she knew wasn't one of her better ones because she hadn't expected to be seduced while feeding the animals in the barn.

"Sorry." Her cheeks warmed up.

"For what?" He pressed a kiss to the generous mound of her right breast, his fingers catching and pinching her already tight nipple. "This is *awesome*."

"I have better bras." And now she was talking to the top of his head as he cupped her breast and sucked hard on her nipple, making her gasp. "Lacey ones, sheer ones . . . *oh*." His thumb slid beneath the cotton and scraped lightly over her flesh. "That's . . ."

He worked the central clasp of her bra free and immediately covered both her breasts with his hands and his mouth like a starving man. Bernie pressed up against him, eager to touch in return, to make him feel some of the exquisite sensations he was arousing in her. She scratched her nails down the back of his shirt, making him straighten, and his hips rolled forward pushing the rock-hard evidence of his desire against her stomach.

She yelped as his fingernail grazed her nipple and grabbed his ass, which was still encased in his Wranglers.

"Let me—"

He raised his head, his breathing uneven, his narrowed blue-eyed gaze focused entirely on her. "Not yet. I have an agenda."

"But . . ."

He took hold of her wrists and set her hands down on either side of the desk. "Hang on."

"Why would I want to do that?"

He winked and dropped to his knees, his face level with her now-soaked panties. He gently touched the lace on the center panel. "Pretty. Can I touch you?"

"Yes, please." Bernie nodded vigorously as his finger slid under the lace. "I'd like that."

She was so ready for him that the slight intrusion of his fingertip made her want to come. She tensed and he looked up.

"Something wrong?"

"Could you just hurry?"

He considered her as he worked his finger in and out of her needy flesh. "Can't rush things like this, Bernie. I'm a thorough man, and I've a lot to learn."

"Maybe next time you could focus on that, because if you just speed up a little right now, I'll come."

"Where's the fun in that . . ." he raised his eyebrows ". . . when I can take it slow and make you come a thousand different ways?" He took off her panties and slowly licked her clit. She shuddered and gripped the desk so hard she hoped she wouldn't get splinters.

"God, that's nice, Bernie."

He disappeared between her thighs, and she experienced the sensation of his clever, clever, tongue inciting her, and the circling of his embedded finger, which made her want to scream. But she couldn't scream, in case someone came into the barn, which somehow made everything even more exciting.

Luke added another finger, and the first tremors of a climax made her go still. Unfortunately, Luke did the same, holding her at a peak of neediness that was half pleasure and half frustration.

"Luke . . ."

His response was to bite her inner thigh and slide his third finger home. Her whole body clenched around him, and she came silently and hard, her breath caught in her throat as she let the sensations roll over her.

"Nice," Luke murmured. "Do it again."

She let go of the desk long enough to shove her hand into his hair and dig her nails into his scalp. He thrust his fingers in and out, which had the desired effect of making her climax for a second time. Bernie didn't care what she looked like now, and even if someone knocked on the door, she wouldn't have the breath left to tell them to go away. She sucked in some air and slowly released her grip on Luke's hair.

"I want to touch you, too. It's not fair."

Luke looked up at her. "I'm good, sweetheart."

"I can hear your knees complaining from here," Bernie said.

"I'm not that old. But maybe next time I'll bring a cushion." He rose to his feet, his expression hard to read. "I want you."

Bernie held his gaze. "And I want you."

"But not here." Luke's gaze swept her makeshift office. "I'd like us to be naked and horizontal the first time we make love."

"How on earth will we manage that? We can't exactly stroll into either of our bedrooms hand in hand without causing a big scandal," Bernie said. She was aware she might sound a bit grumpy. "This place is perfectly fine for me. I'm totally relaxed."

She jumped as a door banged somewhere in the barn.

Luke gave her a look. "Totally."

"Okay, so maybe a locked door and a comfortable mattress would be better," Bernie conceded as she scrambled back into her panties, shirt, and overalls. "I don't want to be responsible for my siblings needing therapy if they burst in on us having wild sex."

She lightly flicked the fly of his jeans and he winced. "But I don't need to lie down and be naked to help you with that."

He caught her hand and pressed it against the hard outline of his shaft. "Are you sure you have time?"

"I'll make time." Bernie pushed gently on his chest until he was backed up against the chair. "Now sit down and start unzipping."

Half an hour later, Bernie sent a very satisfied Luke on his way home and finished off a few tasks in the barn. When she arrived back at the house, Mary was sitting up at the kitchen counter eating cold spaghetti and mayonnaise.

"How can you eat it like that?" Bernie asked as she nuked her own plate of pasta and sauce in the microwave and sat next to her sister.

"It's a texture and temperature thing for me." Mary forked up another mouthful and chewed slowly. "It's quite common when you're on the spectrum."

"So I've heard." Bernie inhaled the glorious scent of her mom's homemade alfredo sauce. "I'm starving."

Mary hopped down off her stool to get them both a glass of water.

"Where's Mom?"

"Upstairs with Dad going over the business accounts." Mary sighed. "I offered to help because I'm a whiz at math, but Dad said I should concentrate on my schoolwork, which I've already done—for the rest of the semester."

Mary had started college at seventeen after graduating high school a year early. She was currently studying online with Stanford University and aiming on double majoring in math and computer tech and possibly nursing. Everyone in the family regarded her with awe.

"You've got that weird look on your face again," Mary commented as Bernie drank her water. "That happy one."

"I can look happy once in a while, can't I?"

Mary studied her. "It's like someone gave you the biggest peach pie in the world all for yourself."

"I do love a good peach pie." Bernie tried to ignore the mental images of what she and Luke had recently been doing in the licking and tasting department. She glanced over at the fridge. "I think we only have apple, right?"

Mary twirled her fork through her spaghetti. She was remarkably hard to shift off a subject once she became interested in it. "You only get that look on your face when Luke's around."

"That would be silly." Bernie fake laughed. "I mean, he's no peach pie."

"I saw his truck down at the barn when I was walking the dogs." Mary continued eating. "I thought about coming to say hello but there was no sign of either of you."

"He wasn't there long." Bernie scooped up more pasta and spent a long time chewing it. "He had something to show me."

"Like what?"

Bernie almost choked and had to grab a quick slug of water and let Mary pat her on the back before she could form another word.

"Just some stuff for the auction."

Mary looked at her. "You're a terrible liar, Bernie."

"Not as bad as you are."

"True. I just don't see the need for it." Mary smiled. "It just makes everything more complicated and people harder to read. Dad says it's because I don't see the grays, only the black and whites, and I'm inclined to agree with him." She hesitated. "I don't like it when people I love lie because it makes me feel bad."

Bernie set down her fork. "I'd never want to do that to you, but sometimes situations aren't clear-cut and talking about them might hurt other people."

"You mean like you saying you're over Luke and dating Oliver while secretly still liking Luke?"

"Um . . ." Bernie blinked at her sister. "Oliver and I are on a break."

Mary smiled. "So the Luke part is true?"

"We're . . . talking things through right now. But you can't tell anyone, okay?"

"That'll be hard for me to remember," Mary said. "But I'll do my best because it's nice to see you looking happy." She finished her meal and put her fork in the empty bowl. "I'm going upstairs to talk to my Discord group. We have a big D&D campaign coming up and I'm the lead writer."

"Sounds great." Even though she had no idea what that meant, Bernie smiled as Mary headed up the stairs. "Have fun."

She placed both bowls in the dishwasher and helped herself to some coffee. So much for no one knowing what was going on. She'd have to try and explain to Luke why deceiving Mary was not in the cards. As her sister didn't always get nuance, she'd also have to be prepared for Mary dumping her in it with her family.

"Hello, love!" Her mom came into the kitchen. "Problems at the barn?"

"Just the usual." Bernie hugged her. "Thanks for the food."

"Mike said he thought he saw Luke's truck going by the house." Linda refilled her coffee mug.

Bernie inwardly sighed. Nothing got by her mom. "Yeah, he was helping me with some auction stuff, and he wanted to show me the photos he took of the puppies, which are adorable by the way."

"You should have asked him up to the house to finish off that pie."

"I did, but he had to get home."

"Did you have a nice hike with Oliver today?" Linda leaned against the counter, her coffee mug cradled in her hands as if she had all night to chat.

"It was really cool going out with someone who knew the forest so well," Bernie said. "He's off to Yosemite for a month of classes."

"That's a shame. He's such a nice young man."

"He is, but we've decided we'd be better off as friends." Bernie met her mom's gaze.

"Which is probably for the best since you're still hung up on Luke." Her mom arched a knowing brow.

"Why does everyone keep saying that?" Bernie asked plaintively. "I mean, Luke and I have been best buds for *years*."

"And there's nothing wrong in wanting to see if there's more to that relationship," her mom said. "Otherwise you'll always wonder."

"Why does everyone keep saying that as well?" Bernie eyed her mom as she got more coffee.

"I guess for my part, I'm worried how you'll feel if things don't go the way you want them to. Your birth dad was very . . . focused on getting me to marry him. In the end, I allowed him to convince me that everything would be okay because he was so relentless. The problem was—once he got what he wanted, he lost interest and went on to the next thing, which in his case happened to be work."

"What does that have to do with me and Luke?"

"Because sometimes I see that all-or-nothing intensity in you, Bernie. I've often wondered whether your fixation on Luke as your one-and-only true love will come back and bite you in the butt."

"My fixation?" Bernie frowned. "It's hard not to be aware of someone who's been in and out of your life since you were five. He's a good person. He's almost like family."

"I *know* he is, but he isn't the only man in the world, sweetheart."

"I have been out with other guys, Mom. I'm not that pathetic." Bernie caught her mom's sympathetic expression and her stomach clenched. "But maybe this is my attempt to get over my 'fixation' before I can find someone new."

"I guess that's one way of looking at it." Why didn't her mom sound convinced?

Bernie raised her eyebrows. "I thought my focus on work was the problem, not Luke."

Her mom smiled at her. "Maybe it's all part of the same thing?"

"You're not helping here," Bernie complained. "I can't change who I am."

"I'm not asking you to do that, sweetie. But if you

aren't aware how far your focus can take you, you might make the same mistakes Brian did."

"I'm not like him, Mom. I barely remember him; he had no part in raising me, and I learned how to be a good person from you and Mike," Bernie said. "I know I've got a lot going on right now, but I'm getting help with the bakery and café, and once the auction is over, I'll have so much free time, I won't know what to do with myself."

"Promise?"

Bernie clunked her mug against her mom's. "Promise."

"Speaking of your birth dad . . ." Linda cleared her throat. "He contacted me again. He'd like to meet you."

"I thought you'd blocked him on everything."

"I have, but he wrote me a letter."

"Who does that?" Bernie frowned. "That's getting into stalker territory."

"I guess he really wanted to reach out to you."

Bernie frowned. "You didn't write back, did you?"

"No, I wanted to give you the letter he included to you first and see what you think." Her mom opened the kitchen junk drawer and handed her a plain white envelope addressed in an unknown hand.

Bernie studied the slanted handwriting but made no effort to open the letter.

"Take your time," her mom said gently. "I wouldn't have passed it on if I didn't think it was worth a look."

"Fine." Bernie put the letter in the front pocket of her overalls. "But I thought we'd agreed Brian had no place in our lives."

"Maybe not in mine, but he is your biological father, and now that you're an adult, it isn't my place to decide how you want to deal with him."

"What does Dad think of all this?"

"Mike wants whatever makes us happy." Her mom

smiled. "But he's also willing to kick some ass if anyone hurts his girls."

"Dad's a gem."

"He is."

"A diamond in the rough," Bernie added.

Her mom chuckled. "I like that. I'll have to tell him." She came across to kiss Bernie's cheek. "You know that whatever you decide to do we'll support you, right?"

Bernie nodded, aware for the millionth time how lucky she was with her family. Her mom was almost out the door before she spoke again.

"By the way, your shirt's on inside out."

Bernie's hand flew to her chest, and she looked down in horror as her mom's chuckles echoed up the stairs.

CHAPTER NINE

"So, I've readjusted our cash flow projections and sent all that info to Joel at the bank," Noah said. "I've also done a series of calculations incorporating some of the schemes and loans we can apply for."

"That's great." Luke studied the spreadsheets. It was way too early in the morning to be discussing finances, but a good reminder of how urgent the problems were. Noah had barely allowed him to drink his second mug of coffee before he'd opened his laptop at the kitchen table and started talking. "Do we need to speak to Joel about adjusting our line of credit?"

"Already on it," Noah said, nodding. "Our current cash flow is inadequate, so the quicker we can access some of these new financial resources the better."

"Good." Luke tried to sound upbeat. "There were some interesting new NRCS schemes that could be implemented here."

"Yeah, there are some great ones." Noah's fingers were flying over the keyboard as he spoke. "Joel's already talking to me about what I've sent him. He wants to meet up with you as soon as possible."

"Can he come out here or do we need to go to his office?" Luke asked.

"I'll check." Noah gave him a sideways glance. "I could go if you'd like."

"Thanks, but I need to be there," Luke said, then cleared his throat. "But I'd appreciate it if you tag along. I don't want to worry Mom too much."

"Sure thing." Noah made another adjustment to his spreadsheet and consulted his text messages, where he was obviously talking to Joel. "Do you want to read these?"

Luke's cell buzzed and he took it out of his pocket. "It's okay, he's cc'ed me into the convo."

He'd begun to hate this side of ranching. It was impossible to survive without having the financial side of things on track, but the work involved with keeping up with the ever-changing ag and government programs was neverending. Luckily, Noah liked the battle more than Luke did, but the ranch wasn't his legacy—it was Luke's, and sometimes it felt like a millstone around his neck.

"How's Bernie?" Noah asked.

"Fine, as far as I know. Why?" Luke looked up from his phone.

"You said you were going to see her last night."

"I did."

"Which is why I asked how she was doing." Noah stared at him. "Everything okay between you two?"

"Why wouldn't it be?"

"Because you've been ignoring each other for quite a while and now you're getting all defensive."

"I'm—" Luke stopped talking.

"Getting it on with another man's girlfriend while he's away?"

"She's not going out with Oliver anymore."

"Which doesn't answer my question." Noah pinned

him with his searching gaze. "Or maybe it does." He paused. "You sure looked happy when you came in last night."

"So what?" Luke crossed his arms over his chest, and Noah pointed at him.

"See? Totally defensive."

Luke tucked his cell back in his pocket and stood up. "I've got work to do."

"Sure, boss." Noah's attention was back on his spreadsheets. "Not like you're running away from me at all."

"Bullshit," Luke said. "I have a ranch to run." He walked toward the door. "I'll check in with Joel about our meeting and get back to you about the date."

"Sure. It's not like my calendar is full." Noah stretched, making his chair creak. "I'm here for the foreseeable future."

"Good to know."

In the mudroom, Luke stepped into his work boots and went out to the barn where Max was waiting with the horses already tacked up and ready to go.

"Did you take another nap?" Max asked. "I've been waiting for hours."

"Noah ambushed me with his latest spreadsheets." Luke checked his horse's bridle and saddle before mounting up. "He's relentless."

"And he's bigger than you." Max looked him up and down. "You're looking very pleased with yourself. Did you get some last night?"

Luke avoided eye contact and wondered if he might be blushing as he eased his horse into a walk. Keeping anything from Max and Noah, who knew him inside out, was proving to be impossible.

"You look happy," Max said.

"Maybe that's because I'm beginning to see some solutions to the many problems of maintaining a financially stable ranch."

"Nah, that's not it." Max kept pace with him, his blue-eyed gaze assessing. "You went to see Bernie last night, didn't you?"

Luke compressed his lips and stared straight ahead.

"While Ollie's out of town?" Max whistled. "I'm surprised at you, boss."

"They're not together anymore." Luke instantly regretted giving away even that information.

"So you hustled over there to stake your claim."

"You've been reading too many Westerns," Luke said. "Bernie and I are—"

"Getting it on." Max grinned. "About time, too."

For a moment Luke wished he had the ability to make his friend disappear, but he knew Max would just keep coming back like some kind of gremlin.

"Is it weird?"

Case in point, as Max just kept talking.

"Is what weird?"

"Getting intimate with someone you've known all your life as a friend."

Luke had thought about that and was shocked at how comfortable he'd felt exploring Bernie's body. There'd been no awkwardness at all.

"I'd say that was none of your business," he replied.

"Sure thing." Max lapsed into silence while they negotiated the gate into the pasture.

"I mean, objectively, she's hot— Not in the same way as Bailey is, obviously, but Bernie has this awesome rack, and this lush, kind of—"

"Shut it, right now." Luke interrupted his friend's musings. "I am not going to talk about this."

"Okay."

Luckily, Luke's cell buzzed. He checked the message from Joel and relayed the information to Noah, who sent back a thumbs-up.

"You talking to Bernie?" Max asked.

"Nope, Joel. I'm meeting him in town this afternoon to go over the bank projections for the rest of the year."

"I can come if you want," Max offered.

Luke looked up as he stowed his cell away safely in his pocket. "That's good of you, Max, but Noah's already offered."

"And I guess I don't add anything of value," Max said.

"You know that isn't true. And you're always welcome to hang out with me."

Max's smile reappeared and Luke wondered whether he'd imagined the flash of hurt in his friend's eyes. "Except when you're getting it on with Bernie."

"Correct." Luke smiled back at him. "Now, should we herd those cows or sit here all day and chat?"

Bernie fished the letter out of her apron pocket and stared at it for the hundredth time. For some reason, she'd kept hold of it since her mom had handed it over, slept with it under her pillow, and brought it into work. It was now lunchtime; she'd been working eight hours straight, and she was on her break. The sun was barely visible through the sullen clouds. Even though it was spring, there was always the faintest whisper of winter in the breeze coming down the street.

She was sitting on the side porch of the coffee shop, out of the wind and away from prying eyes, enjoying her freshly brewed coffee and dithering like a teenager over the letter she didn't want to read. Her mom had asked her to make the effort, and Linda wouldn't have done that unless there was a good reason.

"You're a fully grown woman," Bernie reminded herself. "He can't do anything to you."

With a deep breath, she opened the envelope, drew out the single sheet, and began to read.

Dear Bernadette, I asked your mother to pass this letter on because I would like to meet you. I am aware that you must feel abandoned by me and that I behaved disgracefully when I left you at such a young age.

"Too right," Bernie muttered.

Despite that, I would still like a second chance. I'm older now and wise enough to regret losing the very things I should have treasured and valued. If you don't want to see me in person, perhaps we could arrange a chat over video or something? I'd really appreciate it—even if you just use it as an opportunity to tell me to take a hike. I'd like to apologize to your face and maybe even set things right for the future.

Brian.

Bernie read the letter twice more before putting it back in the envelope. He'd made no attempt to guilt her into seeing him. which was a plus, but he'd also failed to make a case about why things were different enough for her to make the effort to see him. What was going on in his life to make him suddenly reach out?

She took out her phone and googled his name, skimming through the tech articles to find the rare personal details. Okay, so his second wife had divorced him—surprise, surprise—and he'd taken a step back from managing his software company, but no one knew exactly why.

Bernie raised her head and stared out over Main Street. Had he been ill, or had he worked himself to a standstill? If he was anything like her, it was probably a combination of the two, but did it make a difference in whether she wanted to see him or not?

"Hey."

She jumped as Luke's head appeared around the corner.

"Hey!" She waited for him to join her. "I didn't know you were coming in today."

"I wasn't planning on it." He made a face. "I'm meeting Joel."

"From the bank?" Luke nodded. "He works with Dad as well."

"We all need a Joel in this business." Luke sat next to her and stretched out his long legs. "Last year I called him on a Sunday with a heads-up about a piece of equipment I wanted to purchase, and he gave me the go-ahead right away."

"He's a good one."

"He sure is." Luke took her hand and kissed it. "What's up with you?"

"Nothing much." Bernie indicated her coffee and half-eaten croissant. "Just sampling my own work."

"I can tell you that it's the best around," Luke said.

"You're biased."

He smiled. "Maybe."

Bernie showed him the envelope. "I got a letter from my birth dad."

"The tech guy? What did he want?"

She shrugged. "To connect with me, I guess. To apologize for missing out on all my formative years?"

"How do you feel about that?"

"I'm not sure. Mom and Dad have no problem if I want to meet him."

"What about you?" Luke squeezed her hand. "I mean, it's a big ask after all these years."

"I just googled him, and he recently got divorced and took some time off from running his company."

"Sounds like he's going through a few life changes," Luke said. "Sometimes that can set everything off-kilter."

"I don't necessarily want to be part of his great redemption tour. I genuinely have no feelings about him at all because he left before I got to know him."

"Then would it hurt to meet him?" Luke asked. "If you already know your mom's okay with it."

"For what reason?"

"Curiosity? I'd want to know whether we had anything in common."

"Mom already said I'm just like him." Bernie sighed. "He did suggest meeting remotely."

"That might be a good place to start." Luke leaned over and helped himself to a sip of her coffee. "Man, that's good."

She took her mug back and stood. "How about I make you a fresh cup all for yourself?"

He rose, took the mug out of her hand, and set it on the table. "Not until you give me a kiss."

"I can multitask," Bernie murmured against his mouth as he kissed her deep and dirty. "But now I don't want to."

She kissed him back, pulling him against her body, making him groan. His grip tightened.

"I can't go into a business meeting with a hard-on."

"Why not? I bet Noah does. Jen says he totally gets turned on by a good spreadsheet."

Luke laughed and set an arm around her shoulders. "Let's go on in."

"The pet auction website for the animal shelter is going live today," Bernie said as he opened the door to let her go past him. "It usually means more people come forward with dogs and puppies to auction off, so I'll be busy dealing with them over the next few days."

"Too busy for me?" Luke murmured.

"I'll try and squeeze you in." Bernie immediately went red. "I mean, not literally, it was just . . ."

Luke burst out laughing, which made her want to jump his bones and made everyone in the coffee shop look at them.

"Oh, honey, if you only knew . . ."

"Knew what?" Lucy came through the door behind them and stopped short. She wore a white, frilly apron over her pink dress, and her hair was in a messy bun on top of her head. "Why are you standing in the way?"

"Sorry, Lucy." Bernie stepped back. "Luke was just teasing me about something."

"What's new? But I bet he wasn't as bad as Caleb when I tagged along with him and my brother."

"Caleb was horrible to you," Bernie confirmed. "But I guess you've forgiven him, seeing as you're engaged."

"That's because I love my grumpy tech millionaire." Lucy flashed her large diamond ring. "Speaking of which, I need your help."

"I am rather busy right now," Bernie said cautiously, knowing full well how Lucy's mind worked.

"I'm going to Seattle for the weekend to talk through the wedding plans with my parents and Caleb, and I need you to keep an eye on the B&B for me." Lucy paused to breathe. "*Please*?"

"Can't anyone else do it?"

"No one I trust implicitly." Lucy gave Bernie her helpless-little-cousin face. "Please, Bernie. You can eat and drink at my expense, we have great internet thanks to Caleb, and my staff will manage everything."

"Then why do you need me there?" Bernie was slightly distracted by Luke, who was trying to catch her eye and nodding.

"In case there's a crisis." Lucy held her gaze. "You probably won't even need to leave the apartment."

"Oh!" Bernie finally twigged why Luke looked so enthusiastic. "Okay. I'll have to check in with Mom because she'd have to manage all my chores at home."

"I'll make it okay with Auntie Linda." Lucy hugged Bernie hard. "Thanks so much! I knew I could rely on you."

She waved at Luke and practically skipped back out the door, looking like a girl who had won her heart's desire, which Bernie knew she had when Caleb, her longtime crush, had fallen in love with her. Perhaps being a starry-eyed optimist was a good way to live your life. . . .

"A whole weekend, then," Luke said.

"Yes." Bernie looked up into his twinkling eyes. "Maybe you could spare an hour or two to keep me company."

"I'm sure I could."

They were still grinning at each other like fools when Noah and Joel came in.

"Move out of the way, Nilsen," Noah said. "Joel's a busy man."

"I'll get you some coffee." Bernie went behind the

counter, where Anton was covering for her. "Sorry I was
so long."

"Not a problem," Anton said. "I'm leaving now. See
you in the morning, okay?"

"Yes, and thank you."

He winked. "My pleasure. It's nice to get my hands
on some dough again—both kinds." He paused. "I've
asked my buddy to come up and meet you next week, if
that's okay,"

"I'm looking forward to it," Bernie said. "Now, go and
enjoy the rest of your day."

She knew exactly how Noah, Joel, and Luke liked
their coffee and took them on a tray with a selection of
the pastries and muffins she and Anton had baked that
morning.

"Thanks, Bernie." Joel, whom Bernie had known all
her life, smiled as she set his mug by his elbow. "How are
Mike and your mom?"

"Same as everyone around here—trying to keep things
together."

"It's been a tough couple of years," Joel agreed.
"Everyone's struggling." He straightened his spine. "But
it's my job to help make things work, so if Mike needs
anything, tell him to give me a call."

"I'm sure he will." Bernie put a stack of plates on the
table and removed the tray. "I know we all appreciate
how hard you work on our behalf."

"We do." Noah placed his laptop on the table and fired
it up. "Thanks, Bernie."

"Yeah, thanks." Luke looked up at her. "I'll speak to
you soon, okay?"

She resisted the urge to kiss the top of his head and
went to clear some mugs and plates from the empty

booths. Lunchtime was always busy, and as she currently lacked wait staff, the job of bussing the tables often fell to her. As she filled the tray, she considered where to advertise for help. There had to be someone local who wouldn't mind a part-time job when Mary or the twins weren't working.

As there was no one currently at the counter, she went into the back for supplies to replenish the empty glass cabinets. She also checked that the delivery company that distributed her baked goods had left a final list of what they'd picked up and where it was going. Which reminded her, she also needed someone to supervise that part of her business. . . .

Bernie sighed and set about cleaning the work surface and prepping for the following day. Anton had already made the overnight doughs and fed the sourdough starter, so there wasn't too much for her to do. If anyone came to the counter, they could ring the bell to summon her. Her new trainee baker from the culinary college was starting on Monday, which would be helpful. She suspected they'd need a lot of input before they were up to speed, and Anton wasn't the kind of guy who wanted to slow down and teach, so that would be on her as well.

For a moment she wished she could find Luke, take his hand, and disappear—preferably to somewhere with a bed where they could both sleep for a week and forget their problems.

Speaking of problems . . .

She got out the letter and stared at the email address and phone number at the bottom. She was curious as to why Brian had chosen to contact her at this particular moment. But as her life was already a chaotic mess, adding one more element to it couldn't possibly hurt.

She tapped the email into her phone and kept her message short and sweet, adding her cell number with her signature. Knowing her luck, the email would probably go straight to his spam, and she'd never hear from him again, but at least she'd tried.

The bell on the counter dinged, and she went back into the shop. The person wasn't familiar and had the look of a tourist fed up with the endless forest and the lack of civilized facilities.

"Hi! What can I get for you?" Bernie asked.

"Coffee, please." The woman smiled. "Thank God I found this place. I thought I'd have to drive another fifty miles to inhale some caffeine."

CHAPTER TEN

"So, how did you manage to get away?"

Bernie beamed at Luke as he came into Lucy's apartment on the top floor of the B&B. It was nine o'clock in the evening, and he'd sent her a text half an hour ago saying he was on his way. She'd spent the last few hours dealing with a couple of late arriving guests and making sure everything was set up for the morning, when the cook would arrive to start on breakfast. Since Lucy had gotten engaged to Caleb, who was loaded, her monetary worries had diminished significantly, although she still insisted on paying him back with interest. Bernie didn't begrudge her cousin anything when she was so blissfully in love.

"Hey." Luke bent to kiss her forehead and took off his Stetson. He wore his usual shirt over a T-shirt, jeans, and boots, but had recently showered. "I told Mom I had to go to town and would be back late, and she said say hello to Bernie for me, so I guess our cover is blown."

Bernie made a guilty face. "Everyone in my family is totally up to speed as well—except the twins, who never notice anything unless it bites them in the butt."

"Noah and Max are in on it too," Luke added.

"And don't forget Jen." Bernie took his hand and towed him toward the kitchen. "Are you hungry? I made a cake."

Luke fake groaned. "If I eat cake now, I'll have to sit down and digest it for an hour, and I had other things planned."

"Like what?" Bernie looked up at him.

"You naked and horizontal for a start."

"Oh." Bernie's cheeks warmed. "That."

He traced the curve of her lower lip. "I've been thinking about you all day."

"Really?"

He nodded.

"Me, too."

"Yeah?" He lightly brushed her mouth with his own. "Like what was I doing to you in those thoughts?"

"All kinds of delicious things." Bernie sighed as he kissed his way down her throat. She was so glad she'd had time to shower and change into a dress before he'd arrived.

"You're going to have to be a lot more specific than that," Luke murmured against her skin. "You know I'm a details person, and I like to get things right."

"Kissing, touching, saying nice things about me." Bernie's knees went weak as he bit her earlobe. "Anything, really. I just turn to jelly when you touch me."

"I noticed that." He eased back to look at her face, his blue eyes fully focused on her. "I wonder why I didn't notice it before?"

"Because I didn't want you to?" Bernie said.

"Then you're a damn fine actor, because when I get this close, I can feel your heart beating like crazy." He cupped her left breast and bent to kiss it. "Right here."

She grabbed hold of his shoulder as he nuzzled her breast.

"We never got this close before."

"Yeah, we did—when we went camping or sat out in the woods behind my house watching for coyotes."

"That was different," Bernie said. "We were teenagers. And can we not get into an argument right now?"

"No arguing here." He wrapped his arm around her waist and lifted her right off her feet, making her shriek. "Which bedroom?"

"Not Lucy's."

"That would be weird," Luke agreed. "Second door on the left then?"

"That's the one."

He somehow managed to carry her and get the door open. She'd already shut the drapes and lit the fire, so the room was warm, cozy, and inviting. He placed her gently on the bed and stood back to look at her.

"I can't wait to see you naked."

Bernie smiled at him. "I've seen you naked quite a few times."

He put one knee on the bed making the mattress dip. "I thought we weren't going to get into olden times."

"I saw you in the creek a couple of years ago. Nearly swallowed my tongue," Bernie confided as he leaned over her.

"I try and keep myself in good shape."

"I know." Bernie reached out to touch his sharp jaw-line, where more than a hint of evening stubble made him even more attractive. "I wanted to lick my way down over those perfect abs, pause to kiss each hip bone, and then . . ." She paused as he grinned at her. "I guess the water was pretty damn cold that day."

His laughter made everything Bernie was feeling inside flow toward him. She tugged him down toward her.

"Kiss me, cowboy."

He obliged, his warm mouth covering hers as his hands roamed at will over her body. She made sure to do plenty of exploring of her own, her fingers in his short, fair hair, her knee coming up to rest on his hip as he settled between her thighs.

"Too many clothes," Luke muttered.

Bernie tried to sit up. "Shall I—"

"How about you let me?"

"And let you have all the fun?" Bernie pushed at his chest. "We can do it together."

He rocked back on his heels and they both kneeled on the bed facing each other, hands working to remove all their clothing.

Bernie sighed as she gazed at Luke's chest, which was covered in a sprinkling of fair hair. "God, that's *so* . . ."

"Don't say nice." Luke's gaze was fixed on her breasts, his tone rough with need.

"Sexy." Bernie finished her sentence and placed her palm flat on his chest. "You feel so warm."

"Good to know." Luke gathered her close and expertly laid her back on the bed. "Now, where were we?"

They explored each other until Bernie was breathing heavily. Luke's hand cupped her between the legs.

He kissed her breast. "I kept thinking about how you looked when you came for me the other day."

"Probably stupid," Bernie muttered. "I mean . . ."

"Not to me." He flexed his fingers making her clit throb with need as his thumb pressed hard. "Every time I pictured you, I damn near came in my jeans."

"That's"—Bernie gasped as his fingers slid inside her—"beautiful."

"Not half as beautiful as you are." He moved his fingers in and out of her in a fast rhythm, his thumb still planted firmly on her clit. "Do it again for me, okay? I need to see you come apart in my arms."

"I'll—" Bernie came so fast she wanted to scream. "God . . ."

"That's my girl." Luke slowed his stroke as he kissed her mouth, his tongue mimicking the thrust of his fingers. "I could do this all night."

"I'd like a turn." Bernie tried to sound strong, which was difficult when part of her would be very happy if Luke kept giving her orgasms for all eternity.

She reached between them and took a firm grip of his hard cock, making him go still. "Not so cold, now, I see."

He grinned and rolled his hips against the clasp of her fingers. God, he was so sexy . . . "Thank you, ma'am."

"Will you just stop talking and lie down?" Bernie asked.

"Sure." He rolled them over until she was on top, straddling his lean hips. "This good?"

"Perfect." Bernie settled between his spread thighs and contemplated her hard, wet target. She eased forward and licked him like an ice cream, making him groan her name and grab fistfuls of the cover in his hands. "Do you like that?"

He nodded and set his jaw, looking slightly formidable.

She sucked the first couple of inches into her mouth, and he went still, his breathing almost nonexistent. She didn't have time to look up at him to see how he was coping because she wanted to take more, to take all of him and make him feel all the pleasures he gave to her.

Luke groaned as Bernie took him into her mouth and his hips rocked forward, thrusting against the pressure of her lips. He only realized his hand was shaking when he cupped her head, threading his fingers through her thick auburn hair. He hadn't expected to be turned on so fast or to have such little control over his instincts. Who'd have thought his BFF would hold the key to unlocking his uninhibited side? He wanted to roll her onto her back and make her his completely.

"Bernie?"

"Mmm?"

"I'm gonna come if you keep that up," Luke said hoarsely.

She looked up at him and doubled her efforts until he gave it up, groaned her name, and came hard.

He briefly closed his eyes and waited for his heart to slow down while Bernie sat back.

"Are you okay?" Bernie finally asked.

He looked at her and decided a little teasing was in order, because why the hell would she want to listen to him blabbing about her being the best he'd ever had?

"Just contemplating a nap."

Her face fell. "Was I that boring?"

"Hell no! You wore me out." He sat up, wrapped an arm around her shoulder, and drew her close. "I'll be good to go in a few minutes."

She relaxed against him, all warm and smelling of sex and him. "I forget how much older you are than me, sorry."

He kissed the top of her head. "I'm only five years older than you are."

"Yeah, but . . ."

He eased her onto her back and stared down at her. "You're going to make me prove I'm not past it, aren't you?"

Her lips twitched. "I guess I am." She pointed at the nightstand. "There are condoms in the drawer."

Just looking at her lush body and tousled hair spread out in front of him was making him hard as iron again.

"I want you."

She held his gaze, her expression solemn. "I know."

It was his turn to smile. "How did you guess?"

She pointed to his dick.

"Smart woman." Luke got a condom out of the drawer and put it on. "Now we'll see who's going to scream the longest."

She smiled as he fitted himself against her and slid home, her eyes going dreamy as he filled her completely. He gave an experimental roll of his hips.

"You like that?"

She nodded, her hands anchoring themselves on his shoulders as he settled into an easy rhythm. He considered himself a pro at sex, paying attention to his partner's needs, being aware of his strength, and making sure his lover was enthusiastic and fully on board with whatever he was doing. Bernie seemed to have other ideas as she slid her foot up his thigh and set it on his driving hip, opening herself up to longer and harder thrusts that Luke couldn't stop from happening.

He adjusted his position so that he could kiss her throat and breasts, and she followed his lead, her hands on his ass, her fingernails digging in and urging him on. He took several deep breaths and recentered himself on giving her pleasure, while inside him something yearned to reply in kind, to take more, demand more, pound into her until she screamed his name and came so hard, she forgot even that.

"Luke . . ." she whimpered against his throat, and she climaxed, her whole body clenching with need. He allowed himself the luxury to push the pace and came alongside her, his breathing fraught and his heart pounding like a freight train.

"That was . . . wonderful," Bernie murmured as she cuddled into him. "I never thought . . ."

"What?" He leaned in, but she'd gone to sleep with a suddenness he envied. He gathered her close, drew the covers over them, and settled back against the pillows, his body still vibrating. Bernie's hair spilled over his chest, the vibrancy of its color against the paleness of his skin a whole season in one place.

The B&B settled around them, the old roof creaking as if already anticipating the weight of the winter snow, the pipes rattled, and the heating didn't quite make it all the way to the top of the building, defeated by the drafts. He wasn't familiar with the noises, having never slept there before. Unwilling to disturb Bernie, he reached out a cautious hand, found his jeans by the side of the bed, and took his phone out of a pocket. He needed to be back at the ranch by five at the latest so he could start his barn chores without anyone realizing he'd been gone all night.

Like he'd fool anyone.

He set an alarm and put the phone on the bedside table. After a day of hard work and satisfying sex, he should have no problem sleeping, but life didn't work like that, so he'd probably be staring at the opposite wall for a few hours. He slowly smiled and looked down at Bernie's sleeping face. There were some exciting alternatives he might be able to persuade his friend to participate in if he could just nudge her from sleep.

Bernie woke up from a pleasant dream of being cuddled around a naked Luke to find that she was actually doing it in real time—except her BFF wasn't exactly relaxed. He was sitting up in bed, his shoulders rigid and his gaze fixed on the slowly emerging grayness of the dawn. She smoothed a hand over his flat belly.

"Hey."

He glanced down and smiled. "Hey, sleeping beauty."

She fluttered her eyelashes at him. "You could've tried waking me up with a kiss."

"I did that earlier, remember?"

Bernie blushed as she remembered the slow gathering pleasure Luke had given her when he'd kissed her out of her dreams and into his arms.

"I'm glad you're awake because I need to go," Luke said.

"It's still dark." Bernie struggled to untangle herself from the bedsheets so she could sit up.

"Not really." Luke was smiling but there was a remoteness about him that made her uneasy. "I need to get back to start my chores so that no one realizes I was away all night."

Bernie pushed the hair out of her eyes. "Seeing as everyone already knows what's going on between us, does it really matter?"

He didn't immediately reply, and she eased slightly away from him and fiddled with the sheet. "Is there something wrong?"

"Why would you think that?"

"Because I know you, Luke, and you're not being straight with me right now." Bernie held his gaze. "I mean if you don't want people to see you leaving the hotel because they'll think you've been up to shenanigans with Lucy, then—"

"It's not that." He spoke over her. "I just get . . . restless when I can't sleep."

"You haven't slept at all?"

"Not much." Luke's admission came across as grudging. "It's okay, I'm used to it, but I know it's not comfortable to share a bed with someone who can't sleep."

"I don't mind," Bernie said softly. "We can just hang here and talk if you like."

He leaned in to kiss her nose. "I'm sorry. I have to go."

Bernie blinked as unaccustomed hurt hit her hard in the stomach. "Okay. Then why don't you head out?" She moved back to her side of the bed and lay down, her expression anywhere but on him. "I'll be getting up in half an hour to go to work, anyway."

"Thanks for understanding."

"I don't understand, but I guess you're leaving anyway."

"Bernie . . ."

"Night, Luke." She turned onto her side and faced the wall. "Call me when you get a chance."

There was a long silence before the sheets rustled and he got out of bed. She didn't turn to watch his progress toward the bathroom or when he returned to put on his boots and pick up his hat. She held her breath as he paused at the bottom of the bed.

"You're mad at me, aren't you?"

She didn't trust herself to reply because for once she didn't know the answer to his question. She'd spent an amazing night in his arms and some part of her—some small part of her didn't want to let him ruin it. She closed her eyes, faked a small snore, and waited for him to leave—which he did after a long sigh.

After the door closed behind him, she listened for the sound of his truck driving away and then counted to three hundred to make sure he wasn't coming back. With a groan, she rolled onto her back and stared up at the ceiling. Could she have handled that better? If she hadn't woken up, would he have just left without telling her?

He was obviously suffering far more than she or anyone else had realized. He was so good at being the calm, organized one that it was almost impossible to see behind his charming mask.

Bernie bit her lip. If he couldn't even relax in bed with her, did that mean he wasn't really into her either? Or was his desire to flee simply about his other issues?

She groaned, hating all those options. None of them were good for Luke or suggested that their relationship had any chance of succeeding unless he got some help. And now that she'd complicated things by becoming his lover, if she tried to talk to him about what was going on as his friend, he probably wouldn't tell her the truth.

But did that mean she had to regret the night they'd just shared? She smiled as the memories of his touch overwhelmed her. Even if Luke decided he didn't want a repeat performance, she'd still have that.

Her alarm went off and she reached for her cell phone. Lucy's guests wouldn't be up and about until seven, and her kitchen staff arrived at six, which meant that Bernie didn't have to oversee anything from the café until checkout time at noon.

She paused, her brain stuck on the idea of never making love with Luke again. Throwing the covers back, she got out of bed and went into the bathroom. If Luke thought she'd fade into the background and let him struggle alone, then he really didn't know her at all. She had a busy day ahead, but that still left plenty of time to plan for all contingencies, because knowing Luke, he'd try to come up with a logical explanation for them to part and attempt to get her to agree with him.

She wasn't going to make it easy for him because too much was at stake. Whether he realized it or not, he needed her.

"You're up early," Max commented as he came into the barn where Luke was already halfway through mucking out the stalls.

Luke nodded but kept shoveling, his attention on his mother's gelding, which liked to kick out when someone was in the stall.

"But if you've been up all night, I guess you can do that."

"I slept."

"Not in your own bed." Max leaned against the open door of the stall, blocking Luke's exit.

"I had some business to take care of in town." Luke straightened and looked Max right in the eye. "Mom knew where I was. I wasn't aware I had to report back to you."

Max raised an eyebrow. "You're salty this morning. Things didn't go well with Bernie?"

"That's none of your business."

"True." Max nodded. "But let's just say I'm asking as your friend."

"Still nothing to do with you."

"Okay."

Luke had to physically shoulder his way past Max to get out of the stall. He paused to make eye contact. "Could you just for once leave me alone? *Seriously*?"

"That depends." Max didn't look away from the challenge. "You're usually the one telling me to confide in other people. I'm just sharing your own words back at you."

"It's not the same."

"Yeah, it is." Max eased back an inch. "You think you're better than me? That because you're an officer, you're somehow immune to all the shit we went through?"

"I had to be." Luke didn't realize how loud he was until Max winced. "That was my damned job."

"Back then, maybe, but now we're just two old soldiers doing our best to unpack hell."

"I'm good." Luke moved out. "But thanks for the offer."

"Sure."

For once Max didn't follow him, and Luke was more relieved about that than he cared to realize. He dumped the barrowload of manure in the pile and hesitated, unwilling to go back and have Max start again. His gaze fastened on the steaming pile of horse crap, and he reluctantly smiled. Talk about life reflecting the current state of his affairs . . . And he hadn't even seen Noah, his mom, or Jen yet, which meant he still had four separate interrogations to navigate before he got any peace.

He couldn't do it.

Decision made, he went back into the barn, saddled his horse, and sent a text to Noah.

Repairing fence line down at the dry creek. Back at noon.

He waited to see that the message had been acknowledged and put his cell away. He couldn't shut it down
completely because on a ranch that wasn't an option, but
he could ignore it for a few hours. And he needed some
peace, to think about what he was going to do about
Bernie.

CHAPTER ELEVEN

"He just called. He'll be here at nine," Anton said as he passed Bernie on his way to get the blueberry muffins out of the oven.

"Who called?" Bernie looked up from her careful placement of the chocolate chips in the cookie batter.

Anton paused. "Roberto. The guy I told you about." His gaze intensified. "You're all over the place today."

Bernie blushed. "The chef, right." She folded in the chocolate and added another scoop to the industrial-size mixer. "I'm looking forward to it."

"Right. I'll be clocking off around then, so I'll do the introductions and leave you guys to it." He grinned at her. "He's staying at my place, so send him over as soon as you're done."

"Will do." Bernie set out ten large trays for the cookies, which were her bestsellers both in the café and online. "Do you think he'll be okay about the weather up here?"

"I think he'll be thrilled to get regular work with a nice boss who understands where he's coming from," Anton said reassuringly.

"Then let's hope we get along." Bernie scooped the

dough into the cookie shaper. "His resume was impressive."

"Yeah, he's worked at some good places," Anton agreed. "And he has experience in setting up an online bakery business, which would be useful."

By the time Bernie finished with the cookies and had sent all the to-go items out with the delivery service, it was almost nine. There was a tap on the back door, and Anton answered it with a delighted whoop followed by lots of backslapping and murmured conversation. Bernie smoothed down her braided hair and tried to make herself presentable before joining the two men.

"Hey, boss lady. This is my buddy, Roberto Almirez," Anton said.

She studied Roberto, who was about her height. He had tight-cropped black hair, warm brown eyes, and more tattoos than she had ever seen on one person. He also had the look of someone who needed a break. Bernie forgot about politeness and pointed at his forearm.

"Is that a phoenix feather?"

He nodded and pushed his sleeve up past his elbow. "It's the whole bird. It goes right across my back, too."

"It's amazing," Bernie said. "I have like two little tats on my right shoulder, but it was way too much sitting still for me."

Roberto shrugged. "I had the time."

Anton stepped between them. "Casey's manning the counter so I'm going home." He turned to Roberto. "You've got the address, and Bernie can give you directions. It's totally walkable."

"Thanks, bro."

"You're welcome." Anton lightly punched his friend on the shoulder. "Don't screw it up. Bernie's good people."

After making sure they both had coffee, Bernie walked

Roberto through the kitchen and into the shop, where they sat down in one of the booths. It was a quiet time in the morning, so she didn't expect to be disturbed. She patted the folder containing his resume, reports from his case managers, and letters from past employers.

"You come highly recommended."

Roberto half smiled. "I used to."

Bernie met his gaze. "Anton said you'd had some . . . problems recently."

"That's one way of putting it." Roberto looked down at his coffee mug. "I got injured at one of my workplaces, took a load of painkillers, and ended up addicted to them."

"Okay."

"Which led to me losing my job, stealing shit, and ultimately ending up in jail for fraud for bouncing checks."

"That's a lot," Bernie said.

"I'm surprised you're even still listening to me." Roberto set his mug down on the table. "I'm not exactly your regular employee of the month."

"You're not, but Anton says you're a good person and a great cook." Bernie sipped her coffee. "And I trust him."

"I think he's the only person who still believes that." Roberto released a breath. "I just need a chance to prove that I can get back to being the person I was."

"I get it." She considered how much she wanted to share with him. "You might think that out here we don't deal with addiction, but it's a huge problem. Someone I love came very close to making some terrible decisions before they got help."

"Yeah?" He regarded her seriously. "Thank God there was someone looking out for them, and they listened. I wasn't good at doing that."

"I don't think it was easy," Bernie said. "But our local doctor is very persuasive." She smiled at the memory of Luke's mom telling her cousin how things were going to progress and then offering lots of support and love to make sure everything went okay. "Are you clean now?"

"Yup, and I have been for two years," Roberto said. "I still have a sponsor, and I'll be looking to attend any local meetings I can find. I'm willing to work for free for the first month."

"There's no need for that," Bernie said. She was getting a good vibe from Roberto, and she'd learned to trust her instincts. "How about you start on a month's trial instead? If at the end of that time one of us doesn't think things are working out, then we'll go our separate ways."

She took a sheet of paper out of her folder. "I've typed up a list of your responsibilities for the delivery business, the salary, and all the rest of the important stuff, and I'll expect you to step up and work with me and in the café when needed." She handed him the paper. "While you read through, I'll get you some more coffee. Would you like anything to eat?"

"I'm good, thanks." He bent his head to read, his expression slightly dazed. "I can't believe you're actually offering me a job."

"I need good, reliable people," Bernie said. "If you can be that person, then we're gold."

He nodded, his attention back on the sheet of paper. Bernie had learned what made a good employee at the café, and she'd be watching to see how Roberto fit in with everyone before she made her final decision. But with Anton at his side, she had high hopes everything was going to work out fine.

Her cell buzzed as she was getting the coffee, and she saw the name of her father's tech company pop up. Having no desire to read anything from him during her already complex working day, she let the alert go. Luke hadn't contacted her, but that wasn't surprising. He was becoming more elusive than her father.

And she wasn't chasing him down anymore. If he wanted to talk to her, he knew where she lived and worked.

She took the coffee back to Roberto and answered his questions about her rapidly growing delivery business, how it was possible to get anything sent out from the middle of the forest, and how, if the business expanded, she might have to rethink her kitchen space. He was knowledgeable, had interesting ideas, and didn't seem to have a problem with a female boss, which wasn't always the case.

By the time her cousin and sometime employee Pen skipped up to the booth, Bernie and Roberto were already on good professional terms.

"Hey!" Pen smiled at them both. Her hair was blond, and she had dimples, and barely reached five foot two. "I came early, Bernie, because Mom wanted me to do some vacuuming, and I hate that noise so much." She turned her attention to Roberto and waved. "Hi! I'm Pen, I live in town."

"Roberto." He almost waved back.

"It's so cool to meet you!"

Pen's enthusiasm was genuine but quite hard to take on first acquaintance. Bernie hastened to intervene. "This is Roberto. He might be coming to work for me."

"That's awesome!" Pen clapped her hands and bounced up and down on her toes, making her pigtails swing. "I *love* new people. Do you go by Roberto, or Bob, or Beto, or Rob, or . . . ?"

Roberto now looked genuinely terrified, and Bernie couldn't blame him.

"Pen, seeing as you're here early, can you go and take a look over the cookie section and make sure everything's stocked up?" Bernie asked.

"Sure!" Pen blew her a kiss. "It'll cost you two salted-caramel cookies, but I'm worth it. Even Mom says I'm great at fronting shelves."

"You're good at many things," Bernie said.

"I *know*!" Pen waved and went behind the counter. Bernie could still hear her singing when she disappeared into the kitchen.

"Sorry about that." Bernie turned back to Roberto. "She can be . . . a lot."

"She was cool," Roberto said. "By the way, I go by Rob or Roberto."

"Good to know." Bernie finished her coffee and stood up. "I'll send you on your way to Anton's, but please let me know if you decide to take the job."

Roberto rose, too. "If it's okay by you, I'd like to accept right now. Then I can start tomorrow."

"I think you should sleep on it, but if you happened to turn up later today, I'm not going to kick you out." Bernie grinned and held out her hand. "Welcome aboard."

This time his smile was wide and so full of guarded hope that Bernie wanted to hug him.

"Thank you for the chance." He nodded and turned to the door. "Now, if you can just point me in the right direction, I'll go and thank Anton as well."

Luke cursed as he missed the fence post, hit his thumb, and ended up with the wire curled around his wrist. Luckily he was wearing good gloves and his skin wasn't marked, but it took him a while to unhook the coiled wire from the leather. His concentration kept wandering off like a grazing horse because there were a million things to worry about and very few solutions. It was the second day in a row that he'd headed out early to avoid everyone and work on the ranch fences.

"You'd be dead if you were on patrol," Luke muttered to himself as he re-coiled the barbed wire. "And so would everyone under your command."

He let out a frustrated breath and stared out beyond the pasture to the endless forest beyond. It was a constant battle to keep the ranchland free of trees so that the cattle could graze easily. Back in the day, his grandparents' brother had also had a place next door, but after a particularly hard winter, Great-Uncle Finn had given up and gone to live in the city, leaving the forest to reclaim its own.

Even though winter was officially over, the air blowing off the slopes had a hint of ice to it, even at midday. Since fracturing his arm the previous winter, Luke could feel that ache in his bones. He checked the time on his cell and noticed Noah and Patty had been texting him, but there was nothing from Bernie—the only person he'd really like to be hearing from at the moment.

He packed his gear away in his saddlebags. But why would she be calling a guy who'd run out on her at some god-awful time of the morning? She wasn't stupid. She knew something was up, and she'd already made it clear that it wasn't her job to chase him down. When had he turned into such a duncehead? He was usually the one making the life-or-death decisions, and now he couldn't even focus on a basic task like fence repair.

He needed to man up and decide what to do about his best friend and lover. He stared unseeingly at the mass of trees until the green blurred into patches of dense darkness. He didn't want to end things with her. It was as

simple and as complicated as that. She was the only thing
giving him life. But if he did commit—at least for as long
as she wanted him—he'd have to move fast and make
sure he hadn't ended things quicker than they'd started.

Decision made, he untethered his horse and mounted
up. Bernie would be busy at the café until four, so he'd
have to catch her later at home, where he had the perfect
excuse to check in about the puppy auction.

His cell buzzed again as he approached the ranch, and
this time, he checked the message in real time. It was
from Joel, his loan manager.

> Hey, got some figures for you. Come on by the
> office in town and I'll run them by you.

Luke checked the time and sent a quick text to Noah.

> You okay up here if I head straight into town
> to talk to Joel?

> Sure, why not? It's not as if you've been doing
> anything useful anyway.

Luke smiled. Mending fences is always useful.

> Pictures or I don't believe you.

Luke angled himself back in the saddle, snapped a
photo of his horse's ass, and pressed send.

> Nice pic. Noah replied. I'll see the rest of you
> when you get back.

Luke was still smiling as he stabled his horse and went
out to his truck. There was no sign of Max or Noah, but

he could hear Jen and Sky singing along to something they were watching on TV in the house. He loved having Noah's new family at the ranch. Since his sister, Brina, had left for Florida with her kids, it made the house feel like a home again. He got in his truck and started the engine. When he'd been overseas, he'd dreamed about being home so much that he'd often wake up disoriented, with the scent of pine sap and dense forest soil in his nostrils. Now he was afraid to sleep because things had reversed, and he existed in an endless firefight trying to survive.

He shook his head to clear the images that pressed on his skull and turned out onto the main highway that meandered down to town. He'd check in with Bernie, grab a coffee for himself and Joel, and head over to the bank, where he hoped there would be some better news for him.

His cell pinged just as he reached town and parked. It was Bailey who loved to facetime.

"Hey!" She waved at him. She was obviously at work because she wore a white blouse and blue pantsuit, and her hair was styled in a neat ponytail. "Puppy pics?"

"I'm getting them today."

"Great! How's Bernie?"

"She's good." Luke smiled. "We're kind of secretly dating right now."

"Yes!" Bailey punched the air. "Good for Bernie!"

"You could pretend to be sad that I'm not dating you," Luke pointed out.

"Nah, what's the point? I'm not that good a liar. And you two are perfect together."

"You think so?"

Bailey mock frowned at him. "Don't screw this up, Luke Nilsen. I like you both too much for things to be all awkward next time I come to town."

"When will that be?" Luke asked. "Bernie's hoping you'll make it for the auction itself."

"I'm trying, but my boss isn't in the best mood right now." She grimaced. "But if I get this case set up right for her and we prevail, then she might be more amenable to me having a few days away."

"You can do it." Luke grabbed his hat and stepped out of the truck. "I promise I'll send those pictures later."

"Thanks!" Bailey blew him a kiss. "I'd better get back to work."

"Bye, Bailey," Luke said. "Have a great rest of your day."

He went into the coffee shop—where Bernie, Pen, and Casey were all busy working at the counter dealing with the lunchtime rush—and joined the line. It gave him the chance to stare at Bernie without her noticing, which was somehow way more pleasurable than he had imagined. She never looked flustered, even when a customer got their order wrong or took ten minutes deciding what kind of mayo they wanted on their sandwich. She smiled, listened, and got stuff done with the minimum of fuss, which was usually the way he liked to deal with his life.

She also looked kind of cute in her red sweater and jeans. . . .

"Hey!" She blinked as he reached the head of the line. "Was I expecting you?"

"Nope. I'm off to see Joel, so I thought I'd get two coffees to go and find out if I can come see you at your place after you get back?"

She raised her eyebrows. "I suppose it's better than you just dropping in and expecting me to be there."

He tried to look suitably apologetic. "I'm trying not to be that guy anymore."

"And I appreciate it." She nodded and offered him a quick smile. "No one likes being taken for granted."

"Message received, loud and clear." He waited as she got the two coffees. "Thanks for these, and let me know about later, okay? I'll be finished in an hour or so if you want to talk."

"Okay." She waited until he swiped his card and gave him his receipt. "Joel takes three sugars in his coffee so don't forget to take some with you."

"Bernie?" A guy Luke hadn't seen before came out of the kitchen. "Can you show me how to input the order for the delivery company?"

"Sure!" Bernie smiled at the man. "I'll be there in a minute."

"Who's that?" Luke asked as he stepped to one side and picked up the coffees, creamer, and sugar.

"Roberto. A potential new hire who just started today."

"Another one?"

"My business is growing, Luke. I need all the help I can get. Roberto comes highly recommended."

"By whom?"

"Anton." She checked the line behind him and spoke to Pen. "Can you manage the rest of these orders?"

"Totally!" Pen nodded. "And I'm super excited to do that."

Luke lowered his voice and moved closer to Bernie. "You did all the usual background checks, right?"

"Of course." Bernie stared up at him, a crease between her brows. "I always do, and what the heck does any of this have to do with you?"

He frowned. "I'm just looking out for you."

"Then consider your job done and please don't mention it again."

"Fine," Luke said. "I'll see you later."

"I'll have to let you know about that."

She stomped off to the kitchen, and he picked up the drinks and carefully headed for the door, aware that he should've kept his mouth shut after paying for the coffee. Bernie didn't need him being an overprotective jerk. She was more than capable of managing her life and her multiple businesses, but the guy who'd come out of the kitchen hadn't looked like any pastry chef Luke had ever seen before.

God, he sounded like a jerk even to himself. When had he become so judgmental? A few tattoos didn't mean squat these days. Half his marines, including Noah and Max, had them. The only reason he didn't was because he was scared of needles. He paused to wrangle the door and considered going back and apologizing, but Bernie hadn't been in the most receptive frame of mind, and he couldn't blame her. He'd already disappeared on her once today, so she had every right to be prickly.

He'd deal with Joel and take his chances with Bernie after the meeting. Hopefully she'd still be willing to talk to him.

Chapter Twelve

What had started as a good weekend, waking up beside Luke, had rapidly deteriorated into Bernie wanting to kick his ass. He'd walked out on her before dawn the day before with a totally fake excuse and then tried to be all heavy-handed and overprotective at the coffee shop about her business decisions.

"Hey, if you hit that dough any harder, you'll end up with flatbread," Anton said.

She looked down at the dough she was supposed to be knocking down, not knocking out, and winced. "Oops."

"Got something on your mind?"

"Just that I need a bigger kitchen."

He glanced around to where Roberto was perched on a stool in the corner working on the online orders, and Kenya, the new trainee, was washing up in the sink at the back. Pen floated in and out, replenishing the counter and dispensing commentary on her customers, her life, and everything else that occurred to her, whether anyone answered her or not.

"Can't argue with that," Anton said. "You need a separate area for the delivery services, otherwise we're all fighting over this table for the first six hours of the day."

"I guess I should talk to the bank about a loan." Bernie grimaced. "I need more space to become more profitable, but they probably won't lend me the money because I'm not profitable enough."

"Truth." Anton finished what he was doing and slid the heavy tray into the rack against the wall, ready for baking. "Maybe a tent?"

"Funny." Bernie gently molded the dough and set it in the bread pans for its second rise. "Mind you, that British baking show does it."

"And have you seen what happens when the temperature rises?" Anton shuddered. "The chocolate won't set, the ice creams melts, the buttercream dissolves."

"I didn't realize you were such a fan," Bernie said as her cell buzzed in her apron pocket.

"I love that show," Anton declared.

"So do I!" Kenya piped up from the sink. "That's why I decided to train to become a chef!"

Bernie's and Anton's eyes met briefly before they both smiled.

Bernie washed her hands and went to check on Roberto, who wasn't exactly chatty in the mornings but had impressed her with his speed and efficiency.

"How's it going?"

"Good, I think." He half turned on the stool so that she could see the screen over his shoulder. "The ordering system is a little complicated."

"Yeah, I know. I've been meaning to get back into the website and redo it."

"I can do that." He smiled. "I took a website development class when I was in prison. I'll write out a plan and we can go through it together when you have some time."

"That would be awesome," Bernie said. "How are the orders coming along?"

He pointed at the counter in the back kitchen. "The overnight ones are all done and ready to be picked up. Everything else went at ten."

"That's . . . amazing."

He shrugged. "You're welcome. If you want to double-check everything, go ahead." He pointed back at the screen. "It would be great to have a way to alert you as to what has gone out and what's popular so that you can reassess your baking needs for the next day."

"I guess a summary of the orders doesn't give enough detail, does it? I've been dealing with it in real time for the last year, but it's getting harder as orders keep growing." Bernie pursed her lips. "Something else to work on."

"I can print off a list for you after I've finished at ten," Roberto suggested. "At least that would give you something to go on before we can institute automatic reordering."

"I'd appreciate that."

"Or if you like, I could focus on what needs to be baked for the online orders first thing in the morning while you and Anton get on with the rest."

"You could?" Bernie smiled at him. "You're amazing."

Roberto looked like a man who didn't know how to deal with a compliment. "I'm just trying to bring value to your business, boss."

"If you're happy to take that task on, go ahead. Just make sure I still know the quantities and ingredients you're using for my overall ordering."

"Got it." He refocused on the screen. "I'll get back to you when I have that detailed plan."

Bernie checked her cell and found a message from Jen. After making sure everyone in the kitchen was doing okay, she walked into the coffee shop, where she saw her friend waving enthusiastically at her. Sky was standing on the seat beside his mom, and he waved, too.

"Cookie?" Sky asked hopefully. "Please?"

"Absolutely." Bernie smiled at them both. "What will it be today?"

"Chocolate. Always chocolate," Jen answered for her son as he bounced up and down, rather like Pen. "And I'll take whatever you think I need to try today."

"I love your adventurous spirit." Bernie went back to the counter to load up some plates and get Pen to bring them coffee. She also grabbed a handful of napkins because Sky liked to get up close and personal with his cookie.

"How are things?" Bernie asked as she sat opposite Jen.

"All good." Jen paused. "I think Noah's going to propose to me."

"Like for real?"

"Yeah." Jen was blushing. "I mean, he doesn't have to do any of that for me to want to stay with him forever, but he keeps talking about making things legal, being a real father to Sky, which I know means he's already constructed a fifty-point spreadsheet and a plan."

Bernie studied her friend's face. "Are you okay with all that?"

"Yes, I think I am." Jen met her gaze. "After the debacle with Dave, I'll admit I was skeptical about relationships, but I think Noah is a good person, and I love him to bits."

"He adores you."

Jen nodded. "I can't believe how lucky I am, but he does."

"You deserve all the luck after Dave." Bernie was totally up to date on all the ups and downs of Jen's romantic life and had even met Dave on his brief visit to the town. "Noah is his complete opposite."

"I'm trying to pretend I'm not noticing Noah's maneuvering, which isn't easy." Jen laughed. "I'll let you know how it's going."

"Do you think he'll throw you a party or do something private?" Bernie asked.

"He's not into public displays of affection, so I'm thinking private."

"Makes sense. If something does come up, do you want to know or not?"

"Like a surprise party?" Jen asked. "Nah, I'll let him have his way for once, although I don't think that's his style, either."

Bernie pictured the ferocious-looking Noah leaping out with a handful of balloons and a bottle of champagne and shouting surprise, then shook her head.

"Anyway . . ." Jen made sure Sky had eaten one piece of his cookie before she gave him the next. "How's Luke treating you?"

"Honestly? He's driving me nuts." Bernie sipped her coffee. "He's being very inconsistent and un-Luke-like. I can't decide if that's because we're kind of dating or if he's just all over the place generally."

"Noah and Max don't think he's behaving like himself, either," Jen said. "But I've never heard them mention him not treating a woman right in a relationship."

"But he's never gone out with someone like me before, has he?"

"Like a friend?"

"A best friend." Bernie considered how much to share. "One minute I think we're doing okay and we're getting closer, and the next he's distancing himself."

"Men. Noah wasn't exactly the king of communicating, either."

"This is more than that," Bernie tried to explain. "It's like he just ghosts me and shuts me out whenever things get too emotional or too close for him. We used to share everything."

"That sucks." Jen patted Bernie's hand. "I think the only thing you can do is keep being honest and let him know you deserve to be listened to."

Bernie sighed. "I'm doing my best, but it's hard to be sympathetic when I want to kick his ass. Maybe I made a mistake in going for this at all."

Jen studied her carefully. "If you really feel like that then you need to tell him."

Bernie sat back and broke her blueberry muffin into small pieces while she thought through Jen's advice. The deeper she got into things with Luke, the harder it was going to be to recover if things went south. Had she been stupid to even try? The only way to find out the answer to that question was to have it out with Luke.

She got out her cell phone and sent him a text.

I'll be out at the barn at six tonight if you want to come over.

She waited to see if he'd reply and got a thumbs-up. She put her phone away and focused on enjoying her time with Jen and Sky. She had enough on her plate to push all her worries about him to the back of her mind until he was standing right in front of her.

Damn, he was looking good. Freshly showered, dressed in his jeans, shirt, and sheepskin coat with a Stetson on his head and stubble on his chin. How could she resist that? Especially when she knew he looked even better when he took everything off.

"Hey." His smile made her knees weak. "Anything I can do to help before we talk?"

She held up the water bucket. "I'm almost done, thanks. Why don't you go and check on Pandora's puppies while I finish up?"

"Sure." He nodded and set off, the scent of his shower gel wafting behind him, which made Bernie think of him in that shower and didn't help the "play it cool you can go back to being just friends" vibe she might be going for.

She filled all the outside water bowls for the feral cats and night critters and put the bucket back in the tack room. She could hear Luke whistling as he came along the center aisle of the barn.

"Where are you?" he called out.

"In here." She poked her head out the door, and he came toward her.

"Do you ever stop working?" he inquired as he bent to kiss her forehead. "You start at four and you're still going."

"So do you," Bernie pointed out.

"True." He leaned back against the doorjamb and smiled down at her. "You good to talk in here or do you want to go into your office?"

She worried her lip. "My office, I guess."

His smile disappeared. "Don't worry, I promise I won't ravish you without asking first."

She eased past him without replying and headed to the far corner of the barn. She didn't think they'd be interrupted, but you never knew with her family. She went to perch on the edge of the desk, which was her usual habit, but changed her mind and sat on her chair instead.

"How did it go with Joel?"

"Surprisingly well." Luke folded his large frame into the second chair. "He's helped a lot."

"Dad says the same. He's got an appointment with him tomorrow." She paused. "Are things really okay, or are you just saying that to make me stop worrying?"

His eyebrows rose. "You worry about me?"

"Don't be an ass."

He smiled. "Got me in one. It's going to be a struggle, but at least I can literally see the light through the trees. I guess after all our hard work it felt like a slap in the face to realize we'd have to do it all again, but that's ranching for you."

She nodded.

He met her gaze. "I owe you an apology."

She folded her arms and leaned back in her chair. "For what?"

"Getting all overprotective at the café."

"Correct." She made a carry-on gesture with her fingers. "And?"

"Ducking out on you at three in the morning."

"Also correct."

"If I say it's not you, then you're probably going to show me the door, but it really isn't."

"I must have something to do with it. I was there," Bernie pointed out. "If you're having doubts about us being together, then—"

"I'm not." He interrupted her. "Not anymore." He looked down at his boots. "I've never dated my best friend before, and it's kind of awesome, but also scary because you know me so well."

"It's scary for me, too."

"Yeah?" He looked up.

"I've wanted this for years and now I'm living it, and

part of me still thinks it's a dream or some elaborate best friend prank when you'll eventually tell me it was all a big joke, probably on a live TV special."

His eyebrows went up. "That's a lot."

Bernie shrugged. "I've had plenty of time to construct a lot of elaborate worst-case scenarios."

"I thought that was my specialty," Luke said.

"Maybe we're both overreactive."

"That would explain it." He reached over and patted her knee. "Do you want to dump me?"

Bernie scowled at him. "You don't get to ask that question first."

"Seeing as we both agree that I'm the one behaving like an ass, I think I do." He hesitated. "I need to be better."

"You definitely need to stop dicking me around."

"But what if I can't?" His jaw clenched. "I'm not myself right now, I admit that. I'm not behaving like the Luke you think you know."

"But would the old Luke have slept with me?" Bernie had to ask.

"I don't know." He held her gaze, his blue eyes serious. "But this Luke doesn't want to stop doing that."

"Maybe I'm the one who should stop assuming I know you," Bernie said slowly.

He took her hand. "You know me better than anyone alive."

"But you've changed." She studied his familiar face. "You were different when you came back from Afghanistan. I keep trying to push you back into that box, and I shouldn't be."

"Everyone who went out there came back different," Luke said. "But I can't let that ruin everything going forward." He gripped her fingers hard. "I want to be with you and explore what we have together. Can we still do that?"

She looked down at their joined hands, at the calluses on his fingers, and felt the warm strength of his grip.

"I'm not going to keep chasing you, Luke, or waiting for you to explain yourself. If you have a problem or an issue, just *tell* me. Don't walk away."

"That's fair." He nodded. "Even if I don't understand why I'm doing something myself."

"And let me ask the questions I need to ask before you disappear on me," Bernie continued. "Because we are still best friends, and that's important."

He grimaced, his expression uncharacteristically serious. "I agree."

"Then let's keep trying, shall we?" Bernie suggested.

"I'd like that." He kissed her fingers. "Look at us talking things out like mature people." He rose to his feet. "Can I kiss you now? I've been wanting to kiss you all day."

Bernie rose, too, and faced him. "All day?"

"Yeah." He kissed her cheek. "In the line at the coffee shop." He kissed her mouth. "When you were ripping me a new one about being too alpha." He gently bit her ear, making her shudder. "When I saw you standing in the barn when I got here."

She cupped his bearded chin in her palm and brought his mouth back to hers where it belonged. For a satisfactory few minutes, the idea of kiss and make up became a reality. Eventually, she eased back an inch.

"I have to go back to Lucy's place tonight. Her plane was delayed."

"And Caleb couldn't order her up a private jet?" Luke asked. "I thought he was rich."

"Lucy probably wouldn't let him." Bernie smiled up

at him. "But it does mean that I'll be all alone there again tonight." She fluttered her eyelashes at him.

"I could come and keep you company," he offered. "I could even drive you over there when we're done."

She kissed him. "I'll need my truck for work, but I wouldn't say no to a nighttime visit."

"Then I'm your man." He grinned at her. "Do you want to see the puppy pics I took for the website? They're starting to look like little individuals now."

"I know. Three boys and three girls," Bernie said. "I'm wondering whether to give them names before the auction or leave them for the new owners to pick."

"I thought you said names helped on the website," Luke commented, and flipped through the photos on his phone. "Made them more relatable or something."

"That's true." Bernie leaned against his side, and he put his arm around her, pulling her in close while he flicked through the pics with his thumb.

"I'll send you and Bailey the best ones." He paused his scrolling. "I guess their predominate colors are going to be black and white."

"I'd love to be able to afford DNA testing to see how big they're going to be because people always want to know, and this time, I have no clue."

"Bailey said she'd do some sleuthing on the internet to see if she can find any other images that match theirs," Luke said.

"That doesn't always work. One of our rescues looked like a long-haired chihuahua mix, but when her owners did the DNA thing, it turned out she was seventy-eight percent Pomeranian." Bernie was already on the move. "Shall we see if we can get some video of them playing together? Bailey said that would be great for the website."

"Sure!" Luke followed her out of her office. "I was

thinking more about us doing some messing around, but that'll work."

She elbowed him in the side. "Later."

"It's okay, I get it. The dogs come first." He winked at her. "Literally."

"You're so not funny Luke Nilsen." Bernie kept walking.

"You sure about that?" With a whoop he gathered her up in his arms, spun her around a couple of times, and started tickling her. The problem with him knowing her so well meant he also knew all her vulnerable spots.

"Stop it!" she shrieked through her laughter. "You absolute monster!"

He threw her over his shoulder and ran toward the pile of hay at the side of the barn. Before she could even take another breath, he dropped her into the hay and followed her down, still tickling her unmercifully. At some point, she stopped being passive and actively tried to stuff hay down his shirt while energetically fighting off his wandering hands.

"Ahem."

Bernie's horrified gaze fell on a pair of well-worn cowboy boots and then upward to her dad's face.

"Sir." Luke shot to his feet. "We were just . . . having fun."

"So I see." Mike regarded him gravely. "Do you want to give my daughter a hand to get up? She's struggling like a ladybug on its back."

Luke stuck out his hand and hauled Bernie upright. Her hair was covered in hay, the top two buttons of her shirt were undone, and her cheeks were burning hot.

"We were just about to video the puppies," Luke said into the silence. "And we got distracted."

Mike turned to Bernie. "You okay?"

She nodded vigorously. "Totally."

"Then I'll leave you to it." Mike touched his hat to Luke. "Don't keep her up too long. She has an early start, just like we do."

"Yes, sir, Mr. Murphy," Luke said. "I was just leaving."

"You do know you're welcome up at the house?"

"Yes, sir."

"Then don't forget to pop by. Linda would love to see you." He paused. "Why don't you come to dinner tomorrow night?"

"I'd love to do that, sir."

"Good."

Bernie slid her hand into Luke's as they watched her dad make his leisurely way back up the drive.

"He must have seen your truck." Bernie patted her flushed cheeks. "And he came down here to make a point."

"Which I have taken on board. Next time I come over, I'll stop at the ranch house first and be polite." Luke glanced down at her. "Are you okay?"

"About my dad finding me fooling around in the hay with my best friend?" Bernie brushed hay off her shirt. "I feel like a teenager again."

"You and me both. I guess the barn really is off limits."

"Which means we have even less places to . . . get together."

Luke kept hold of her hand and pulled her along to Pandora's stall. "I had a thought about that. You know the barn where we keep the snow equipment?"

"The one with the loft-space apartment?"

Luke nodded. "We could meet up there if you don't mind coming over to my place."

Bernie considered her rapidly shrinking options. "I'm sure I could manage it. I mean, who needs sleep?"

"Have you ever thought of slowing down a tad?" Luke asked as she unlocked the stall and they went in.

"It's not in my nature," Bernie replied. "I'm either full on or off."

"Because you're dealing with a hell of a lot right now."

"I'm trying to fix that." She met his gaze. "Delegating has never been easy for me, but I'm learning how to find good people I can trust and letting them get on with what they do best."

"Like your new hire with the tats."

"Yeah, Roberto. He's basically taking over the running of the delivery part of the business. He's only just started, and he's already come up with some great ideas."

She waited to see if Luke had any pushback for her, but he just nodded, took out his phone, and crouched down to pet Pandora, who had come out of her crate to see what all the fuss was about. Thirty seconds later, her puppies spilled out from behind her. Bernie sat on the floor and encouraged them to come and say hi. Soon she had a lapful of puppies and was in heaven. She didn't realize Luke was videoing her until he started asking her questions.

"Any names coming to mind?"

She picked up the puppy who was attempting to gnaw on her wrist and scrutinized his adorable tiny face. "No idea, except maybe Mischief."

"What about the speckled white one on your left?"

"She's a darling." Bernie gave the puppy a hug. "Probably the best behaved of the bunch."

"Who's the worst?"

She pointed at his feet. "The one who's chewing your boot—except he's not bad, he's just super advanced and curious."

Luke took her through all the puppies, and she talked

about their personalities, which were emerging even at an early stage, and about how they would be old enough to leave their mother by the time the auction started. After a few awkward moments, she totally forgot he was filming her as she concentrated on showing off the puppies and simply enjoying their antics.

After a while, the puppies were worn out and retreated into the crate, where Pandora went to lick and snuggle them. Bernie rose to her feet to find Luke smiling at her.

"What?"

"I'll add amazing video personality to your long list of accomplishments. That was awesome. Bailey's going to love it!"

"You will tell her to edit most of me out, right?" Bernie asked. "It's the puppies that everyone needs to see."

He stroked her cheek. "I never thought of you as shy."

"It depends on the venue." She met his gaze. "I mean, the things that I'd like to do with your naked body aren't exactly the thoughts of a maiden aunt."

"Yeah?" His thumb rubbed over her lip and dipped into her mouth. "Maybe you can show me some of your moves later."

"Oh, you can count on it." She turned her head to suck the tip of his thumb. "Don't forget to bring the ropes."

CHAPTER THIRTEEN

It wasn't until she'd arrived at Lucy's and stowed her stuff in the spare bedroom that Bernie remembered the message Brian, her birth dad, had left her earlier in the day. The B&B was quiet as everyone was either tucked up in their beds or out on the town, which meant Bernie had time to read the message before Luke turned up.

She opened her messages and clicked on the latest one from Brian.

I'd love the opportunity to facetime or call you. Let me know your schedule and I'll put the appointment in my calendar.

Bernie considered what to do as she reread the message a hundred times. His tone was businesslike, which suited her fine, but did she actually want to look at his face while they talked—and to let him see hers? Would a phone call work better? She'd googled him and from what she could see, he didn't look anything like her. Would she be searching for that resemblance while she tried to make small talk with the man she'd never been given the opportunity to form a relationship with?

"Stop overcomplicating things," Bernie told herself. "Make a decision."

Her fingers hovered over the keys. She'd let him make the decision as to whether he wanted to see her face or not.

> Hi! I can do most workdays between eleven
> and twelve noon when I take lunch, or after
> six in the evening when I get home. I'm at
> work at four in the morning so I tend to go to
> bed early.

She was just about to put her phone away when he replied.

> Great! I'll put it in for tomorrow at eleven.
> Can't wait to speak to you and appreciate the
> opportunity. B.

Bernie stared at the text. Tomorrow? That was way sooner than she was prepared for—but maybe it was better to get it over with so she could get on with the rest of her far-too-complicated life.

She sent a text to her mom, who was usually quick to reply.

> I'm talking to Brian tomorrow. How much
> does he know about me?

> He's up to date on most things. I haven't told him
> about Luke yet.

> Any more thoughts about why he's so keen to talk
> to me? And don't tell him anything about Luke.

Her mom sent a thumbs-up. I haven't spoken to him since you contacted him, it's your business now. x. But let me know how it goes!

Bernie rolled her eyes. Her mom was a terrible gossip. Anything Bernie told her would be known by the whole family by the end of the day.

I hear Luke's coming to dinner tomorrow night. Does he like beef?

Mom, he's a rancher, of course he does, it's obligatory.

Mike said he seemed a little flustered when he saw him in the barn. ;)

Bernie grinned. They'd both been flustered. There was nothing like your dad turning up to throw cold water on your heated passion. She knew Mike would've told Linda all about it.

Mike said it was hard not to burst out laughing.

Bernie decided not to indulge her mom's obvious fishing expedition.

Beef will be fine. I'll see you tomorrow after work. Love you, Mom.

This time she did put the phone away and walked downstairs to the kitchen to make herself a hot drink before Luke arrived. She loved the B&B and had many happy memories of running through the rooms with her cousins in the long, hot summers, when everyone came home. The only sounds now were the hum of the industrial refrigerators and the gentle ticking of the clock above the large kitchen range.

She decided to make hot chocolate the old-fashioned way, with boiled milk, and soon had a mug full of chocolatey goodness topped with whipped cream in her hands. She sat at the scrubbed kitchen table and let out a sigh. It was good that Luke was coming over because it would distract her from thinking about the conversation with her dad the next day.

She yawned so hard her jaw clicked, reminding her that she'd hardly slept the night before because of Luke, and that she probably wouldn't be sleeping much again that night. Setting her mug on the table, she propped her head against her hand and yawned again. Leaving her phone upstairs hadn't been the smartest idea because now she had no clue when Luke would turn up.

Her eyes closed and she hurriedly picked up her mug. She'd best drink her hot chocolate and make her way back upstairs to wait for Luke in Lucy's sitting room before the warmth and the peacefulness of the kitchen sent her off to sleep. But it was almost too nice to move. . . .

Max fixed Luke with a penetrating stare across the dinner table. "I guess we'd all like to know if you've taken on another job, boss."

Luke frowned at him. "What the hell are you talking about?"

"You keep disappearing," Max said as he forked up a

piece of roast pork and slowly chewed. "It's like you're never here."

"Bullshit. Sorry, Mom."

"It's a good thing Sky's already in bed," his mom said. "Because your language could do with some cleaning up, son."

"Like Noah never curses," Max said.

"Not in front of Sky." Noah leaned in a little as he spoke, his expression not friendly. "I promised Jen."

"And he's keeping his promise." Jen intervened before Max and Noah got into it. "Which I appreciate." She stroked Noah's arm until he sat back in his chair.

"Anyway, back to you, Luke." Max obviously wasn't done. "What's going on?"

"Are you saying I'm not pulling my weight on my own ranch?" Luke asked, aware of an unaccustomed tide of anger rising through his gut.

"Maybe." Max glanced at Noah. "What do you think?"

"None of my business."

Max raised an eyebrow. "One little comment about your cursing and now you won't back me up. We were talking about this earlier!"

"One, I'll always back you up even when you're being a complete jerk, and two, I said I was worried about Luke, not that he wasn't doing his share of the work." Noah held Max's gaze. "Don't twist my words."

"You said it was hard to allocate work when you weren't sure where the boss would be," Max replied. "That's exactly what I'm asking him."

"Hey." Luke raised his voice over the others as they both spoke at once. "I am here, so don't talk about me as if I'm not. If you schedule the work, I'll do my share. That's all I have to say about it."

Noah folded his arms. "Good enough for me."

"I'm trying to restructure our debt, get new loans and opportunities, talk to Joel and Patty, and run this god-damned place," Luke continued. "If it's not good enough for you, Max, you don't have to stay."

Silence fell around the table as everyone looked at him. Luke kept his attention on Max, who was glaring at him.

"Nice attitude, boss. You really know how to motivate your workforce."

Luke held up his hands. "I can't deal with you right now, bro. I don't have the time or the energy to work through all your shit."

Max stood up, threw his napkin onto the table, and walked out.

Luke let out his breath. "That went well." No one said anything, and he glanced around the table. "You think I was too harsh?"

His mom nodded. "You know what Max is like—"

"Yeah, I do, and I know why, but that doesn't give him a free pass to question and insult everything I do." Luke wasn't in the mood to back down. "Noah and I were right there with him through everything. I don't see anyone making the same kind of allowances for us as we constantly make for Max."

"But—"

Luke turned to his mom. "Please don't make excuses for him that you wouldn't make for me."

"That's not fair." She met his gaze.

"Neither is everyone coddling Max, but I'm obviously the only one who feels this way."

"With all due respect, boss," Noah said, "you're usually the one stopping me from punching Max's lights out."

"Then maybe I've changed my mind." Luke stood up and started clearing the plates. "And for the record, once

I've finished up here, I'm going to see Bernie. Anyone have a problem with that?"

There was no sign of Max when Luke went out to the barn to check that everything was good for the night. Max had obviously been there because all the chores were done, and the place was as spotless as a barn could be. Max's truck was still in place, but his horse was gone. Luke considered whether to text him and decided to wait until he was certain his temper was under control. He had no idea why he'd lost it so badly earlier, but sometimes Max got under his skin and wouldn't stop digging. And he was tired—tired of all the shit he was dealing with, and he truly didn't need his friend undermining him in front of the people he loved.

Luke blinked as he found his keys and got into the truck. He hadn't expected everyone around the table to treat him as if he was the bad guy. The trouble was, they were all so used to tiptoeing around Max's delicate sensibilities that Luke being the one telling him to knock it off had come as a shock. He started the engine and stared out into the darkness. Either he should've toughened up sooner or he *was* the bad guy. Maybe Bernie could help him sort it out.

He drove to town, breathing a sigh of relief when he emerged from the all-encompassing forest into the lights on Main Street. He still wasn't comfortable driving even these familiar roads after dark, and venturing farther than town gave him chills. The B&B was lit up like a Christmas tree, which was just how Lucy liked it. She said it had to be a beacon of warmth and welcome just as her grandma would've wanted, and Luke couldn't argue with that. He parked around the back and made his way to the kitchen door. He tried the handle, but it was locked.

He could see into the room through the glass-paneled door. A large cat sat on a cushion beside the range. Bernie was at the table, her head lowered into the cradle of her arms.

Luke frowned and tapped gently on the glass. She didn't move, and he knocked harder. Gripped by a sense of urgency, he made his way around to the front of the hotel and went into the lobby. There was no one at the reception desk, so he kept on going right through to the kitchen.

"Bernie, what the hell?"

He paused as he registered that she was breathing steadily and not in any apparent distress. He gently touched her shoulder, and she responded with a muffled squeak and an attempt to raise her head.

"It's only me." Luke decided to leave his lecture about the hotel being open to all callers for when Bernie was more awake. "You fell asleep in the kitchen."

"Oh . . ." She yawned and lowered her head again. "Sorry. I need to . . . lock up I guess."

"I'll do that." He took a firm hold of her elbow and eased her to her feet. "Go to bed. I'll join you in a minute."

"Okay." She leaned hard on his arm as he helped her toward the door. "The guests all have their own keys to the front door, but don't set the alarm."

"I won't." He gave her a gentle push in the direction of the stairs.

It didn't take long to check the doors and make sure they were secure. The rush of adrenaline that had coursed through him when he'd been unable to rouse Bernie had retreated, leaving his legs heavy and his head fighting the beginnings of a headache.

By the time he got upstairs, Bernie was fast asleep in bed. He contemplated driving back to the ranch, but he was exhausted, and the thought of curling up next to her while she slept was appealing. He took a couple of painkillers, stripped down to his boxers, and got in bed. She sighed and patted his hand as he wrapped himself around her. She didn't like him suggesting she'd taken on too much, but he was starting to worry about her. Experience told him that she wouldn't listen to a word he said until she hit her own wall.

Which reminded him of somebody. . . .

They were both remarkably stubborn in their own quiet ways. Noah was brutally honest about how he felt and not shy about telling you. Max was the complete opposite—always hiding behind a smokescreen of jokes and jabs that made him exasperating to deal with. Luke had always prided himself on being the calm center of his friends' extremes, but was he still that man? His current behavior wasn't calm or rational. He was making ultimatums, upsetting his mom, dating his best friend, and getting angry for no apparent reason. He didn't like himself much right now, but he wasn't sure how to get back on the right path.

He turned onto his back and stared up at the ceiling, all desire to sleep suddenly deserting him. He'd told everyone he was looking for a therapist, and he hadn't done that, either. . . . He wasn't used to lying, and he really had meant to reach out to one of the contacts his mom and the VA had offered him—except life had gotten crazy and he hadn't done it.

He needed to make those calls. The people who loved him deserved to get the best of him, not the worst.

He yawned and allowed his eyes to close as he reached out to touch Bernie's auburn hair, which streamed across the pillow. If he could get through the night without any nightmares, he'd make amends to everyone in the morning.

"Oh my God!" Lucy's screech woke Bernie with a jolt. "I didn't realize—I mean you two are *dating*? Luke Nilsen's naked in there with you?"

Lucy was practically vibrating with a mixture of embarrassment and enjoyment as she hovered in the doorway, her hand pressed to her cheek.

Bernie gazed blearily at her cousin. "Can you go away? Just for a minute?"

Lucy nodded energetically. "I'll get the coffee on."

Bernie grabbed her cell and realized they'd slept in. She sent a hurried text to Anton and leapt out of bed.

"Dibs on the shower!"

"What?"

Luke's blond hair was sticking straight up, he had the best stubble, and he was half-naked and warm in her bed, and she had to leave him there like a beautiful, unwrapped present.

"I'm late for work," she shouted over her shoulder as she rushed into the bathroom.

"Crap!" Luke wasn't far behind her. She barely had the shower on before he joined her in it. "I forgot to set my alarm, too."

She grabbed the shower gel, slapped a handful on his chest and rubbed energetically. "Get moving. I don't have time to wash my hair."

His hand slid over her hip, stilling her frantic motions as he crowded her back against the wall.

"Why the rush? We're both late, we can take a few minutes to enjoy each other."

"With Lucy likely to pop in with some coffee?"

"I locked the bathroom door." Luke's callused fingers continued their downward glide. "And I really, really want to be inside you right now."

Bernie's knees trembled as he leaned in and kissed her with a slow thoroughness that made her reach for his shoulders and hang on. His thumb pressed against her clit in a circular motion as he pressed his thrusting fingers upward.

"Okay," she murmured against his neck. "I think I can . . . fit you in for a few minutes."

"That's very good of you." He lifted her and fitted himself against her with one smooth upward thrust of his hips, pinning her against the wall. "I promise I'll make it worth your while."

A few frantic minutes later, Bernie started to come for the second time and Luke groaned. "I need to pull out, I don't have a condom on."

She dug her heel into his muscled ass. "I'm on the pill. Don't you dare stop now."

"You sure?" he said hoarsely. "I mean . . ."

"Yes!" She kicked him hard for emphasis. "Just do it!"

After a quick toweling off, Bernie got dressed, kissed Luke goodbye, and let him out the front door before going into the kitchen to find Lucy. Her cousin had already poured her a mug of coffee and set two slices of raisin toast on a plate beside it.

"Thank you." Bernie sat down, drank half the coffee, and started on the toast. "Just how I like it."

Lucy tapped her forehead. "I like to remember my guests' requirements."

"I try and do the same at the café," Bernie said.

Lucy sipped her own coffee and stared intently at Bernie. "Are you going to tell me about you and Luke?"

"Not much to say, really."

Lucy's eyebrows rose. "I never knew you had a crush on him. I mean, everyone knew how I felt about Caleb—except him—but I thought you and Luke were genuinely just best friends."

"We are friends." Bernie drank more coffee. "Just with benefits, right now."

"So it's not a permanent thing? Just a hookup?" Lucy frowned. "That's not like you."

"It is what it is." Bernie shrugged. "We're just enjoying the moment."

"Still so not like you." Lucy pursed her lips. "I don't want you to get hurt, Bernie."

Bernie smiled at her cousin. "I don't intend to. I guess we're trying to see if it sticks."

"But what if it doesn't and you destroy your friendship? You'll have to see each other for the rest of your lives."

"I think we're mature enough not to let that happen." Bernie finished her coffee. "And it would be nice if you could be happy for me rather than reminding me of all the things that might go wrong. You're usually the most positive person I know."

Lucy rose to her feet, rushed around the table, and bent to hug Bernie. "Of course I want you and Luke to live happily ever after! I just worry about you so much!"

Bernie patted her cousin's arm. "I have to go."

Lucy held on. "Only if you forgive me."

"I forgive you, now let me go."

"Sorry." Lucy kissed the top of Bernie's head and got out of the way. "I love you so much, and thanks for looking after the B&B for me."

"My pleasure." Bernie stood up. "How did the wedding planning go?"

Lucy made a face. "As badly as I expected now that my mom is involved. I just want to have the wedding here, and she wants some elaborate ceremony in Seattle so all her friends can come."

"Doesn't Caleb have friends there, too?" Bernie asked as she put on her coat and grabbed her backpack.

"He's a nerd; his friends don't emerge in daylight or have the social skills to deal with a public occasion."

"Harsh. I'm sure some of them would risk it for Caleb."

Lucy sighed. "I hadn't thought of that. I'll ask him whether he wants the Seattle thing as well as a celebration here. He didn't say much when my mom was getting into it, but that's just how he is. And to be fair, neither of us got much of an opportunity to talk while Mom was in full flow."

"Then talk to Caleb and tell your mom what you both want for your wedding," Bernie said firmly. "It's about you, not her."

Bernie's aunt was a formidable organizer who tended to think she knew what was right for everyone. Lucy had always struggled to express herself against her mother's wishes.

"This time I will do that." Lucy kissed her cheek. "Now, go to work and don't forget to send those doughnuts over. My guests love them for breakfast."

"I won't." Bernie smiled at her cousin.

"And if you and Luke ever need a quiet corner to . . . sleep . . . or simply be together, you can always ask if I have any spare rooms," Lucy suggested.

"That's very sweet of you." Bernie blew her cousin a kiss and went out the kitchen door. Her café was literally across the street, so she'd be at work in no time.

There was little traffic in town at this early hour and Main Street was quiet. It was far busier in the summer when the tourists came through. Bernie didn't mind them. Most of the town's businesses relied on that income to see them through the lean snowed-in winters. She tried to keep her café open year-round for the locals, but sometimes she couldn't make it into town when the snow came down too hard.

She checked the time, noting she was two hours late and hoped her new team had coped without her. A year ago she would've been screwed because she'd been doing almost everything herself. To her relief, the lights were on at the front of the café, Kenya was stocking the counter with freshly baked goodies, and the smell of baking bread wafted through from the kitchens. Maybe this whole delegating thing was a good idea.

"Hey, boss lady!" Kenya called out as she came toward the counter. "You okay?"

"I forgot to set my alarm," Bernie confessed as she went past Kenya into the kitchen. "Sorry I'm late."

Anton and Rob briefly looked up when she entered and then returned to their work.

"What do you want me to start on?" Bernie asked Anton.

"Check the ovens. The first batches of bread should be coming out any minute now." He grinned at Bernie. "Good night?"

"The best. I fell asleep over my laptop, forgot to set my alarm, and slept like a baby for eight hours."

"I'm jealous."

Bernie washed her hands and put on her apron. "I was taking care of the B&B so at least I was close."

Rob cleared his throat. "Ms. Smith at the B&B will want her usual two dozen doughnuts, right?"

Bernie nodded.

"They'll be done by eight. I'll walk them over."

"Awesome." Bernie checked the ovens, put on her protective gloves, and started sliding trays out of the fiery heat and onto the cooling racks. "Everything looks great."

"We can manage without you, boss," Anton said.

"Good to know." Bernie slammed the oven door shut and made sure it was secure. "What's going in here next?"

Five hours later she was sitting on the side porch of the café with her laptop and phone in front of her, waiting for Brian to call. Because she'd arrived late, she'd been far too busy to worry about what she was going to say, but the longer she sat there, the worse her nerves became. Why the hell had she agreed to talk to him? They had zero in common, and she had nothing she wanted to say to him. She jumped like a newborn fawn when her cell buzzed with his number, and then she hit accept.

"Hi!" His face filled the screen. "Bernie."

"Yup!" Okay so they were facetiming. She stared at him, searching for anything she might see in her own mirror every day and finding nothing. He had short brown hair that was graying at the temples, blue eyes, and a narrow mouth.

"You look like your mom." He'd obviously been making his own observations as he studied her. "I always loved her auburn hair."

Bernie patted her head. "It's somewhere between a blessing and a curse."

He laughed, and something about his smile was very familiar. "I hear you're running multiple businesses out of your coffee shop."

"Well, they're all variants of the same thing—my love of baking. I just thought that considering the current climate, it would be good to diversify."

"Excellent thinking. I've been trying to do something similar in the last couple of years." He paused. "That's probably why I'm on my second divorce. I tend to hyperfocus and forget to nurture my other commitments and relationships."

Bernie had a moment of sympathy. "Mom says I'm the same. She thinks I'm doing too much as it is."

"She might have mentioned something along those lines." His smile was wry. "But I can't exactly tell you not to do anything that I'd do myself."

"I didn't realize you guys talked so much."

"We reconnected a couple of years ago when I needed some information for my new will."

Bernie considered how much she wanted to know about that and why her mom had downplayed it. Would she sound mercenary or simply nosy? Better to wait and see what he wanted to tell her.

"Okay." She nodded. "Makes sense."

"Linda didn't tell you that?"

Bernie shrugged. "She might have mentioned it at the time, but to be honest, I wasn't interested in hearing anything about you at that point."

He grimaced. "I guess I deserved that. I haven't exactly been father of the year, have I?"

"Mom said you always made your monthly child support payments on time."

"That's the bare minimum I could've done." Brian

sighed. "I was in such a hurry to be successful that I forgot everything else that matters."

"It's okay." Bernie wasn't willing to feel sorry for him in the slightest. "Mom married a good man who's been the best dad ever."

"I'm glad about that. Linda and you deserved way better than me."

Bernie just looked at him, and he surprised her by laughing.

"You remind me so much of Linda right now. She could always see right through me." His expression sobered. "I guess you'd like to know why I wanted to connect with you."

"I'm sure it wasn't to talk about my business. And I don't even know what you're doing with your life. Google seems to think you disappeared two years ago."

"Actually, that's a really good stepping off point for the rest of this conversation," Brian said. "As I mentioned before, a couple of years ago, the public story goes that I decided to step back from my company. That wasn't quite the truth. I was forced to do so because of my health. At the same time, my wife, who didn't sign on to deal with a burned-out basket case, decided to divorce me." He shrugged. "I don't blame her. We didn't have any kids, and she's about to remarry a mutual friend of ours. We're all good with that outcome."

Bernie wasn't touching any of that. "Mom said you were in tech."

"Yeah. After a few doomed startups, I created a data analytics company about ten years ago, and it's done really well."

"Doing what exactly?" Bernie couldn't help being curious. It was such a different world.

"To put it in layman's terms, every time you click on something on the internet, my software takes that information and feeds it back to the companies that want to know all about you."

"So it's basically spying."

"In a way, but these companies legally buy my software to get that feedback and use it to better market their products to you."

"Which is why if I click on a pair of boots, I immediately get four hundred ads for more pairs of boots."

"Exactly." Brian nodded. "I wrote the original code, so I'm the founder of the company, and I still own the majority of shares."

"I guess that means you can take a few years off."

"I can if my board is okay with it." He paused. "In this instance, I also had a medical issue that had gotten worse because I refused to take time off and deal with it when it was far more treatable. The board and my doctors insisted I stop acting as CEO and, for the first time in my life, outvoted me."

"This was because you were burned out and sick?"

"Yeah, I had testicular cancer. Kind of a double whammy." He sighed. "I'm on the mend now, but it sure was a wake-up call."

Bernie decided to be honest. "That's all very . . . interesting . . . but I'm still not sure what any of it has to do with me."

"You're my only child. The treatments I had means the likelihood of another kid are minimal."

"Didn't you, um, freeze your sperm?" Bernie blushed. "I can't believe I just said that."

"I did, but the chances of me wanting to be a father at

my age are relatively low, and I'm gun-shy of marrying again and going through another costly divorce."

"That's hardly a positive attitude," Bernie pointed out. "You might meet someone who makes you change your mind."

"But I don't need to. I have you."

Bernie folded her arms. "Okay, I don't want to sound rude, but I'm not some late-in-life consolation prize because I'm your kid. You've had nothing to do with raising me or making me the person that I am."

"I'm well aware of that. Linda made it very clear that neither of you owed me anything." He hesitated. "I have made financial settlements for both of you in my will, but that's something you'll have to deal with when I'm no longer around to argue."

"So what do you want?" Bernie asked.

He shrugged. "Just a connection. I'd like to be someone you might occasionally check in with if you have good news, or if you wanted to have dinner with me when you were in the Bay Area . . . anything you want really."

"That's super vague."

Brian smiled. "I'm trying not to scare you off."

"I'm still not getting the point of this. You've apologized for not being around, I've told you that I had great parents who brought me up right—surely that's all we need to say to one another."

"If that's all you need from me then yeah, I suppose we are done." He hesitated. "But to circle back to your original question, I think your mom hoped I might offer you some business advice."

"Wait—are you saying she reached out to you?"

Brian held up his hands. "I'm not suggesting anything of the kind. I just got the impression she thinks we're similar and that I might understand your drive to succeed better than she can and stop you from making the same mistakes I did." He paused. "She's worried about you, Bernadette."

"Bernie. No one calls me that unless they're mad at me."

"Sorry, Bernie."

"I think I need to talk to my mom."

"Sure." Brian nodded. "It was nice talking to you—I really mean that."

"Same," Bernie replied automatically. "Bye."

She ended the call and sat there staring at the wall as her brain danced a complicated jig around a wide chasm filled with emotions. Her cell buzzed, and she saw a text from Luke and opened it.

See you at the snowmobile shed at 8?

No can do, you're having dinner at my place at six, remember? Bernie typed back.

Dammit. I forgot. See you there.

She flipped through to her mom's text thread and paused. This wasn't a conversation to be having over text. She'd have to hold everything in until she got home, and they could speak face to face.

It wasn't until Luke sat down for lunch that he realized something wasn't right. Jen was quiet, Sky was behaving himself, and Noah was muttering under his breath a lot.

"Where's Mom?" Luke asked.

"She's out on call," Jen answered as she handed Sky some toast and jelly.

"She's not supposed to be doing that anymore." Luke

ate his ham sandwich and tried to ignore the pleading looks from his mom's dogs, Winky and Blinky.

"It got busy today," Jen replied. "And it was one of her favorite patients."

"That figures." Luke chewed his food. "Where's Max?"

Noah looked at him. "No idea."

"I thought we had a schedule these days."

"We do, but it's hard to schedule someone who hasn't turned up for work."

"He's not here?" Luke stopped mid bite. "Have you checked all the usual places?"

"No, boss, I've just sat here on my ass all morning twiddling my thumbs," Noah said. "Of course, I've checked. There's no sign of him anywhere."

"He had his horse with him last night." Luke remembered.

"I found Bouncer in the pasture behind the stables this morning. His tack and saddle were on the fence."

"What about his truck?" Luke asked.

"It's gone, and his room is empty." Noah scowled at Luke. "He didn't leave a note."

"You're blaming me?" Luke glared right back. "Max is a grown-ass man. If he chooses to get offended about being called out and disappears, then it's on him. And it's not exactly the first time he's done a midnight flit, is it? He always turns up in a day or two."

"Luke's right, Noah," Jen chimed in. "I'm sorry, but this is a crisis that's been brewing ever since I got here, and it's totally on Max."

Noah sat back and ran a hand over his bearded jaw. "Okay, fine. You've both convinced me. Now, what do we do?"

"I'm not sure we can do anything," Luke tried to sound more confident than he felt.

"We could drive over to some of the towns close by and see if he's been through," Noah suggested. "Max always makes a splash."

"We don't have time," Luke said quickly. "And I don't want to be stuck on the road at night."

Noah gave him a look but didn't comment, and Luke continued.

"Max will make his own mind up in his own time. We can text him to check if he's okay and make sure he knows he can come back whenever he wants, but after that, it's on him."

"This is going to screw up my spreadsheet," Noah growled. "We'll have to get extra help now, and I didn't budget for that this month."

"We'll manage," Luke said. "We always do."

Noah fixed him with a steely stare. "Only if you commit one hundred percent to being here right now and not disappearing on me, too."

"I will." Luke crossed his heart. "It's my ranch. I won't let you down."

He was still pondering that promise when he walked over to the barn to bring Max's horse, Bouncer, from the pasture into his stall. It wasn't a great time for Max to walk out, and Max knew that. But as Jen had pointed out, there was a feeling of inevitability about Max imploding at some point. Luke just wished it hadn't happened right now, when everything else was up in the air. He'd sent a text to Bernie asking her to meet him at eight and been re-minded he was due for dinner with the whole Murphy clan. After their exploits in the shower that morning, he wasn't going to miss that meeting, so he needed to get on with Max's share of the chores before Noah started breathing down his neck.

Bernie opened the door to Luke and despite her smile, he noted she seemed tense. She went on tiptoe to kiss him and cupped his jaw.

"I'm glad you didn't shave off your beard."

"I wouldn't dare." He kissed her back. "How was your day?"

"Busy and complicated." She took his hand and drew him into the kitchen. "I spoke to Brian."

"Yeah?" Before Luke could ask anything more Linda came toward him, her arms open wide, and gave him a big hug.

"It's so good to see you, Luke!"

Mike offered him his hand. "What she means is that it's better than the rear end of your truck disappearing down the drive."

"I apologize for that, sir. I was trying not to disturb you." Luke shook Mike's hand. "I'll make sure to pop in more regularly."

Absentmindedly, he tried to pet Bernie's cat, who made a low growling sound in the back of her throat, which made him whip his hand back. Cleopatra still had it in for him, and he had no idea why. She retreated to the back of the couch and glared at him. He didn't dare sit down.

He turned to the kitchen where Mary and the twins were busy getting food out of the oven. "Can I help?"

"No, you just sit yourself at the table and we'll be done in a minute." Linda pulled out a chair for him. "Mary? Don't forget the gravy."

"How could I forget it when it's right in front of me?"

Mary asked as she went past Luke carrying a large jug. "Hi, Luke."

"How's college going?" Luke asked as he moved a mat out of the way to let Mary set the jug down on the table.

"Great, although I've already finished my coursework for the year, and no one seems to know what to do about that." Mary frowned as she readjusted the napkins. "I want to go on to next year's work, but apparently that's not possible."

"I guess they've never dealt with someone like you before," Luke said. "You'll have to forge a new path and take them along for the ride."

"That's my intention. I'm planning on staging a sit-in at the dean's office starting tomorrow."

"That's my girl," Mike murmured.

Mary beamed at him. "You'll bail me out of jail if I get arrested, right?"

"Sure I will, honey." Mike patted her shoulder as she walked past him. "Anytime."

Luke concealed a smile as the rest of the Murphy family pretended that Mary was just an average teenager rather than a fast-developing genius.

"If I finish this coding degree this year, I can focus on my master's or PhD, and maybe take the nursing qualifications as well," Mary said as she set a warm plate in front of Luke. "In fact, I might start applying now."

"Good idea." Luke breathed in the smell of roast beef with all the trimmings and unfolded his napkin. "The food looks great, Mrs. Murphy."

"You can still call me Linda, you know." Bernie's mom took her seat at the other end of the table, the twins to her left and Mary to her right. Bernie sat opposite Luke

on her dad's left hand. "I know you and Bernie are officially dating now, but there's no need to be formal."

"You're dating?" Mary looked up. "What about Oliver?"

"Olly and I are just friends," Bernie said as the twins
nudged each other and grinned. "I already told you that."

"Maybe he'll date me." Mary cut a piece of beef and
chewed thoroughly. "I like a man who is passionate about
his work."

"He's too old for you," Bernie said. "And you need to
finish your education."

"I can multitask," Mary said. "I'm quite good at it."

Luke glanced over at Bernie, who didn't look her normal
happy self. She was frowning down at her food as if she
thought it was poisoned and was not really eating. The
twins chatted with each other and put away quantities of
beef Luke couldn't imagine eating anymore. Linda kept
the conversation going with help from Mike, and Luke
played his part, answering ranch questions and family
stuff when called upon.

It wasn't until the twins and Mary were given permission
to leave the table to do their homework and Mike was busy
cleaning up in the kitchen that Luke nudged Bernie's foot
under the table.

"Are you okay?" he asked quietly.

"She's always tired these days." Unfortunately, Linda
who had brought the coffeepot and mugs over to the table
overheard him. "I keep telling her she's doing too much."

Bernie looked up. "I hear you've been telling a lot of
people that."

"It's no secret that I think you're overdoing it." Linda
sat down and poured them all coffee.

"Is that why you asked Brian to talk to me?"

Luke tensed as Linda frowned. "I beg your pardon?"

"Brian accidentally let on that you told him I was too focused on my work."

"I might have mentioned it." Linda looked inquiringly at Bernie. "Why wouldn't you want his advice? He's a very successful man who happens to share half your DNA, which means he knows what makes you tick."

"He doesn't know me at *all*, Mom. He walked out when I was three."

"But—"

"Can you stop defending him?" Bernie held up her hand. "I'm kind of mad at you about this."

It was the closest Luke had ever seen to the two women falling out. His gaze met Mike's, who had gone still in the kitchen, his attention fixed on the discussion at the dining table.

"I thought you said he initiated contact." Bernie obviously wasn't ready to let it go.

"He did! He was rewriting his will and contacted me to let me know that we'd both be included."

"That was two years ago," Bernie said flatly.

"And there was a lot of legal stuff to sort out, which meant we kept in touch." Linda raised her eyebrows. "I was only trying to make sure he got some sense of the amazing person you'd become."

"Except you also told him that I was overdoing it. You said I was turning out to be way more like him than you had imagined, and that you didn't know how to stop me repeating his stupid mistakes."

"It wasn't like that at all." Linda clutched her coffee mug. "We just got to chatting, and of course you came up in the conversation, and I knew he'd understand my concerns because I'd said the same things to him." She looked over at Mike. "Can you back me up, here? You heard everything I said."

Mike turned to Bernie. "Your mom meant no harm. She's just worried about you. We all are."

"Yet none of you have noticed all the changes I've made in the past six months? The new people I've employed, the new software for the automatic ordering process?" Bernie looked between her parents. "The way I've been delegating so that I'm not the one doing everything? Has anyone asked me about that?"

She placed her napkin on the table. "No one has because you've all been too busy repeating that Bernie isn't good enough, isn't capable enough, is doing too much, and is heading for a disaster, to actually appreciate how much I've achieved." She stared at her mom. "I'm not Brian, and I don't appreciate you involving him in our lives after telling me that he wasn't worth it for the past twenty-three years."

"That's not fair," Linda protested. "Everything I've done has been in your best interests, I swear."

"Including asking Brian to give me business advice even though he's never been worthy of being a father?" Bernie stood and looked at Luke. "Can you take me over to your place? I feel like I need some fresh air."

"Sure."

"Thank you." Bernie turned to her mom, who looked shell-shocked. "I'm sorry if I hurt you, but I really need you to stop making assumptions about me that just aren't true. If you can believe Mary will have her PhD done in a year, why can't you believe I'll have three successful businesses?"

"That's different," Linda said. "Mike—"

"Mike's her father, and he isn't mine," Bernie said, interrupting her mom. "I get it." She smiled at Luke. "Shall we go? I won't stay out late, I promise."

* * *

Bernie only realized she was shaking when Luke reached across and draped his spare jacket around her shoulders. She'd never been good at confrontations, and she and her mom usually got on so well that calling her out was hard.

"Not the first time I've wished I had one of those fancy new trucks with the seat warmers," he commented. "It's still cold out here when it gets dark."

"I'm not cold. It's just how my body reacts when I get angry." Bernie grabbed the edges of the jacket and held them tight. "Sorry I ruined your evening."

"You could never do that." Luke turned out onto the county road and headed back toward his ranch. "Now, if you'd gone off before I got to eat that delicious beef, I might be mad at you, but you had the decency to wait until we got to the coffee."

"You're welcome." Bernie tried to find a smile somewhere. "Was I totally out of line?"

"Not for me to say."

"You were right there," Bernie pointed out. "You heard every word."

"Yeah, but you know I can't comment on your family. The moment I say anything, you'll turn it around and make me the bad guy."

"True," Bernie conceded. "But did I sound really mean?"

"You sounded upset and angry." He paused. "And I get why you felt like that."

"I've probably made Mom cry. Mike's going to be mad at me."

"I think Mike's wise enough not to get involved between a mother and her daughter."

"But he's her husband and I'm only his stepdaughter." There it was—the painful thing that could never be changed no matter how much she wished otherwise.

"He adopted you, right?"

"Yes."

"He didn't have to do that."

"Mom probably made him."

Luke glanced over as he turned off the main road and stopped at the upper gate to his place. It was hard to see his expression when his face was in shadow, but his voice was calm. "I don't think anyone could make Mike Murphy do anything he didn't want to do."

His answer was surprisingly comforting.

"He's probably regretting it right now," Bernie said gloomily.

"I doubt it." Luke put on his high beams as the forest closed in around them. "Do you want to come up to the house or would you prefer some privacy?"

Bernie groaned. "If I can't deal with my own family, I hate to think what I might say to yours."

"Then we'll stop at the snowmobile barn." Luke craned forward to see over the next ridge and down into the flat valley below where the main ranch buildings were situated. "I left the outside light on so it should be easy to spot."

Bernie sat back and let him drive, her thoughts so jumbled that speaking or even pretending that everything was okay was beyond her. The good thing about Luke was that because he'd seen her get mad before, he knew how it affected her.

"I've always been scared that Mike would decide I wasn't good enough for his family."

The words escaped her before she realized it. Luke stopped the truck in front of the building and turned off

the ignition. He reached for her hand and held on to it in
the darkness.

"Bernie . . ."

"I'm a grown-ass woman and it still makes me shake
with fear."

Luke squeezed her fingers. "It doesn't matter how old
you are, sweetheart. Some things just drag you right back
into the worst moments of your life."

After a long pause, she managed a shaky laugh. "Okay,
let's get out before we freeze to death."

He released her hand and came around the truck to
help her down, carefully rearranging his jacket over her
shoulders.

"It's not that cold." Luke murmured and kissed the top
of her head.

She looked up at the millions of stars in the night sky
and made herself breathe slowly. She reminded herself
that her entire life span represented a minute speck in the
universe and that it was a privilege to be alive and expe-
riencing anything.

"Come on." Luke reclaimed her hand and led her
toward the door. "I left the fire on so it should be nice and
warm upstairs."

The lower half of the barn contained three snowmo-
biles and various supplies to see the people and animals
on the ranch through the harsh winter months. It smelled
faintly of motor oil and fertilizer—a smell so familiar
Bernie hardly noticed it. She took off her boots, followed
Luke up the stairs, and paused at the top.

"I'd forgotten how nice it is up here."

There were two couches, one of which looked like a
sleeper, a wood burning stove, a small kitchen, and thick
rugs covering the wooden floorboards. A big window

looked out toward the unending forest, and most of the walls were solid piled rock.

"We made some improvements in the last year." Luke took off his coat, checked the wood burner, and went into the kitchen. "Noah and Jen like to get away from Sky sometimes, and this is nice, close, and private."

Bernie set Luke's spare jacket on the back of the couch and unzipped her own. In the blur of leaving, she didn't even remember putting it on.

Luke held up the coffee jug, and she shook her head. "I'm already anxious. Do you have anything else?"

Luke checked the refrigerator. "We have beer, milk, bottled water, and hot cocoa."

"I think I'd like a beer."

His eyebrows rose but he took two bottles out of the refrigerator, opened them, and handed one over.

"Here's to us."

She clinked her bottle against his. "Because no one understands us?"

"Works for me." He sighed. "Max has gone AWOL, and everyone's blaming me for being too hard on him."

"What did you say?"

"Told him not to question my commitment to my own ranch, and that if he didn't like the way I was handling things, he didn't have to stay."

"Ah." Bernie drank some beer. "I bet that went down well."

"It needed to be said." Luke wasn't smiling. "I've poured everything I have into the ranch, and Max suggesting I'm never here was just the last straw."

"He certainly knows how to hit all the tender spots."

"He's a master at it." Luke sighed. "And this time he got me on the wrong day, and I let him have it." He walked over to the couch and patted the seat beside him.

"Come and sit by the fire. It's way more comfortable than the kitchen."

"He usually comes back, doesn't he?" Bernie asked as she settled against Luke's side.

He immediately put his arm around her. "Eventually. And then he pretends nothing happened, which grinds my gears."

"Sally says he needs therapy."

"We all need it in our own ways." He cleared his throat. "I am actively doing something about that for myself."

"That's good." She took a sip of beer and tried to relax, which only meant that all the horrible things she'd said to her mom came rushing back to fill the void.

"Hey." Luke hugged her. "It's okay. I know it's not my place to say anything, but you spoke your truth." He hesitated. "And I guess we've all tended to downplay your abilities over the last few years because you just get on with shit."

"When you have an actual genius in the family like Mary, everything else must seem ordinary." Bernie tried to be fair. "But sometimes . . ." Her words caught in her throat as tears threatened. "I just wish I was enough."

Luke took the bottle out of her hand, set it on the table, and took hold of her shoulders. "You are enough. You're amazing, and talented, and funny, and . . ."

"Fantastic in bed?"

"Absolutely the best lay I've ever had." Luke held her gaze. "I mean it."

"That's"—her breath hitched—"a really sweet thing to say."

"You don't make me feel sweet." Luke kissed her with a rough thoroughness that left her gasping. "You make me hot and hard as hell. I want to strip you naked, tie you to my bed, and never let you leave."

Bernie gazed at him and fluttered her eyelashes. "But what about work?"

His lips twitched. "Maybe I'd let you get up to bake your bread. It's so damn good."

She bit his lower lip. "I like a man who is willing to compromise." She fiddled with the top button of his shirt. "Can we get naked?"

"I wasn't sure if you'd be in the mood to—" He abruptly stopped talking as she cupped his groin. "Okay, I obviously misjudged you."

She attacked his shirt buttons and wrestled with the top of his jeans while he cursed and reciprocated until their clothes were flying everywhere and they were tangled together and laughing. She pushed him over onto his back and straddled him.

"That's better."

"I like the view." He raised his head to lick her nipple, and she shuddered. "I've got a condom in the pocket of my jeans if you want to put it on me."

"Then I'd have to move." She rocked against him, her wet panties catching on the hardness of his dick.

"Better you than me." He leaned down and somehow found his jeans. "Here you go."

Two seconds after she'd covered him, he tore off her panties, and she climbed on board, making them both gasp with the swiftness of their joining.

"That's . . ." Bernie squeezed her internal muscles, and his hand came up to grab her hip and hold her down ". . . just what I needed."

"I feel so used," Luke murmured. "But I kind of like it."

She rose over him and established a fast rhythm that made her forget about anything but him, her need, and the pleasure he was sharing with her. For a few minutes nothing else mattered, and that was just what she wanted.

She climaxed with a scream and fell forward, her hair streaming over his chest as he fought not to come with her, her heart pounding as waves of intense pleasure coursed through her.

"Dammit," Luke growled. "I can't hold on—" He joined her in a fiery climax, his fingers biting into her waist as he thrust upward to fulfillment.

Bernie gently rolled off him and fell onto the rug.

"Hey." Luke looked down at her, his blue-eyed gaze intense. "Where did you go?"

"I forgot we were on the couch." She smiled back at him. "It didn't hurt a bit because I'm so relaxed."

"I'm glad to hear it, but I can't leave you down there." Luke rose from the couch and offered her his hand. "Do you want to shower together, and then I'll make us some hot chocolate?"

"Wow, you really are the perfect twenty-first-century man," Bernie marveled as he helped her up. She smoothed her hand over his chest. "I appreciate that."

"Good. You can make it up to me in free doughnuts." He put his arm around her and drew her toward the bathroom. "For life."

"For life?" Bernie rallied. "That's a big ask."

"Hey, come on. I'm worth it."

Half an hour later, Bernie was tucked up against his side, drinking her mug of chocolate, and he was falling asleep. It had been a long, hard day without Max doing his share of the work. Until Noah could rustle up a replacement or Max returned, the days wouldn't be getting any easier.

"I don't know what to do about Brian," Bernie said out of the blue.

"What's the issue?" Luke shook himself back to consciousness. "I mean, if you want to discuss it with me."

She punched his arm. "If I didn't want to, I would've kept my mouth shut. You're still my best friend, and you know my family better than anyone."

"Fair enough." Luke fought off a yawn and focused his attention on her.

"To summarize, Brian said he just wants to keep the lines of communication open between us. But I think he wants more."

"Like what exactly?"

"To act like my father. And I told him I already have that person in my life. Even though he claimed he got that, I wonder whether he really did."

"I thought," Luke said carefully, "that he wants to help you out with the business part."

Bernie nodded. "That's what Mom asked him to do."

"So, correct me if I'm wrong here, but it doesn't sound as if he wants to replace Mike in your life. It sounds like he's trying to find some way he can connect with you and maybe help you succeed," Luke suggested.

Bernie stared at him and nibbled her bottom lip. "Are you saying I should take him up on his offer even though Mom asked him to since she thinks I can't cope?"

Aware that he was treading on dangerous ground, Luke chose his next words with great care. "It doesn't matter what Linda thinks, because we both know you're supremely capable. The question is, would help from a man who has successfully run his own business for years be useful to you?"

"I hadn't thought of it like that." Bernie frowned. "But wouldn't Mom now think I'd done it because I'm desperate for help because I'm failing?"

"You don't need to tell her anything, and you could ask Brian if you could keep any conversations you have between yourselves," Luke pointed out.

"Hmm . . ." Bernie set her empty mug down on the coffee table. "I guess that's one way of looking at it."

"Free advice from a highly successful entrepreneur who wants to help," Luke repeated. "Advice you don't have to take if it doesn't work for you."

"He's no longer the acting CEO of his company. He got sick and burned out, and the board suggested he take a back seat."

"That's tough." Luke was dying to make a point about what overwork did to people but held his tongue because he knew Bernie would take it the wrong way. "He did get to keep his money though, right?"

Bernie smiled. "He still owns the majority of the shares. He said they gave him some bullshit title with no responsibility for the day-to-day running of the company, but he's still officially there."

"Sounds great," Luke mused. "All the money and none of the responsibility. No wonder he's bored."

"If he's anything like me, he'll hate having nothing to do. Maybe he sees me as his little side project."

"Nothing wrong with that if it benefits you."

It was the first time she'd mentioned any similarities between her and her birth father, and he wasn't going to say anything about that, either. Over the years he'd learned that the best thing to do was plant the seed, walk away, and let Bernie work things out for herself. He yawned hard enough to crack his jaw and slapped a hand over his mouth,

"Sorry."

She kissed his cheek. "It's late. I'd better get back."

"You can stay the night here if you like," Luke offered.

She winced. "I'm sorry. I know you hate driving in the dark, but I need to get home. I don't want them thinking I've run out on them or anything."

"I'm happy to take you," Luke said quickly. "It's only ten minutes up the road." Farther into the forest and pitch black, but he'd cope. The fact that she'd noticed his aversion to driving at night was worrying, though.

"Or I could take your truck and get Dad to drop it back to you tomorrow morning," Bernie suggested.

"That might be a hard ask after what happened this evening."

She groaned. "Yeah, I guess it would be. I've never been good at forgiving people and giving in graciously."

"You're telling me that?" Luke rose from the couch and stretched. "The guy you pushed in the pond about three months after I did it to you?"

"You deserved it."

She picked up the mugs, brought them to the kitchen, and washed them while Luke made sure the fire was out and the lights in the bathroom were off. He was glad she looked more relaxed, but sex would do that for anyone. He could only hope she'd taken some of his advice to heart.

He helped her into her coat, nuzzling her neck as he reached around to zip her up. "You smell good."

"We showered together, doofus; I smell just like you." She leaned back against him. She was a delightful mix of the practical and the magical. "Thanks for everything you did tonight."

"You're welcome." He turned her around and wrapped her in his arms, suddenly reluctant to leave the warmth of their shared space. "I wish I could take you home to bed."

"And scandalize my parents even more?" Bernie eased out of his arms. "We'd better go or Mike will be organizing a posse."

"I'd like to see that." Luke ushered her in front of him, turned off the lights, and followed her down the stairs. "Big Mike on his horse with a flaming torch in his hand."

She chuckled as they left the building and he locked up. The stars were bright in the black sky and the moon was almost full, which would help him navigate the roads without worrying about what was concealed in the depth of the forest.

With the lack of traffic and no dawdling tourists, it didn't take long to arrive at Bernie's. The curtains twitched as Luke drew to a stop and Bernie put her hand on his thigh.

"You don't need to come in. I can handle this."

"You sure?"

She patted his cheek and then kissed him. "Thank you."

"You're welcome." He kissed her and waited until she was safely through the door before driving in a slow circle and heading back up to the county road. Whether she realized it or not, Bernie was a strong, resilient woman. He had no doubt she'd make the best of the opportunities life gave her. He wished he had half her strength.

Alone in the truck, the darkness closed around him, and he wished he'd brought one of the dogs for company. On his own, everything became a threat, and he hated the way he reacted to every damn shadow.

He focused on his breathing and following the cat's eyes in the center of the road. In the winter, there would only be the whiteness of the snow against the blackness of the forest, but he wouldn't be driving much because it got dangerous. Some part of him yearned for the days when they'd be cut off from everything, when the ranch became the center of his universe and no one wanted him to go anywhere.

He shook off the sensation of being watched and turned into the Nilsen top gate, activated the code, and went down the drive. Last winter he'd gone out to search for Max, fallen off his horse, and broken his arm. He'd spent several hours alone in the snow until Noah had found him, brought him back, and Jen had set his arm.

It hadn't been fun.

In fact, that fear had stayed with him, growing and spreading inside him until it was becoming hard to contain. He took a deep, steadying breath and set his gaze on the distant lights of the barn and ranch house below him. Time to stop imagining shit, put on his game face, and make sure his mom and his friends thought everything was absolutely fine.

CHAPTER FOURTEEN

"Go look at it!"

Bailey was so excited she was practically yelling, or maybe that was just because Bernie hadn't slept much the night before and had a tension headache to prove it.

"I'm just going to do that." Bernie took her phone and laptop out onto the porch of the café and sat down to check the puppy-auction website. "Give me a sec."

She propped her phone up against the condiments so that she could still see Bailey's face and miraculously clicked all the right keys on her laptop.

"Wow!" She blinked as the vibrant front page came up. "This is awesome!" It was about a hundred times better than her previous attempts. "You have to let me pay you for your time."

Bailey's expression softened. "Nah, consider it my gift to the humane society." She made a shushing motion with her hands. "Click the links! There's one for each dog and puppy, and there's also a sign-up page for coffee with your pet with a suggested donation for the shelter!"

"It's beautiful." Bernie wanted to cry. "I don't know what to say except thank you from the bottom of my heart."

"Aww . . ." Bailey blew her a kiss. "It was more fun

than anything else I do, and I enjoyed using my skill set."
She beamed at Bernie. "How's Luke?"

"He's good." Bernie smiled back. "We're kind of dating."

Bailey clapped her hands. "I told Noah Luke had the
hots for you, and he looked at me like I was crazy!"

"He only came after me when you politely turned him
down," Bernie reminded her.

"Get out of here." Bailey wagged her finger at Bernie.
"He was totally into you all the time. He just needed a
nudge in the right direction to realize it."

"Like me blurting it out to his face, you mean?"

"Don't knock it." Bailey chuckled. "It worked, didn't
it, girlfriend?"

"Are you and your sisters coming to the auction?"
Bernie asked, eager to get Bailey away from the subject
of Luke.

"We're doing our best to make it. If the case I'm
currently working on doesn't go to trial, I think I'm
good, and the twins' work schedules are more flexible
than mine."

"You can stay at the B&B in town."

"I'd love that!" Bailey said. "Your cousin Lucy is so
sweet." She glanced behind her. "I must get back to work,
but I wanted you to see the finished result. Will you go
through every page, click every link, and let me know if
there are any issues? I tried it in several browsers, and it
was very consistent, but you never know."

"Will do, and thanks again." Bernie waved as Bailey
ended the call. She put her phone back in her pocket,
took her laptop into the café, and plugged it in on the
shelf she laughingly called her office. Her gaze swept
the crowded kitchen. What would it be like to have the
money to expand her business? She had enough space
behind the shop to do it. All she needed was a set of plans,

permission from the town council, and the finances to go ahead.

Like she'd find a bank to lend her money . . . She had no idea how to write a business-loan proposal, and her business plan was mainly in her head.

She washed her hands and went back into the main kitchen where the ovens were full and her employees were taking a well-earned break. Casey was dealing with the front of house, Anton and Rob were chatting at the table, and it was one of Kenya's days at college.

Rob had already dealt with all the online orders and wanted to talk to her about increasing her product range. Anton had decided to stay another month and had offered Rob the spare bedroom in his apartment until he found something more permanent. Bernie got some coffee and joined the guys.

"Okay, dream-kitchen time. What would you want in here if money were no object?"

She got out her cell and started typing as the ideas flowed and they discussed how to set up the perfect kitchen for all her current projects.

"Did you win the lottery or something?" Anton asked.

"I wish."

"What you need is some good financial advice on how to achieve your goals," Anton continued. "Like you didn't already know that."

"You had great advice and things still didn't work out," Bernie said.

"Nope, that came from the other guy's lawyer and business manager. I should've gotten my own." Anton grimaced. "You should ask Kenya if any of the people at her college could hook you up with someone who knows what they're doing."

"That's a good idea." As Bernie put away her cell, she flipped past Brian's name and paused, remembering

Luke's suggestion from the night before. "I might have another source of help as well."

She stood up. "I'm going to take over from Casey out front so she can have lunch. Let me know if you need anything."

"I think we've got everything in hand." Anton looked at Rob, who nodded. "We can take care of it."

Bernie went into the café and was immediately immersed in the early lunchtime rush. As the snow melted on the high mountain passes, a steady trickle of tourists started coming through, which made things busier. Bernie didn't mind. She enjoyed meeting new people and finding out where they had come from and where they were headed. As a child she'd always felt hemmed in by the forest, and she had gone to college in southern California, where the weather was consistently warm and the only trees were palms.

She'd never imagined she'd end up back home running the local coffee shop, but when the opportunity had come up to take on the lease, she'd leapt at it, and she didn't regret a thing. She loved her community and her family—even when they were arguing.

When there was a lull, she got out her phone and sent a text to her mom, whom she hadn't seen since dinner the night before.

Hey, just checking in. I'm sorry I got mad last night.

She waited, but there was no reply. With a sigh, she tucked her cell into her apron pocket. Her mom was big on face-to-face apologies, so she'd make sure to offer one when she went home for dinner. Luke had checked in with a smiley face, and she'd thanked him for his support again, which he'd brushed off with a joke. He was good at offering up suggestions without ruffling her feathers, which was a skill, because she could be stubborn.

"Hey!" Jen came in with Sky balanced on her hip. "A latte for me, something sweet for Sky, and black coffee for Noah, who's at the post office getting the ranch mail."

"Coming up."

Knowing Sky's tastes well, she put a cinnamon doughnut on a plate and cut it into small segments. She suspected he'd prefer the cinnamon roll but guessed Jen wouldn't want him covered in cream cheese frosting and sticky on the ride back home. She put four of the rolls in a box and took it over with her.

"Here you go." She smiled at Sky who was staring at the plate and licking his lips. "This is for you, buddy. And here are some cinnamon rolls for later."

"Say thank you," Jen said.

Sky bobbed his head. "Nank noo."

"That's good!" Bernie grinned at Jen. "His speech is really coming on."

"Not surprising with all the yacking that goes on at the ranch." Jen sipped her milky coffee and sighed with bliss. "Luke's looking a lot happier these days, so thanks for that."

Bernie tried not to blush. "I think I'm making things worse. He had to deal with me having a meltdown with my mom last night."

"He looked okay this morning. In fact, I'd go as far as to say he was smiling like a fool when texting a certain someone."

"Then it was probably Bailey."

Jen held her gaze. "Will you stop putting yourself down and accept a compliment? You make Luke happy. That's a good thing for both of you, right?"

Bernie nodded. "I guess."

"Stop assuming the worst." Jen obviously wasn't done. "There is no reason why you and Luke can't stay together and be happy for the rest of your lives."

"Don't jinx it!" Bernie couldn't help herself.

Jen laughed as she wiped cinnamon and sugar from Sky's face.

"Has Max come back?" Bernie asked.

"Not yet. He hasn't replied to anyone's texts, either. Even Sally, whom he adores. They haven't said anything, but I think Luke and Noah are worried."

She turned her head as the door to the café opened and Noah came in. The way her face lit up made Bernie want to smile.

"Nono!" Sky stood up and waved enthusiastically at the tall man coming toward him.

"Hey." Noah acknowledged Bernie and slid into the booth opposite Jen and Sky. "Hi, little buddy. What are you eating there?"

Sky frowned and placed his hand palm down on the remaining two segments of doughnut squashing them into the plate. "All gone, Nono."

"So I see," Noah said gravely. "I guess I should get one for myself."

"Des." Sky nodded.

Jen burst out laughing, and even Noah smiled.

"He's a smart kid." He looked up at Bernie. "Any more of those around?"

"I'll get you one with your coffee, along with some wipes for Sky." Bernie went back to the counter.

When she returned, Noah was sorting through the mail he'd picked up at the post office. He'd opened an envelope and was examining a set of keys.

"These are for the ranch." He shook the envelope. "There's nothing else in there."

Jen touched the pile of keys. "The key ring has an M on it."

"Then I guess they belong to Max." Noah stared down at them. "Or should I say they belonged to him."

"Luke's going to be gutted," Jen said.

Bernie set Noah's coffee and plate well away from Sky and stepped back. She wasn't part of the conversation, but she wished she was.

"Thanks, Bernie." Noah who noticed everything, glanced up at her. "You okay if I tell Luke about this first?"

"Of course!"

"I think it would be better coming from me," Noah hesitated. "Luke's going to take it personally."

"He takes everything personally," Jen said. "That's why he was such a good officer. It's a shame Max didn't think to include a note."

"That's Max for you." Noah picked up the envelope and examined it. "This was sent from Reno, and there's no return address." He searched through the rest of the mail. "And there's nothing else from Max here, so I guess we know where we stand."

"What's up?" Luke was filling in an online grant application with a Californian wildlife trust when Noah came into the farm office and closed the door behind him. "Jen left you?"

"Nope." Noah stopped in front of the desk and tossed something to Luke who instinctively caught it.

"Keys?" Luke asked. "You *and* Jen are leaving?"

"They're not mine."

Luke, who had been straightening them out stopped as he recognized the dangling key chain. "They're Max's. Where did you find them?"

"He sent them back in the mail. No return address and no note."

Luke felt like someone had punched him in the gut. It took him a moment to speak.

"This is my fault."

"Nah." Noah pulled up a chair, sat down, and faced him. "This is on Max."

"You all told me I was being too harsh, and you were right." Luke set the keys on the desk, his fingers slightly trembling.

"Bullshit." Noah leaned forward, his expression intent. "Max ran away because he couldn't deal with the slightest criticism. That's always been the problem, not what you said on that particular day."

"I got angry with him and that's not like me."

"Someone had to." Noah shrugged. "If it had been me, he'd have ended up flat on his back with a black eye. He's like a burr under your saddle that just won't stop rubbing you up the wrong way. Sometimes I think he provoked us to give him the excuse to leave."

"That's messed up."

"Max is messed up." Noah grimaced. "Maybe without us protecting him, he'll have to get some help. That's the only good thing I can take from this entire clusterfuck." He rose to his feet. "Jen's getting lunch. We stopped at Bernie's and got doughnuts and cinnamon rolls. Are you coming?"

"Was Bernie okay?" Luke asked.

Noah stopped in the doorway. "She was worried about you."

"She would be." Luke turned his attention to his laptop.

"I must finish this application. Can you tell Jen I'll be there in ten?"

"Sure." Noah still hesitated. "You're not at fault here, boss."

Luke nodded but kept his head down. He heard Noah sigh before finally leaving and walking down the hall. Luke tried to refocus on the questions, but nothing made sense anymore. *He'd* done this. He'd run one of his best friends off his ranch, and nothing anyone said would make him feel good about that.

He saved the application and pressed his fingers over his eyes. The headache from the day before was making a comeback, and he'd need painkillers to get through the rest of the day. He picked up Max's keys, put them in the top drawer, closed it with a bang, and got to his feet. Just before he left the room, he took out his cell phone and started typing.

Got the keys. Thanks. You are still welcome here anytime you want.

He paused to read back his words. Did he want to apologize or was that something best left until Max came back? Because Luke had to believe his friend would come back, or he wouldn't be able to go on. He pressed send without adding anything and didn't wait for a reply he sensed might never come.

He went into the kitchen where everyone was gathered around the table eating lunch. They all stopped talking to look at him, and he shrugged.

"No point trying to tell me this isn't my fault, so can we just eat?"

His mom looked like she wanted to cry. She'd always been very fond of Max.

"Fine by me," Noah said, biting into his sandwich.

As usual, Noah had his back, and Luke was especially grateful for that right now.

"Bailey's finished working on the puppy auction website." Noah kept talking, which wasn't like him at all. "It looks amazing. She said Bernie was thrilled."

"I bet." Luke helped himself to soup and a ham sandwich and sat down at the table. "It was good of Bailey to put in all that work."

"She said she enjoyed it." Noah was well into his second sandwich while also helping Sky manage his. Luckily the kid had gotten over the drop-everything-over-the-side game, which meant the dogs were very disappointed, but leaner. "She wants me to send her pics of you, me, and Sally with the dogs for the coffee-with-your-pets thing."

"I love that idea," his mom said, her voice determinedly cheerful. "Jen should do it, too."

"No thanks." Jen smiled. "I'm already up to my elbows in cat adoptions."

"I told Bernie it was a terrible idea. I doubt she'd want me to participate." Luke forced down a bite of sandwich.

"I'm sure she'd love to see you stripped down to your boxers holding Blinky and Winky," Jen said.

"She can see that anytime she likes," Luke said. "I'll even skip the boxers."

His mom snorted with laughter, and after a second, everyone joined in.

"Oh, Luke." Sally wiped a tear from her eye. "You're such a romantic."

"Bernie's a lucky woman," Jen added, and looked around the table. "That's better. We can't be miserable all the time." She reached for Luke's hand across the table and squeezed it hard. "We're going to get through this together, and when Max sorts himself out, he'll be back." She met Luke's gaze. "I *know* he will because this is his home."

Bernie took a deep breath and started typing.

Hey Brian. If you were serious about wanting to offer me some business advice, I'd like to talk about that.

She watched the little dancing bubbles, which showed he was replying, with intense interest mixed with fright.

I'd love to. Let me know what you need.

She stared at the screen for a long time. Was she being mercenary asking him for advice, or was she simply being practical? If she made it clear that she wasn't seeking anything else, would he be okay with that? He was still a human being with feelings, and maybe he didn't deserve to be exploited. She typed a reply.

I want to be clear that this is all I need from you right now. Are you okay with that?

I understand. I'm starting to miss my business so this will help with the boredom. ☺

Bernie made one last attempt to make sure he got it.

I don't want you to feel like I'm using you.

Her phone rang, and she accepted the call.
"I appreciate you trying to make sure my expectations

are low, Bernie, but I'm more than willing to help you."
There was a hint of amusement in Brian's voice.

"I don't want you to feel used," Bernie said frankly.
"Even though I'm aware that's what I'm doing."

"Maybe I'm okay with that. After all, I did offer to
help you." He paused. "In fact, I'm way more comfortable with transactional relationships than emotional ones.
Ask my ex-wives."

Bernie laughed and he joined in.

"Okay, so what can I help you with?" he asked.

"General business stuff? How to get loans, whether to
expand my premises, whether I really am doing too
much?" She paused to breathe. "I mean, is that too basic
for you? It's not exactly high tech."

"It's the foundation of every good business model, and
I know how to do that. The best way to understand what
you need would be for me to visit you, see your working
conditions, and talk things through face to face. Would
you be willing to do that?"

Bernie considered what he was asking her. Was she
ready to see the man who'd abandoned her and Linda
over twenty years ago? And if she was, what on earth was
she going to tell her mom?

"I think I'm ready to risk it," Bernie said. "You can
stay at the B&B in town, which is just across the street
from the café."

Even if she kept Brian well away from the ranch, her
mom would still find out because Lucy couldn't keep a
secret to save her life. And Pen, who sometimes worked
at the B&B as well as the café, was even worse.

"I'll check with my admin, and she can send you my
availability," Brian said. "Looking forward to it. Have a
great day."

He ended the call, leaving Bernie staring at her phone. What had she done? She'd gone against her original instincts not to get involved with her birth dad—done exactly what her mom had wanted her to do, albeit for different reasons, and would have to eat crow when her mom found out.

But if Brian could help her successfully grow her business and remain a sane and loving person, wouldn't that be worth all the hassle along the way?

Her cell buzzed and she looked down, expecting it to be something from Brian's admin, only to see Bailey's number and a text all in caps.

CALL ME

Bernie checked the time and clicked on Bailey's number.

"What's up?"

"That video of you playing with the puppies Luke took?"

"What about it?"

"It's kind of gone viral."

Bernie frowned. "Define viral."

"Okay, well I set up all the social media apps on all the available sites for the auction with links directing them back to the humane society page and your café, and some big influencer must have picked up on the video because you're everywhere right now."

"But it's just me playing with the puppies." Bernie frowned as she picked up her coffee and headed back into the café. "And I told Luke to cut me out of most of it before he sent it on to you."

"He didn't do that and to be honest, I thought you were

just as adorable as the puppies, so I left you in," Bailey confessed.

"If it helps get interest out about the auction, then I guess I'm okay with it. We might get a few more online bids, which would be great."

"Bernie, I don't think you're quite getting the magnitude of this," Bailey said. "There have been over two million views of your video, and it's still rising. I gotta go. Congrats!"

Kenya looked up as Bernie came into the kitchen.

"Did you know you're famous?" She patted the front pocket of her apron where her phone was located. "I couldn't believe what I was seeing this morning when I got up. I literally shrieked to my roomie that my boss was an internet star."

"I . . ." Bernie shook her head. "I don't know what to do about any of this."

"What you need to do is make some follow-up videos talking about this place and your online bakery business," Kenya said. "Ride that wave and do your business a solid. I can take some video right now if you like?"

"While I'm standing here with my mouth open from the shock?"

"I was thinking more that you just get on with your day and I'll take some sneaky shots and share the insider point of view as to what it's really like to work for the famous puppy girl."

Casey came in from the front of store.

"Wait—you're *puppy girl*?" she gasped. "I thought they looked familiar!"

Kenya rolled her eyes. "How could you not know?"

"Well, because Bernie's not exactly the kind of person I'd expect to be uploading content to social media sites," Casey said. "No offense, Bernie."

"None taken, and it wasn't me. It was the person who created the humane society website and outreach campaign."

"Then she's doing a phenomenal job. Whoever took that video made you look amazing." Casey took a fresh tray of muffins out of the rack. "We should exploit this while it lasts."

"That's exactly what I said," Kenya agreed with a nod.

Bernie made a face. "It'll all blow over in a few hours."

"Why would you want that to happen?" Casey and Kenya looked at each other and then to Bernie. "This is your chance to be famous."

"I don't want to be famous," Bernie countered.

"That's . . . nuts," Kenya said. "Can I just do one video of you in your natural work environment? Because if you don't want the attention, I'll gladly take it for you."

"Actually, that's a great idea," Bernie said. "Anyone watching me work will be so bored that they'll forget about me even quicker."

"Then you'll let me?" Kenya grinned. "That's awesome! I won't forget to mention the name of the café and the website at least ten times."

"I'm not talking directly to the camera or making any effort to look cute," Bernie said, clarifying her position as Kenya took out her phone. "If those idiots want to see how boring I am when not surrounded by a pile of puppies, then this is their chance."

CHAPTER FIFTEEN

"Four million views now," Bailey said in hushed tones. "And I just got a text from your local news center in Reno. They want to come and interview you."

Bernie groaned as she walked over to her truck. She'd had to turn off her phone for most of the working day because of the constant pinging. She wasn't sure if it was her imagination, but it felt like the café had been busier than usual, and that her customers were staring at her a lot more. She'd even noticed a couple of them surreptitiously videoing her when she'd walked by. The effort of smiling and not noticing anything weird was exhausting, and her staff hadn't helped. They'd all been totally into her transformation into a viral celebrity.

"Do you think we should take it down?" Bernie asked, climbing into her truck.

"I don't think it will make much difference at this point. It's taken on a life of its own," Bailey said. "Just think of the positives!"

"I'm trying to." Bernie started the engine and backed out of the small parking lot at the rear of her café as Bailey continued talking on speakerphone. "I just wish I hadn't been in the video."

"But you were so cute!"

"I was just messing around with the puppies and chatting to my best friend."

"About that . . . A lot of people want to know who the mysterious guy shooting the video is," Bailey said. "Luke's got quite a little fan club of his own."

"Hopefully, Luke never has to know about it." Bernie looked both ways before turning out onto the county road, which was getting busier as the tourists returned. "Don't you think it's weird that four million people have been staring at me goofing around in a barn?"

"Bernie, people love stuff like that."

"I have no idea why, but if it helps with the auction, I'm just about okay with it."

"Have you seen the hits on the website today? Those stats are huge," Bailey said.

"I'll take a look when I get home."

"The bids for coffee with your pet are also insane."

"Awesome." Bernie stopped to allow a logging truck to slowly pass across the road from one area of the forest to another. "I still can't get my head around it."

Bailey chuckled. "And I can't decide if I should give up my day job and just do promo for you and your many businesses."

"I'd keep doing what you're doing. This will all be forgotten by tomorrow."

"Probably," Bailey agreed. "Are you okay if I give the local news outlet your info?"

"Sure, why not?" Bernie was convinced they'd never get in touch. "I can hype my business at the same time."

"By the way, I loved the videos Kenya posted of you today."

"They're up already?"

"And getting thousands and thousands of views."

Bernie put on her signal and slowed down to navigate the turn into Murphy Ranch.

"I think you should do one with Luke," Bailey said.

"*So* not happening." Bernie leaned out of the window to punch in the gate code.

"I could ask him if you like."

"I know he'd do anything for you, Bailey, but can we wait on that? I'm hoping things will get back to normal soon, and that he'll never need to know a thing."

"Fair enough. I've got to get back to work. Speak to you tomorrow, puppy girl!"

Bernie parked her truck in front of the barn and went into the house. She took off her jacket and boots and walked into the kitchen to find her whole family lined up in a row staring at her.

"What? Did someone die?" Bernie asked.

MJ pointed at her. "You're famous."

Mary nodded. "You're everywhere!"

Bernie rolled her eyes. "Hi, everyone, I had a really interesting day at work, what's for dinner? Can I help set the table?"

"The twins said you've 'gone viral.'" Her dad made bunny ears. "Sounds nasty."

"I'm beginning to think you're right about that." Bernie eased past her gawking siblings and helped herself to a mug of coffee. "Is something burning, Mom?"

"Oh! My pie!" Her mom hurried over to the oven. "I forgot."

"So, what's it like being famous?" Bill asked. "I mean everyone was sharing that video of you at school today. You're kind of like a hero."

"Great." Bernie sipped her coffee. "All I had to do was play with a few puppies and suddenly I'm a god?"

"It was quite cute," Mary chimed in. "I just wish we'd

seen more of Luke, and I think a lot of the viewers would agree with me."

"You haven't been reading the comments, have you?" Bernie asked as she hung her keys on the hook on the wall.

"I like reading them," Mary said. "One gets a very interesting glimpse at the variety of human experience."

"This is all Luke and Bailey's fault. I didn't mean to be in a video at all," Bernie grumbled as she drank more coffee. "Are we going to eat, or are you all going to keep staring at me? It's getting old now."

"Of course, we're going to eat." Her mom herded them all toward the table. "I had to get Mary to show me how to create an account on that ticky tocky thing, which slowed me down a bit with making dinner."

If Bernie hadn't been so hungry, she might have been tempted to grab something and run for the hills, but the smell of roast chicken was making her stomach growl. And she had worse things to worry about than some silly viral video. She somehow had to explain to her mom that her ex-husband would be coming to town to offer business advice to his only daughter.

"Can I talk to you after dinner?" Bernie asked her mom.

"Is it about our family being in your next video?" Linda beamed at her. "We're all willing to go down to the barn and talk about anything you want!"

"It's not about that." Bernie took her plate of chicken and added a large pile of mashed potatoes and green beans. "But if you want to help get animals adopted, I'm totally up for it."

Mike smiled at Bernie. "I'm going to take a rain check on that, being camera shy."

"That's all right." Linda blew him a kiss. "The twins will make enough noise to get everyone's attention."

"Well, Bill will," Mary said. "MJ is way calmer with the animals."

"Me and MJ together will totally be a hit," Bill said. "Everyone loves identical twins."

Bernie looked at her dad, the only sane one at the table. "How was your day? Did you manage to move all the cattle onto the new pasture up the hill?"

"Yup." Mike cut into his chicken. "It all went very well."

"Did you help him, Mom?"

"Of course, I did." Linda flashed a smile at Mike. "I've always got his back."

Mary cleared her throat. "So, to get back to what I was saying earlier, will you ask Luke—"

Bernie spoke over her. "I don't want to be rude, sweetie, but I'm not going to talk about the video over dinner, okay? It's bad enough that everyone else in the world is talking about it and, quite frankly, I could do with a break."

"That seems counterproductive," Mary objected. "When we could help you strategize to gain the maximum exposure and financial benefit from the experience, and I'm fairly certain that getting Luke involved would only enhance that."

Bernie fixed her sister with a look. "I'm a real person, Mary, not a theory to be tested and adapted, and I've asked you not to talk about it while I eat my dinner."

"There's no need to be unkind, Bernie," her mom said. "Mary can't help how she thinks."

"I am well aware of Mary's abilities and her tendency to hyper focus, Mom, I'm just asking her to lay off while I eat my darn meal."

Mary's smile faded. "I'm sorry, Bernie. I wasn't trying to be mean. I just wanted you to ask Luke if he'd do a video with you. It's a totally reasonable request."

"Mary," Mike spoke up. "That's enough, okay? Let your sister eat her dinner."

Bernie reached across the table to touch her sister's hand. "You're never mean, sweetie. Can we talk about this later?"

Mary nodded, and a blessed silence fell around the table as everyone concentrated on the excellent food. Bernie hadn't eaten much at work because she'd been too stressed and managed two helpings of everything. Then, while Mike and the younger kids handled the clean-up, Bernie and her mom went upstairs to her bedroom to talk.

Linda sat on the bed beside Bernie.

"If this is about our spat the other day, I want to apologize. Sometimes I do forget to acknowledge how well you've done." She sighed. "I guess you always seem less vulnerable than the other kids, and I take your self-sufficiency at face value and forget to ask how you're really doing."

"I appreciate you saying that, Mom," Bernie said carefully. "But you're right; I can handle my own stuff, which is why I get upset when you worry about the wrong things for me. I might have Brian's DNA, but you and Mike brought me up, and I'm a reflection of that care, love, and work ethic."

"Yes you are, and we're both very proud of you."

Bernie smiled. "Which brings me nicely to what I wanted to talk to you about because I owe you an apology, too."

"For what?"

"For not understanding, as you pointed out, that Brian might actually have something useful to offer me."

"Such as?"

"His business experience."

Her mom grinned and waggled her finger in front of Bernie's face. "Ha! I told you!"

"You did, and I wanted you to know that I reached out to him, and he's agreed to help me formulate a better business plan."

"That's awesome." Her mom clapped her hands.

"We talked on the phone and the thing is, he wants to come here and see how things work in real time," Bernie rushed on. "He won't be coming to the ranch, just to the B&B in town, and I don't intend for him to have any interaction with anyone from our family—"

Her mom put a hand on Bernie's arm. "Hold up. I'll need to talk things through with Mike, but I don't see why we can't be welcoming if he's coming to town."

"Mom, you've spent years talking shit about him!" Bernie exclaimed.

"But now he's doing something to help my daughter, and I approve of that."

"Only because you got him involved."

"I suppose I did." Linda made a face. "I shouldn't have interfered, but I'm kind of glad it worked out so well for you."

"It still might crash and burn," Bernie said gloomily. "He might be unbearable in person."

"Do you really think I would've fallen in love and had a child with someone unbearable?"

Bernie shuddered. "I don't even want to think about that."

"Then don't." Linda got off the bed. "What an exciting day you've been having."

"So exciting that I'm going straight to bed." Bernie followed her mom to the door. "Can you tell Mary I'll talk to her tomorrow when she comes into the café for her shift?"

"Will do. And don't worry about the animals, MJ's already done all your chores." Linda kissed her cheek. "I'll go and speak to Mary before I square things with Mike."

Bernie was just about to get into bed when her phone buzzed with a text from Luke that was identical to the one Bailey had sent her except for the caps.

Call me x

And the kiss. Bernie lay on her back, picked up her phone, and FaceTimed Luke.

"What's up?"

His smile was warm. "I think you're the one who should be telling me that."

"Is this about Max?"

He raised an eyebrow. "Good try, to throw me off, but no."

"It's just that I overheard Noah and Jen talking at the café about him returning his keys, and Noah asked me not to say anything to you, and—"

"Bernie . . ."

She sighed. "How did you find out?"

"One of the cows told me. How do you think I found out?"

"Sky? He's about the right age group."

"Close—Jen." He grinned at her. "Hey, puppy girl."

"Stop that."

"But it's funny."

"Not to me."

His expression immediately sobered. "Are you really not okay with it?"

"I'm just . . . overwhelmed?" Bernie tried to answer him honestly. "Like, how does that happen, and what am I supposed to do about it when it's totally out of my hands?"

"I kind of get that." He hesitated. "It's like being stuck in the middle of a battle or a walking into an ambush. All hell breaks out and you're fighting, and yelling, and trying to find a way out of complete madness."

"I appreciate the sentiment, but I think what you and your troops went through was way worse," Bernie said gently. "At least this will go away fairly soon."

"Yeah." He swallowed hard and she kicked herself for resurrecting those shadows in his eyes. "I guess that was a stupid thing to say."

"What happened to me will fade away in a couple of days when something else takes off," Bernie said. "I just need to figure out a way to get through it."

"Bailey called me."

"Of course, she did."

"She told me upfront you didn't want her to."

"I asked her not to, which is a totally different thing," Bernie replied. "I can't stop her doing anything."

"She wants us to do a video together with the puppies and talk about the auction and what it means to our town and valley. She thinks it would be a great fundraiser."

"She's probably not wrong," Bernie said cautiously. "But don't you think doing that will stir the pot?"

"If it was just to make us famous, then sure, but it is for a good cause. It depends on what you want." He hesitated. "More money coming into the animal shelter means you could hire more people."

"Because I'm doing too much."

Luke sighed. "I'm not getting into that with you again, okay?"

Bernie studied his face. He looked worn out. She knew how hard it was to work a ranch when you were suddenly shorthanded, and it was even worse for Luke because the person who'd gone was one of his best friends.

"Okay, then let's do a video." She smiled. "I guess it would be nice to have at least one permanent member of staff to keep things running smoothly. And I talked to Brian today—he's going to come and assess my business potential."

"That's awesome." His smile was so warm she wished she could crawl through the screen and right into his lap. "Can I say I'm proud of you without you biting my head off?"

"Absolutely." Bernie fluttered her eyelashes. "I guess this is what being all mature and stuff feels like."

"I guess so," he said, his voice deepened. "Man, I wish I could see you right now."

"You can see me."

"You know what I mean."

Need pooled low in her stomach, and she shivered.

"Don't do that," Luke murmured. "You're just making it worse."

"I can't help how you make me feel," Bernie confessed. "Can you meet me at the puppy barn tomorrow evening? We can make the video and then maybe we can make out?"

"I can't wait."

She blew him a kiss. "I'm so sorry about Max."

He shrugged. "Nothing I can do about that right now. He'll come back when he's ready, or he won't."

"Does he have family nearby?"

"I've no idea. He never talked about anyone, and I never really asked."

"How can you be besties with someone for so long and never asked those basic questions?" Bernie wondered.

"Max made it quite plain that his family was off limits, so I stopped asking."

"Sounds like Max."

"Yeah, he's an ass, but I miss him." Luke sighed. "Sometimes his honesty was useful."

"And sometimes he caused a lot of hurt," Bernie reminded him. "Especially to you and Noah."

"Yeah, I'm not trying to make him out to be a saint. If he comes back, we're going to have to set down some ground rules."

"That's a great idea." Bernie yawned. "Excuse me."

"Go to bed." He blew her a kiss. "Wish I was with you."

"Me, too." Bernie air kissed her phone. "I'll see you tomorrow."

Just after she closed the link, a text flashed up on her phone with a calendar date. It appeared Brian was keen to come and see her and had set up a meeting in a week's time. She accepted the invite, sent his admin details of Lucy's B&B, and collapsed into bed.

She really needed to get some sleep and hoped that when she got up the next day her viral video would be forgotten. . . .

"What the hell?" Bernie muttered as she looked out the coffee shop window. It was seven in the morning, she was just about to open up, and a line had already formed outside the door. There was also what looked like a film crew interviewing people in the line and getting shots of the town.

Kenya came up behind her and peered over her shoulder. "This is so cool!"

"What do they want?"

"Coffee, I guess." Kenya grinned at her. "Good thing ours is superior."

Bernie turned tail. "How about you open up, and I go hide in the kitchen?"

"Fine by me." Kenya smoothed her hair. "I'm so glad I wore my new sweater today—not that you can see much of it under my apron. But I still look good."

Bernie was almost behind the counter before Kenya had finished speaking. She had a weird sense that she was under siege.

"What's going on?" Anton looked up as she came into the kitchen at a breakneck speed. "You look like we've been robbed."

"There are loads of people lined up outside the door, and there's a film crew," Bernie said breathlessly.

"Then we'd better make sure we have enough to feed everyone and send them away with great things to say about the café." Anton looked over at Rob. "You okay to stay a bit longer today? We might need to do a second round of baking."

Rob nodded. "As soon as I've finished the online orders—which have tripled, by the way—I'm happy to help."

"And I'll stay all day to help you deal with front of house," Casey, who had just arrived through the back door, called out. "I just got interviewed by some news crew from Reno!"

"Make sure you lock that door," Bernie called out to her. "We don't want anyone wandering in the back."

She took a deep breath and faced her kitchen staff, aware of a rising rumble of voices from the café as Kenya let everyone in the front door.

"I'm so sorry about this. If anyone wants to bail, I won't blame you."

Anton raised his eyebrows. "Bail? I think it's great for your business, and you should go for it." He grinned at her. "You'd better call Pen to come in as well. I think we're going to need all the help we can get."

Luke checked the time on his cell and strolled over to look up the road that came down past the main ranch to the pet barn. Bernie had told him she'd be there by six. It was way past that now, and she hadn't responded to any of his texts except to say that the café was super busy and she didn't have time to talk. He'd stopped off to say hi to Mike and Linda, who knew all about the video and were thrilled on Bernie's behalf.

A cloud of dust rose above the road and seconds later Bernie's truck appeared, silhouetted against the dipping redness of the sun. He shaded his eyes and watched her bumpy descent to the front of the barn. She parked at a haphazard angle, shut off the engine, and flung open the door.

"Hey." Luke walked over to her. There was no one else around. "How's it going?"

She practically ran into him. "Can you just hold me for a sec?"

"Sure." He wrapped both his arms around her and rested his chin on the top of her head. "That better?"

She nodded but didn't speak, and he continued to hold her and inhaled the heavenly scents of baking bread, cinnamon, and coffee he always associated with her. Silence settled around them, broken only by the evening birdsong and the occasional faraway howl of something feral emerging to wreak havoc as darkness swiftly covered the forest.

"You okay now?" She looked up at him and he smoothed his thumb along the curve of her jaw. "Bad day?"

She turned into his touch, her lips touching the pad of his thumb, and suddenly nothing else mattered other than his urgent need to kiss her and be welcomed into the sultry warmth of her mouth.

"Bernie . . ." he murmured against her mouth as she went on tiptoe and kissed him back. "We're at the barn, remember?"

"I don't care."

He cupped her head and eased back so that he could see her face. "I can't afford therapy for your siblings, or risking getting shot by Mike, so give me a safe place and a locked door, and I'm all yours."

She grabbed his hand and dragged him toward the coolness of the barn and her corner office. He didn't need to be told to shut the door and barricade them inside. He'd barely turned around before she crashed into him, her hands urgent on the zipper of his jeans, her mouth hot and needy, just how he wanted it.

There was no time for finesse. He turned her until her back was against the wall, stripped her out of her jeans and panties, and picked her up until he could thrust upward into her wet heat. She grabbed hold of his shoulders and came so fast he almost lost it, but it didn't matter, because she urged him on, faster and faster, until he came with a guttural groan, pinning her hard against the wall as she climaxed again. He lowered his head to her shoulder and drew in great gasps of air, aware of her body continuing to pulse around his dick.

"More?" He rocked his hips.

She bit his throat and his body roared back into life. He meant to go slow, but that wasn't happening, and it was all over again in five minutes. She sagged against him, and he gently lowered her to sit on her desk and set about cleaning himself up. He waited until she was decent again before crouching in front of her. Her hair was all over the place, her lips were swollen from his kisses, and her brown eyes were languorous.

"Better?"

She nodded. "Much."

"Me, too." He paused. "Jen's going to be here at seven to do the video—if that's still what you want."

"What time is it now?"

Luke checked his watch. "Six forty-five."

"Dammit!" Bernie jumped off the desk and then winced.

"You okay?"

"I guess I'm getting too old for upright sex." Bernie pulled open a desk drawer, took out a brush, and started frantically brushing her hair. "My muscles can't take it."

Luke stood up and swaggered toward her. "Or I make your knees go weak."

"You do." She glanced up at him as she bullied her hair into submission. "Do I look okay?"

"You look like you've just been . . ." Luke grinned at her. "Satisfied? Is that a good word?"

"I forgot Jen was coming."

"I did let you know at lunchtime, but I guess you were busy." Luke took the brush and took over taming her hair. "Jen said she went past the café today on her rounds and there was a line out the door."

"It was crazy." Bernie leaned back against him as he combed through her hair. "Mmm, that's so nice."

"I guess it's all good publicity."

"So everyone keeps telling me." Bernie closed her eyes. "It's exhausting being famous."

He braided her hair and used a piece of twine he found in his pocket to tie it off.

"You're good at this."

"I used to do Brina's hair when my parents got busy." Luke turned her around to admire his efforts. "I could probably manage a French braid if I had more time."

"Showoff." She cupped his chin. "Thank you."

"You're welcome." He gestured at the door. "We should open this up, or Jen will think she's not wanted."

"To be honest, I wish her timing was better." She gave him a tired smile. "It's been a hell of a day."

"I bet." He opened the door and wrapped his arm around her shoulders as they went out into the barn. There was no sign of Jen's truck yet, but the sun had gone down, and the barn lights were the only thing keeping the darkness at bay. "Mom said you were interviewed on the six o'clock news."

"Yeah, it was the only way I could persuade them to go away," Bernie confessed. "To be fair, they were really nice about it and didn't ask any awful questions. I got to promote the humane society, the auction, *and* my business."

"The triple threat," Luke said. "You're amazing, you know?"

"I'm . . . too exhausted to even think about it." She looked up at him. "I want all these things to go well, but maybe not this well?"

Luke was still chuckling when Jen arrived and parked her truck. She came toward them, a big smile on her face.

"You two are positively glowing!"

"We've been hauling hay bales around," Luke said quickly.

Jen rolled her eyes. "Sure, you have." She grinned at Bernie. "Let's go see the puppies!"

Five minutes later, Jen was sitting on the floor cooing to the dogs while Pandora took a much-needed break and got fussed over by Bernie. When neither of them was watching, Luke took a couple of photos of Bernie just for himself. There was something about her that just made him want to stare at her all day. He must have watched the video he'd taken of her with the puppies a thousand times.

Man . . . he was in way too deep for comfort. How had that happened? When had he stopped seeing her as his best friend with benefits and fallen in love with her?

"Luke?"

He started as Bernie called his name.

"What's up?"

She was smiling at him. "You looked worried."

"I'm good," he hastened to reassure her. She knew him far too well for him to get away with being insincere, but his mind was doing cartwheels. "I was just thinking about the grant application I filled out today."

"That's enough to give anyone indigestion," Jen commented as she took out her phone. "Now I wish I could stay here all night and pet the puppies, but I promised Noah I'd be back in an hour. Can we get this done?" She pointed at the bales of hay in the corner. "Why don't you two sit over there and let the puppies play around you, and I'll ask the questions." She took out a piece of paper. "I made a list."

Luke mock groaned as he scooped up two of the puppies and took them over to where Bernie was sitting.

"Come on then, puppy girl. Let's get this over with."

* * *

Hours later, Bernie was tucked up in bed trying to sleep but finding it impossible. She hadn't told Luke about the many horrors of her day—the incessant questions, the constant staring, the way people she'd never met before acted as if they had the right to ask her anything or thought that they knew her from a three-minute video. It made her feel vulnerable, but because everyone else seemed to think it was okay, she'd played along, promoted her business and her pet causes, and done her best to appear unaffected in front of the public and the cameras.

But it was exhausting, and she wasn't sure she could keep doing it for another day, let alone forever. Arriving at the barn and finding Luke there ready and willing to help her forget her terrible day had saved her soul. Her mind drifted back to the intensity of the sex—how he'd literally held her up and given her exactly what she needed without even asking. The thought of not having that—of losing him in the middle of this mess—was terrifying. He'd come to mean so much more to her than her best friend. He was everything.

But she couldn't deal with that right now. It wasn't what he wanted, and she had far too many calls on her time to be deciding that Luke Nilsen really was her one true love after all. He was just being his usual kind, considerate self.

Kind . . .

She shivered, her hand drifting down to the slight soreness between her legs where he'd filled her so completely and so thoroughly that she'd come twice in five minutes. He hadn't been kind then; he'd been as relentless and driven as she was. But what did it mean, this strange alchemy between them? Was it all her? She certainly wasn't behaving like herself right now, in many ways. Was Luke simply responding to her desires at the expense of his own? It wasn't exactly something she could just ask him when she was depending on him to keep her sane.

She needed him right now, and if he was willing to fulfill her desires, wasn't that enough? She closed her eyes and pictured the clenching of his muscles as he drove into her, the barely restrained strength that had pinned her to the wall and kept her there until he'd come undone along with her. None of that was her sweet, charming friend; it was all a different, more feral Luke—the warrior, the man who'd commanded troops in battle and had an iron will. She liked that core of steel within him and couldn't help but respond to it.

She turned onto her side and resolutely closed her eyes. She had a lot to do, and worrying about Luke wasn't helping. Once the video died its natural death and the auction happened, there would be plenty of time to find out whether her feelings for Luke were the forever kind or just a symptom of the crazy journey she was currently on. And she was still assuming Luke felt the same, which wasn't a given, because it was supposed to be an experiment.

She reminded herself not to be pessimistic and finally allowed herself to fall asleep.

CHAPTER SIXTEEN

Luke sat back in his chair and immediately groaned as his bones creaked. It was almost a week since he'd had sex with Bernie up against a wall, and his back still hadn't forgiven him. He hit send on his latest grant application and consulted his list. It was the last one, which meant it was now a waiting game to see which organizations and government departments might decide to help him out. Joel had been in touch about the bank refinancing, and that was looking better than Luke had expected.

It would still take a long time to recover from the previous winter, but Luke was cautiously optimistic that they would survive. He was deeply thankful that his fear of being the Nilsen who lost the family ranch wouldn't come to pass. The tightness around his chest had eased slightly, allowing him to worry about all the other things going on in his life.

Noah had found someone to cover full time for Max, but his absence still left a hole in the family. He hadn't contacted them, and Luke was beginning to lose hope. He hadn't seen much of Bernie since they'd appeared in the video together. He checked his phone, noting that there were well over three million views of them talking about the auction and the humane society. Several people in the comments had offered to donate large sums of money to the cause if Luke would take his shirt off, which Bernie had firmly nixed.

After the video's success, they had decided to stay away from each other until things got back to normal—which didn't seem to be happening. She'd texted him last night asking if he'd like to have dinner with her and Brian at the B&B that evening, and he had already decided to go. He was intrigued to meet Bernie's birth father and knew she'd appreciate the support.

There was a tap on the door, and his mom came in.

"Everything okay?" She smiled at him. "It's my day at the medical center. I'll be back around six."

"You work too hard." Luke rose from his seat and came around his desk to give her a hug.

"So do you," she pointed out. "When are you going to invite Bernie up here for dinner? I haven't seen her since this whole video thing exploded."

"She's not feeling very sociable right now, but I'm sure I can persuade her to come over."

His mom cupped his cheek. "She's good for you, Luke."

"Yeah."

"Really good." She paused. "I hope you're serious about her."

"Mom . . ."

"I know it's none of my business, but I can't think of anyone who would suit you better. Why go to all the bother of dating if you don't mean to get married at the end of it? I'll never understand you youngsters."

"You've just turned sixty. You're not that old," Luke objected. "And these days we do dating, not instant courtship, and we take our time."

"I am aware of that," Sally said tartly. "Your sister went from 'going out' with Tom, to being 'exclusive' with Tom, to half living in his house, to moving into his house, and then only getting married when their first child was about to be born."

"That's the way it's done these days, Mom." He kissed the top of her head. "But I'll try and keep the fuss to a minimum just for you."

"I'd appreciate that." She turned toward the door. "Do you think Bernie would mind if I popped into the café and asked her to come for dinner next week?"

"I'm sure she'd love to see a familiar, friendly face," Luke reassured her. "She's fed up with being stared at by strangers."

"I wonder if anyone will know I'm your mother?"

Luke grinned at her. "Now you want to be famous? Just stand alongside Bernie for a few seconds. I can guarantee someone will take your picture, find out who you are, and have your name plastered all over social media in a nanosecond."

"I'm not sure I'd like that. Noah said there are people hanging around at our top gate trying to catch a glimpse of you."

"Which is why I haven't been anywhere for a week."

His mother studied him. "I get the sense that doesn't bother you as much as I think it should."

"There's nothing wrong with appreciating the comforts of home." Luke strode over to the door and held it open. "If you're planning on seeing Bernie, you'd better go, or you'll be late for your shift."

"Fine, but we really do need to talk about this, Luke." She went past him into the hallway.

"I'm already taking about it with my therapist, okay?"

"You are?" She smiled. "That's great! Are you doing it online?"

He nodded. "Yeah, it seems to be working out fine."

"I'm very proud of you. If we could've just gotten Max hooked up with someone who could've helped him, he wouldn't have felt he had to leave the only home he's ever known."

Luke winced. "Thanks for reminding me."

"For the millionth time, it's not on you." His mom looked him right in the eye. "It's on Max. Stop obsessing." She blew him a kiss. "Have a good day."

"I'm having dinner with Bernie at the B&B this evening," he called after her as she marched briskly away. "I'll probably pass you on the road this evening when you're coming back."

She waved to show she'd heard him and continued out into the yard. Winky and Blinky came down the hallway, collapsed at Luke's feet, and sighed deeply. Luke nudged one of them with his toe.

"Come on guys, you can ride out with me today and earn your keep."

Bernie had agreed to meet Brian at the B&B rather than at the café. She wanted to see him in person before she allowed him access to her business or to herself. If he gave off a weird vibe, she hoped she'd pick up on it, and would send him on his way.

She went out the back door of the café, ignoring the curious bystanders who had become a feature of the place in the week since the video had gone viral. She was aware that she was being filmed from the glint of the reflecting sun on the screens lifted to follow her path. She'd already learned not to look around or stop because if she did, she'd immediately be surrounded.

It wasn't that people were unkind; it was just the constant presence of onlookers made her feel like she could never be alone. Mike had changed the security code on the gate at Murphy Ranch three times to stop people from getting in. There was nothing more disconcerting than to be eating your dinner and discover a whole family staring at you through the window.

Mike had also started letting the dogs out at night because they were the best at spotting intruders. No one in her family seemed to mind at this point, but Bernie did. She'd specifically asked Luke to stay away because she didn't want him subjected to the same scrutiny. Though she had asked him to meet her at the B&B for dinner with Brian because she wanted some honest feedback, and she knew she'd get it from Luke.

She fixed her gaze firmly on the B&B, crossed the street, and entered through the rear of the property into the kitchen, where Lucy was chatting with her chef.

"Hey!" Lucy came over to give her a kiss. "Brian's in the lounge, but I thought you'd probably prefer to talk to him privately, so I've set you up in here. I'll just go and get him." She smiled. "By the way, thanks for all the extra guests coming my way. I wish I'd thought of a way to make myself an internet celeb."

"Be my guest," Bernie said. "I hate it."

Lucy laughed and disappeared down the hall while Bernie stood by the table, trying to decide whether to sit or stay standing. She'd stuck her hands in her pockets because they were shaking so much.

"Hey."

She turned to see a dark-haired man with glasses

standing in the kitchen doorway. He wore a sweatshirt with the Stanford logo on it, khaki pants, and soft, brown lace-up shoes. He looked like a thousand other Californian tech dudes.

"Hey!" She gave him a stupid little wave. "You must be Brian."

"That's me." His smile was wide and generous like hers. "Shake hands, high five, or a hug?"

She regarded him carefully and then nodded. "I think we can risk a hug."

He laughed and stepped forward. "It's great to see you, Bernie."

"I've probably grown a bit since the last time you saw me."

Bernie indicated that they sit down at the table. The chef had disappeared into the back half of the newly extended kitchen, and they were alone. She waited to see whether Brian would mention the viral video.

"Your mom has sent me pictures over the years." Brian settled into a chair. "And your grades."

"She never mentioned that." Bernie poured them both some coffee and let him stir in his own cream and sugar.

"It was part of our divorce agreement. It's about the only thing I'm proud of asking for."

Bernie stirred her coffee and considered what to say next. He seemed warmer in person, and more awkward in a nerdy, tech-guy way. She didn't know how to reconcile that with the person her mom had told her about, who had chosen his career over his family.

"How could you just walk away from us?" Bernie blurted out before she could think it through.

Brian blew out a breath, looked down at the table, and spread his hands wide before answering her.

"I was so hyper-focused on my career goals that I assumed everyone had to prioritize them. Linda wasn't on board with that, and at the time, I didn't have the emotional skills to understand why, so I cut and run." He looked Bernie right in the eye. "It doesn't excuse the fact that I screwed up, but I'm trying to be as honest as I can here. I was a selfish, immature jerk."

Bernie nodded and waited for the, "but," which never came. Okay, so her birth dad knew how to apologize, which had to be a good start.

"Did you know Linda contacted me about my visit here?" Brian asked.

"I know she was threatening to do so."

"I must admit I was quite surprised, especially when she reassured me that she wouldn't meet me with a gun and a list of grievances but with thanks for finally taking an interest in you."

"You only took an interest because she prodded you into it."

"It didn't take much prodding, Bernie. I was already looking for ways to make up for what I did to you both when I redrafted my will." He cleared his throat. "I've been invited to the ranch for lunch on Sunday."

"Holy hell." Bernie blinked at him. "Mom didn't mention that."

"Do you think it's a good idea?" He frowned. "I really don't want to ruffle anyone's feathers."

"If she's asked you, you'll be quite safe. And it's a good opportunity to show you around the humane society barn so you can see what I do with the rest of my time."

"Okay, I'll take your word on that." He opened his laptop. "Now, do you want to talk me through your business plan before we hop over to the café for a look around?"

His swift change of subject reminded her of Mary, but she was more than willing to climb out of the murky waters of her family history to discuss the future of her business.

She took out her own laptop. "Sure. I can't wait to hear what you think about it."

Three hours later, and after an extensive tour of the café, she was exhausted from his rapid-fire questions, and lightning-fast ability to grasp not only what she did well, but the parts she tried not to think about. After leaving the café in the capable hands of Kenya and the excitable mystery of Pen, they returned to the B&B, where Lucy provided tea, coffee, and privacy in her office where there were two comfy chairs.

"Business appears to be booming," Brian remarked as they settled in. "I'm surprised your bank won't agree to a loan based on your current revenue."

"To be fair, it isn't normally like this. We get the tourist trade in the spring, summer, and fall, and then basically shut down in the winter." Bernie sat opposite him and helped herself to a strong cup of tea. "It's super busy because my friend posted a video of me with some of the auction puppies that went viral, and all these people keep turning up to stare at me."

"You went viral?" Brian frowned. "That's interesting. Any idea why?"

"Nope. Just one of those things I suspect," Bernie said. "You could ask Bailey how she did it if you really want to know."

He nodded, his keen gaze intent. "I'm interested in

social media as a means of spreading information fast. I'd like her email."

"I'll check if she's okay with me handing it over."

"Sure." Brian returned his attention to his laptop. "Do you want to go through this now? I think I have a decent idea about how things stand outside the viral phenomena."

"Why not?" Bernie sighed, kicked off her shoes, and curled her feet underneath her. She'd sent him her year-to-date financial statements before his visit, and he'd obviously read them. "Go for it."

"First, I think you should can the coffee side of the business."

"Can, funny." Bernie sat up straight. "I love roasting my own coffee, and it's very popular with my customers."

"But it's the least cost-effective part of your business. It also takes up a lot of your time that could be spent elsewhere. There are dozens of coffee roasters around here whom you could contract with for half of what it's costing you to do it yourself."

She crossed her arms. "I like doing it."

"Okay, let me explain it another way." He turned his screen so she could see the graphs and charts on it. "Your mail-order business is thriving and needs investment. Your café is also doing well and could do even better if you expanded the kitchen size and took on more staff."

"I know all that."

"But if you look at the time you spend on the coffee-making part of the business, and the space it takes up in your facility, you can see they aren't cost productive hours. I mean, you could partner with a different independent coffee roaster every month and still have great variety in the store and all kinds of opportunities to promote the product between you, halving your marketing costs."

She hadn't expected him to go after that part of her business. "I'll have to think about it."

Brian showed her another graph. "If you use the space the coffee-roasting equipment takes up and re-lease the hours you spend at it, you'll have more room in the kitchen for the revenue-generating areas of the business and more time to put into improving it."

"I'm surprised you didn't tell me to give up my work with the humane society."

He considered her. She couldn't decide if his straight delivery was refreshing or maddening. "I haven't seen what that entails yet, but I'm sure I'll have notes. Maybe you could think about which would be easier to let go— the coffee roasting or the humane society."

"Okay, you've got me there. What else?"

"Your staff are hardworking and motivated."

"Thank you."

"You're a good boss and you encourage a pleasant working environment."

"I know," Bernie said.

He smiled. "You need more space. In fact, you really need two kitchens—one for the café and the other for the online business, which I think you should expand to include savory items and maybe even full meals."

"I don't have the oven capacity to do that," Bernie objected.

"But you can add it if you get the kitchen extension done."

"Do you know how hard it is to get staff out here?"

"Yes, I did look at that before I came to see you. You'll have to offer excellent wages and benefits."

"Duh. Even that doesn't work sometimes. Some people are afraid to move out here because of the wildfires and the snow. Affordable accommodation would be useful, too."

"Yeah?" Brian looked interested. "I have a good friend who specializes in converting underutilized buildings into affordable apartments. I bet there are places in and around town that could do with a makeover."

"I'm sure there are, but I don't have the money to convert anything."

"I understand. That's not your priority, but it is something I can look into for you if that's okay." He moved his laptop to one side and faced her. "In my opinion, your number one priorities are to increase the size of your kitchen and take on more staff—maybe even start your own delivery crew for the online business."

"Which requires heaps of money and personnel that I don't have."

Brian sat back. "Which is why I'm going to help you draw up a comprehensive business plan that will have the banks fighting over who gets to fund you."

"So, you don't think I'm overdoing things, like Mom says?"

He grinned at her. "If you ditch the coffee roasting and focus on the other parts of the business, I'd say you're doing just fine."

Bernie smiled back. "If you say that to my mom's face at lunch on Sunday I might even consider going along with your suggestions."

"You're on."

She checked the time. "I have to go back to the café and make sure the new shift is ready to clock in."

"We're having dinner here, correct?" Brian took off his glasses and wiped them on his handkerchief.

"Yes, my boyfriend, Luke, will be joining us, but you

have plenty of time for a nap before he gets here. You drove a long way."

"I might just do that." He put his glasses back on. "I've enjoyed today."

"It's certainly been . . . interesting."

He rose to his feet. "Remember that you don't have to do a single thing I suggest. You're the boss. I'm just offering advice here."

"Don't worry, I get it." She stood up, too. "Thank you."

"You're welcome." He smothered a yawn. "I guess I'll take that nap."

Luke parked in his usual spot at the back of the B&B and made his way to the rear door, which was locked. He tapped on the glass, and Lucy appeared to let him in.

"Hi!" She kissed his cheek. "You're having dinner with Bernie and Brian, right?"

"Correct."

"You could've come through the front door like a regular guest."

"Bernie told me to be discreet. She says there are still a lot of strangers hanging around town."

"Most of them have gone home now, thank goodness." Lucy linked her arm through Luke's and walked him through to the front hall, where the dining room was located. "They're sitting by the far wall."

The dining room was full, which was unusual this early in the season. He had the weirdest sensation that some of the guests were whispering and pointing as he passed, which was confirmed when a teenager suddenly stood up right in his path and thrust her phone at him.

"Can we do a selfie, please?"

Luke took an involuntary step backward and almost collided with one of the servers.

"What?"

"You're Luke, aren't you?" She smiled. "From the video."

Luke glanced wildly toward Bernie, who was talking to her dad and hadn't noticed his arrival.

"Uh, sure."

"Nice!"

He faked a smile and stood next to the girl, who pulled him in close.

"Thanks so much!" She was blushing now. "Are you and puppy girl dating?"

"Yeah."

Her face fell. "I thought so. You look good together, but if anything goes wrong, you can always call me, okay? Can you put your number in my phone so I can send you the pic?"

Luke gently eased away from her. "I'm good, thanks."

"Okay, thanks again."

He managed to get to the table without being accosted again and unceremoniously interrupted Bernie.

"Did you see that?"

She looked up at him. "Luke, this is Brian."

"Nice to meet you, sir." Luke offered his hand to Brian, who shook it. "I've heard a lot about you."

He sat down and addressed Bernie. "I just got asked for a selfie with some teenager, and then propositioned."

Bernie sighed. "In here?"

"Yup."

"I'm going to have to ask Lucy to tell her guests not to bother us. It probably wasn't a good idea to eat publicly."

She looked around the packed room. "Shall we hightail it to the kitchen and eat there?"

"Might be easier if the chef doesn't mind," Luke agreed. "This is getting old real fast."

"Welcome to my life," Bernie muttered. "Let's go."

Chef was delighted to have them sit at the kitchen table so that he could explain all the intricacies of his dishes, which didn't bother Luke half as much as internet fans did.

Brian poured them all a glass of wine. "I hear you're a rancher, Luke."

"Fourth generation."

"It's a tough life, especially out here."

Luke shrugged. "Every job has its good and bad points, and I love mine. What do you do?"

Brian smiled. "I'm basically a software engineer who did well for himself."

"You should talk to Bernie's sister, Mary. She's totally into all that stuff."

"Mom invited Brian to lunch on Sunday, so he'll get to meet the whole family," Bernie said brightly.

"Your mom invited him?" Luke blinked at her. "I mean, I'm sorry, of course she did."

"It's okay, I was surprised myself. We didn't exactly part on good terms," Brian said. "But we're both determined to do the best we can for Bernie."

"She deserves that." Luke held Brian's gaze. "She's amazing."

"So I'm finding out." Brian held up his glass. "Here's to Bernie and the continuing success of her multiple business ventures." He clinked his glass against Luke's and then Bernie's.

When Bernie went to the restroom, Luke was left alone with Brian for the first time. He wasn't at all how

Luke had pictured him, and Bernie seemed quite relaxed around him, which was surprising.

"I hear you and Bernie have been friends since you were kids."

"Yeah."

"Then you probably know her better than anyone." Brian paused. "I'm going to run this by her parents on Sunday, but I'd appreciate your opinion. If I offered her a loan for her business, would she take it?"

"A personal loan?"

"Yes."

Luke sat back. "I think she'd prefer to get a loan on the merits of her business rather than as a handout. She might see it as a bribe or some kind of guilt thing."

"That's what I thought." Brian nodded. "Do you think she'd be more receptive to the idea if the banks turned her down—not that they will."

"I think that would make it worse. She's very stubborn."

"I noticed." Brian's smile was warm and reminded Luke of Bernie's. "We've been disagreeing all day."

He looked up as Bernie returned and took her seat. "Is Luke coming to lunch on Sunday? It might be nice to see another familiar face."

"Linda invited me today, although I didn't know there would be a surprise guest of honor," Luke said. "I was going to ask you if you wanted me to come, Ber."

"I'd love it." She reached over and took his hand. "You're my rock."

Luke smiled at her, and for a moment he completely forgot that they weren't alone.

Brian cleared his throat. "If you'll excuse me, I just need to make a call." He stood up. "Can you order me some coffee? I think I'll skip dessert."

Bernie barely waited until he was out of earshot before she leaned toward Luke.

"What do you think?"

"He seems like a nice guy."

"Seems?"

"I guess I don't understand why someone like him would walk out on his family."

"I did ask him about that," Bernie said.

Luke groaned. "Of course, you did."

"He basically said he was an immature, selfish jerk who didn't realize what he was throwing away."

"Can't argue with that. The fact that he can admit it means he's learned something."

"I think he has." Bernie nodded. "It will be interesting to see how he gets on with Mom and Mike on Sunday."

Luke checked the dessert menu and relayed his and Bernie's choices to the chef along with a request for coffee.

"How did it go today with the business advice?" Luke asked as the plates were cleared off the table.

"Brian was very clear about what he thinks works and what doesn't."

"And how did you feel about that?"

She raised her eyebrows. "I hated it, but he's right—about a lot of things."

"That's my girl, stubborn to the end."

"You know me so well." She paused. "He wasn't asking about your intentions toward me, or anything was he?"

"When you were in the restroom?" Luke shook his head. "Nope."

"Good, because he's still not my dad." She sipped her water. "It's been an exhausting day."

"But worth it?"

"Yes, because he made me see the *possibilities*. And he didn't doubt I could be successful." Her smile made him want to lean in and kiss her. "I wasn't expecting that."

"You're amazing."

She blushed. "Duh."

"Maybe he'll tell Linda not to worry about you so much."

"I asked him to." Bernie grinned. "Although, I'm not sure how she'll take that news. He was supposed to tell me all the bad things about being super focused, impatient, and too greedy."

"You're none of those."

She reached over and punched him gently on the arm. "Stop being so nice."

"I'd be a lot nicer if I could get you alone for more than five minutes," Luke said.

"I know. It's been horrible with everything going on right now. But Bailey said the hits are falling on the videos, and there were slightly fewer gawkers around town today."

"Good, because the pet auction is in a couple of weeks, and I'd especially like the puppies to go to local people," Luke said.

Bernie frowned. "I don't mind where they go as long as they are going to be part of a warm and loving family."

"Which is why it's better to go local, because we know everyone around here."

"Just because they are local doesn't mean they are the best match. You've traveled all over the world; you know there are good people everywhere."

Luke fake shuddered. "Not usually in the places I went to."

"You're beginning to sound like one of those people who've never left their hometown," Bernie said.

"There's nothing wrong with knowing where your home is."

He wasn't sure why he sounded so defensive, and he didn't like the way Bernie was looking at him. It reminded him of the conversation he'd had earlier with his mom. He was almost relieved when Brian reappeared and sat down.

"I was just talking to that friend of mine who specializes in renovating old buildings. If you're okay with it, Bernie, I'll send him some information about the town and its current infrastructure, and he can take it from there."

"Fine by me." Bernie slowly tore her gaze away from Luke.

Their desserts and coffee arrived, and they all dug in, giving Luke much-needed breathing space. After the meal, which Brian insisted on paying for, Luke got up to leave.

"I must get back. With Max gone, I share lock-down duties with Noah."

Brian held out his hand. "It's been a pleasure to meet you, Luke."

"Likewise." Luke shook his hand.

"I'll walk you out," Bernie said.

"No need," Luke said lightly. "I'm parked right outside."

Bernie started walking, and he followed her out through the kitchen to the back of the B&B. He stopped beside his truck and unlocked the door.

"I guess I'll see you on Sunday, then?"

"Yes." She looked up at him. "Are you okay?"

"Why wouldn't I be?"

She hesitated. "Sometimes you can be a little . . . stubborn about certain subjects."

He knew damn well what she was talking about, but he wasn't going to admit it. "Like what?"

"Anything to do with yourself?"

"I know we're dating, Bernie, but that doesn't mean I have to tell you everything."

"You used to when I was just your best friend." She angled her head to look at him, her brown-eyed gaze suddenly wary. "Or maybe you didn't."

"Do we have to get into it right now?" Luke asked. "I don't know where you're going with this, and I'm too tired to give you the answers you obviously think you deserve."

"Okay." She took a step back. "Understood." She blew him a kiss. "Have a great rest of your evening."

"Bernie . . ."

She was already walking away but looked back over her shoulder. "Don't you dare 'Bernie' me when you just told me to butt out."

"I said I was tired."

"*I'm* tired, Luke, but I'm not the one throwing up barriers because I can't handle my girlfriend asking me a personal question." She shook her head. "And you're right. Let's not do this. I've had a great day up until now."

She went back into the B&B and slammed the door with a bang, leaving Luke feeling stupid. He was the one who was supposed to have his shit together and he was acting like a fool. He got into his truck and started the engine. If everyone would just leave him the hell alone so he could pretend everything was fine, life would be a whole lot easier.

CHAPTER SEVENTEEN

Bernie spent Sunday morning helping her mom cook an enormous lunch that would easily feed the whole town. Linda had gotten her hair and nails done so that Brian wouldn't think she was "just some rancher's wife" and wore her tightest jeans, best bra, and flattering top, just to make sure he knew what he'd lost. Bernie had spent as many hours reassuring her mom that Brian was okay as she had cooking and was already exhausted.

She hadn't spoken directly to Luke since their argument at the B&B. Sometimes his refusal to admit that he had problems was infuriating. She'd hoped their increasing intimacy would help bridge the barriers he'd erected against her, but he couldn't seem to do it, which didn't make her feel great about their future together. And she wanted a future with him. When they were in tune, he was everything she had ever wanted in a man.

Had it been a colossal mistake to get involved with him? Would he ever let her in completely?

"Bernie? Will you quit staring out the window and get on with those carrots?" Linda called out, making her jump.

"Sorry, Mom." Bernie hurried over to the sink. "What time are we expecting everyone?"

"In half an hour, so we'd better hurry up."

Only fifteen minutes passed before Bernie spotted Luke's truck pulling up outside. She was strangely reluctant to go out and greet him, which wasn't a good feeling.

"Luke's here!" Mary rushed toward the door and went outside, followed by the dogs.

"I think your sister's got a little crush on your boyfriend," Linda murmured. "He's always so good with her."

"What am I supposed to do about that?" Bernie asked as she watched Mary hug Luke, take his hand, and drag him toward the front door. He was wearing his best shirt, jeans, and boots, and had trimmed his beard. He carried a bunch of flowers and a bottle of wine.

"Nothing. He's a good role model for her to practice her charms on."

"Lucky old Luke," Bernie said as she set the carrots in a sieve on the drainer while the water boiled on the stove.

"Everything okay with you two?" Linda asked.

"We're good, thanks." Bernie turned toward the door as Mary came through with Luke and walked over to her. "Hey! You made it!"

She kissed his cheek and stood aside as he handed the wine and flowers to her mom, who then hugged him.

"Do you want to see the puppies?" Mary asked. "I'm quite sad that they'll be leaving us in a week or so, are you?"

"As long as they go to good homes, I'm happy for them," Luke replied as he edged cautiously around Cleopatra, who was definitely stalking him and already growling under her breath. "Maybe we can check out the puppies after lunch? I think Brian wants to see them, too."

"Bernie's birth father?" Mary frowned. "Why would he want to see them?"

"Because he's helping me with all aspects of my businesses and the humane society is one of those reasons."

"But it's a nonprofit," Mary said.

"Which means it's a lot of work and it needs constant fundraising to keep it going," Bernie reminded her.

"I would've thought you'd earned enough money from the videos to fund it for the next ten years." Mary turned to Luke. "It was my idea that you do one with Bernie. I knew everyone would love it. I've watched it twenty times."

"It was a great idea," Luke agreed. "But I think we're all glad things have started to go back to normal now."

"Yeah, the latest sensation is a toddler feeding a giant koi fish and singing to it in Japanese while it makes bubbles." Mary nodded. "It's way funnier than Bernie."

"Thanks." Bernie heard a car outside. "That's probably Brian. I'll go and say hi."

She walked out into the weak sunshine and inhaled a deep breath. She still wasn't sure how things would go between her mom and Brian. If her mom told him to take a hike, would Bernie have to say goodbye to his input on her business ventures? Not that she'd even hesitate to ditch him if her mom wasn't happy, but it had been nice to talk to someone who totally got her.

"Don't be selfish," Bernie muttered to herself as she approached Brian's car and he got out, also carrying flowers and wine. "Hey! You found the place."

"Thanks to your excellent directions, which became vital when my navigation system quit on me halfway along the county road." He smiled at her. "Everything okay?"

"Yup! Come on in, we don't bite."

Well, her cat might. . . . She could only hope Cleopatra would like Brian more than she liked Luke, which wouldn't be hard. She took him through the front door and out to the family room and kitchen, where her mom and Mike stood together holding hands and waiting for them.

Brian cleared his throat. "Thank you both for inviting me." He held out the flowers and wine. "These are for you."

"That's very sweet," Linda replied, a faint tremor in her voice betraying her nervousness. "You are welcome in our home."

"I appreciate that."

Mike stepped forward to shake Brian's hand. "Good to meet you."

"Likewise."

Mary stepped in front of Brian. "You don't look much like Bernie. Are you quite sure you're her father?"

"One hundred percent," Brian said, nodding.

"Have you investigated DNA testing? I've heard it's very accurate these days."

"Mary." Linda put her arm around her daughter. "Brian is definitely Bernie's father."

Bill and MJ came forward to meet Brian and then retreated into the family room with their phones. Luke stepped up with his usual easy smile and helped smooth things over while the last preparations for the meal went on in the kitchen.

Halfway through the meal, Bernie started to relax. Her mom's stress level had visibly reduced, Mike and Luke were calmness personified, and Brian was dealing with all the questions without getting offended at all.

"Bernie was telling me that the town lacks affordable housing," Brian said as he helped himself to more gravy.

"It's definitely part of the reason why it's hard to get workers up here," Mike said. "There's also the isolation, the risk of forest fires, the cold winters . . . You've got to be okay with being on your own."

"I'm not sure I could live here full time," Brian said. "It's great to visit, but I prefer being in a city."

"Where do you live?" Mary asked.

"Near San Francisco, in a place called Saratoga." He glanced over at Bernie. "I'm hoping I can persuade your sister to come and visit me there."

"That would be cool." Bernie kept her tone light, as if she didn't really believe he meant it.

"And you're all welcome, too." Brian's attention went around the table. "I have plenty of guest bedrooms."

"I'm considering colleges for my PhD near you, so I'd appreciate that," Mary said.

"Your . . . PhD?" Brian raised his eyebrows.

"She's a nerd genius," Bill said, and Mary stuck out her tongue at him.

"She finished high school early, and she's almost finished with her undergraduate degree," Linda said proudly. "She'll need scholarships and grants to go further, but I don't think that will be a problem."

"And you're only seventeen?" Brian asked. "That's incredible."

Mary nodded. "I know I'm not technically your daughter, but I'd be more than willing to allow you to use your influence to get me into the right college."

"Mary!" Linda said. "That is not an appropriate thing to ask any guest."

"Why not?" Mary frowned. "You're all okay with him helping Bernie even though he left when she was three."

Everyone at the table went quiet.

"That's a different conversation entirely, and neither of

them will be happening at my dinner table!" Linda said strongly.

"Okay." Mary returned her attention to her food.

Brian caught Linda's eye. "I would be more than happy to have a private conversation with you about anything you want before I leave—if everyone is okay with that."

"Thank you," Linda said. "I'll think about it. Now, why don't you finish up your meal and Bernie can take you down to meet the puppies in the barn."

Luke glanced over at Bernie as they followed Mary and Brian down the path to the lower barn. She'd been quiet during the meal, and he wasn't sure what was up with her.

"That went well."

"Better than I expected." She wasn't really looking at him as she walked, her hands tucked into the pockets of her best jeans.

"I thought it was about to go off the rails when Mary got involved, but your mom got it right back on track."

"That's Mary for you."

"Brian's a decent guy."

"He seems to be." Bernie stopped to kick a stone off the path.

"Will you take him up on his offer to visit him in Saratoga?" Luke took the opportunity to pause alongside her. Mary, Brian, and the twins had disappeared down the trail, chattering away like they'd known each other forever.

"Maybe." She finally met his gaze and took a deep breath. "Will you come with me?"

"I would've thought you'd prefer to go alone—what

with it being a business meeting and not a vacation," he said carefully.

"Okay, so what if I added a vacation element to my plans. Would you come, then?"

"Why are you being so insistent that I have to be involved?" Luke asked. "You're perfectly capable of handling Brian and your business on your own."

"That's not what I'm trying to establish here. The question is whether you'd be willing to accompany me."

"And what if I don't think it's right to suddenly make this all about me?"

She pressed her lips together. "When was the last time you went anywhere, Luke?"

His gut clenched and it took him far too long to come up with a reply. "That's got nothing to do with what we're discussing right now."

"You know it does." She reached out to touch him, and he stepped back. "When, Luke?"

"I've been to plenty of places." He only realized he was glaring when he saw the hurt blossom in her eyes. "Just because I don't go around listing them off or telling you doesn't mean I don't get out."

"I don't think you've been more than ten miles from the ranch since you left the marines." She held his gaze, and he was the first to look away.

"This is stupid. We should catch up with the others."

"So you won't come with me."

He'd already started moving on, and he swung back to look at her, his voice rising. "Can you just let it go? Maybe I don't want to come because I have a ranch to run, I'm shorthanded, and everyone depends on me to see them through another goddamn year!"

She swallowed hard. "Okay." A tear glistened in the

corner of her eye before she quickly nodded and dashed it away. "I'm sorry. I guess I was being selfish."

It was her turn to start walking, and she brushed past him. "I'd better find Brian before Mary persuades him to offer her a scholarship to Stanford."

Luke waited until she disappeared before letting out a stream of curses and punching the nearest tree, which didn't help at all. There was nothing like seeing the person you loved literally give up on you in real time, and it was all his own damn fault. He'd pushed her away, and she'd listened to his stupid excuses, accepted the blame, and left him to it.

Probably for good.

She wasn't going to cry. Bernie almost stumbled down the hillside as she hurried to get away from Luke. He'd let her know exactly where they stood trust-wise, and she should be grateful to him for laying it out so plainly. He didn't want her to get close to him, and he had better things to worry about than a stupid trip to Saratoga with her.

The thing was—his excuses for not going were entirely valid, but their entire conversation felt wrong somehow. Maybe she shouldn't have baited him. Was she trying to convince herself that his reluctance to travel more than a mile or so from his ranch was just her imagination? She should have asked Sally or Noah whether they'd noticed the same thing before rushing in to perform her own stupid single-handed intervention.

No one liked to be cornered, and hurt animals often lashed out. She just hadn't expected such an extreme reaction from normally even-tempered Luke.

She stopped at the entrance to the barn, blew her nose on a tissue in her pocket, and went inside. She had to pretend everything was fine. The last thing she wanted was for Brian or her siblings to wonder what was up with her.

She could hear Mary's voice coming from Pandora's stall and went to join her family. She had no idea how she would deal with Luke if he chose to come to the barn; her hurt was still too raw to manage much more than the pretense of politeness.

"The puppies are cute." Brian was sitting on one of the hay bales, well away from the dogs who were currently swarming all over the twins and Mary.

"Not a dog person?" Bernie asked.

"I prefer cats, but I can see the attraction of these for a charity auction. How do you make sure the potential owners are a good fit?"

"Everyone who wants to be part of the auction is preapproved before they're given a bidding number. I personally vet all the applicants."

"That must be time consuming."

"It was this year because of all the outside interest, but normally I handle it along with Mom."

"Can I see the rest of the place?"

"Sure. We do have lots of adoptable cats if you're interested."

He smiled. "I'm not home enough to be a responsible owner right now, and paying someone to look after my cat when I'm not there seems to defeat the purpose of having one."

"Understandable." Bernie turned to MJ. "Will you make sure to lock up behind you when you leave Pandora's stall? I don't want any puppies getting out."

"Will do." MJ, who was the most responsible of her siblings, nodded. "I don't think we've had any trespassers today, but it pays to be careful."

"Trespassers?" Brian asked as he shut the door behind them.

"Trying to see the puppies before the auction," Bernie explained. There was no sign of Luke. She hoped he'd have the sense to leave her in peace and go back to the house. "Not the locals who have more sense than to get in the middle of a working ranch, but the internet crazies."

"Is that still a thing?"

"It's dying down. I think by the time we have the auction we'll be back to normal again. Now, let me show you around so that you can see what I do in my leisure time."

Luke didn't appear, and after Bernie gave Brian the VIP tour, they headed back up to the house through the early evening shadows. Bernie loved this time of the day, as the sun set and a chill crept down the hills to fog the hollows and obscure the forest.

"What you're doing here is admirable," Brian said.

"I sense a 'but.'" Bernie turned to look at him as the path widened.

"You know what I'm going to say. It's a lot to take on along with your very ambitious business plans."

"So, you're siding with my mom after all."

"No, I'm simply saying that you need to prioritize your time. If the animal-rescue stuff is important to you then something else has to give."

"I've always considered sleeping overrated anyway," Bernie said, noticing the lack of Luke's truck parked outside the house. She wasn't sure whether to laugh or cry.

"Just don't be me," Brian said. "I got my priorities so out of whack that I forgot what was important and lost you and your mom."

"Luckily, I'm not married."

"You are in a relationship," Brian said.

"Luke's even busier than I am. He understands." Bernie pushed open the door to the mudroom and shucked off her boots. "Have you got time for some coffee or do you need to get back?"

"I've got time." He took off his jacket and shoes. "I might need to call the B&B to let them know I'll be in late, but that's easy to do."

"Go ahead. I'll let Mom and Dad know you're here and put the coffee on."

She checked her phone; there was a text from Luke.

Thought it was best if I stopped ruining your
day with your family and went home. I apologize
if I upset you.

She stared at his text for a long time before putting her cell away without answering it. What was she supposed to say? She'd already apologized for making assumptions about him and their relationship, and there was nothing to add. He'd drawn his boundaries, and she'd walked right into them. Maybe it was time she stopped chasing him and draw some of her own.

Luke walked in on his family having dinner and immediately checked the time.

"Sorry I'm late."

Noah frowned. "We weren't expecting you. You said you'd be out at the Murphy place."

"I think Bernie wanted Brian to spend some time alone with her family without me hanging around." Luke got himself a plate and took the smallest helping of chicken casserole he could get away with without drawing his mother's attention. He'd already eaten a full meal at the Murphy place.

"Did she actually tell you to leave?" Noah asked.

"Not in so many words, but I know her well enough to get the context without her having to tell me to my face."

Jen smiled. "You and Bernie are almost psychic. That's probably why you make such a great couple."

Luke stuffed his mouth full of food so that he had the excuse of chewing and not answering. He wasn't sure they were a couple any longer. He'd texted Bernie an apology after he'd explained to her parents that he had to leave, but she hadn't replied, and he wasn't certain she would. She was probably sick of him running away when things got tough, and he couldn't blame her.

"How's the auction prep going?" Jen asked. "I'm all set up for the feline part of the day."

"Great!" Luke said. "We have about thirty dogs, and Pandora's puppies. Everything is set up and ready to go."

"I had a text from Bailey earlier. She says that she and the twins will be here." Noah drank his glass of water in three gulps.

"That's awesome." Luke tried to inject some enthusiasm into his voice.

Noah looked at Luke. "Bailey wants to know if there will be any cats at the auction."

"Bidding or just hanging out?" Luke asked.

"I don't think she cares." He paused. "I already told her not to bid or buy anything with four legs, but she never listens to me."

"Who does?" Jen asked, and kissed Noah's cheek, which earned her a reluctant smile. "Just remind her that I'm taking care of the kitty adoptions and I'll treat her right."

"I volunteered to build a platform in front of the barn,

so I'll be there, too, making sure no one falls through it,"
Noah said.

"And I'm taking care of Sky!" Luke's mom added.
"We'll arrive in time for the actual event after his nap."

Luke forced down his food and took an active part in
cleaning up because anything was better than being alone
with his thoughts. It was strange how everyone was just
going on with their lives when he'd just blown a major
hole in his own. Part of him knew that the best thing he
could do was to go to Bernie and tell her the truth about
why he'd freaked out.

He went down to the basement, threw the damp dish-
cloth in the laundry basket, and went back up the stairs
into the kitchen. His mom smiled at him.

"How did it go with Brian meeting Mike and Linda?"

"Good. They all acted like mature human beings."

Sally sighed. "That's great."

"You were hoping for drama?" Luke asked.

"Maybe." She winked at him. "Would you like some
hot chocolate? I'm making some for me and Jen."

"Thanks, but I've got some stuff to do in the barn."
Luke went over to give her a hug. "I'll get some when I
come back."

He put on his boots and fleece-lined jacket and headed
out. There wasn't much to do because Noah had obviously been out and done most of it earlier. He still checked
all the stalls and topped up a few water buckets before
ending up in the feed room decanting huge bags of grain
and dog food into sealed containers.

It was quiet in the barn, apart from the odd hoof scrap-
ing against the concrete floor or the rustle of hay. Luke
almost missed Max's terrible whistling and insistence on

talking even when it was obvious that the person he was talking to didn't want to hear what he had to say.

Luke leaned back against the counter and got out his phone. There was nothing from Bernie. He almost wished Max was standing right in front of him because he could sure do with some honest feedback right now at the moment. He tapped on Max's profile picture and started typing in a text.

Hey, I know you're not talking to me, but I've really screwed things up with Bernie and this time I don't think I can fix it. I know you'd tell me to get over myself and beg but I'm not sure that would work.

There was no reply—not that he'd expected one—but he could already imagine what Max would say anyway. Seeing his own failure in black and white made it worse somehow. He checked the time and went out to his truck. Bernie deserved to hear the truth, and he was the only person who could deliver it.

"Bernie?"

Linda put her head around Bernie's bedroom door. "Luke's back. He said he forgot to give you something important."

"I'm in my jammies," Bernie said. "Can't it wait until tomorrow?"

"He's downstairs, honey. Why don't you go and tell him yourself?"

Her mom walked away, leaving Bernie staring after her. She didn't want to talk to Luke right now. In fact, she wasn't sure if she ever wanted to talk to him again, and certainly not until she'd sorted out her own feelings.

She sighed, put on her dressing gown and slippers, and went down the stairs to find him alone in the kitchen.

"Hey." He nodded stiffly at her.

"What's up?"

He set his Stetson down on the counter and shoved a hand through his hair. "I wanted to clarify something."

"Okay." She walked toward Mike's office. "Come in here so we can have some privacy."

She waited until he closed the door and turned to face him, her arms crossed tightly over her chest.

Luke looked down at his boots. "I shouldn't have gotten mad at you."

She didn't have anything she wanted to say to that and waited for him to go on.

"When you suggested I come with you to Saratoga, I kind of panicked and lashed out." He grimaced. "I guess you already knew that."

"I was right there." She paused. "I shouldn't have pushed you into a corner."

"Maybe you needed to. It wasn't because my life is busy and you were being selfish. It was because I . . . *am* struggling with getting out of my comfort zone right now." He briefly met her gaze.

"I kind of knew that, Luke," she said gently.

He looked away from her. "I guess you did."

"I think it's more important that you are honest with yourself, because if you can't even say exactly what's going on with you, then how can you expect me to believe you get what the problem is?"

A muscle twitched in his jaw. "Okay, I'm a goddamn coward. Is that what you want to hear?"

"I don't think you're a coward," Bernie said, choosing her words with care. "You're a retired marine who fought in a terrifying war."

"Yeah, a marine who's scared of his own shadow." He let out his breath. "But that, as they say, is a me problem, and it's not on you." He finally met her gaze. "I just want you to know that."

"Thank you," Bernie said.

He rubbed a hand over the back of his neck. "So, are we good?"

"About what?"

"Everything." The wariness returned to his blue eyes. "Us."

"I hope we'll always be friends."

"And what about the rest of it?"

She took in a labored breath. "I don't think that's working for me."

"Why the hell not?"

"Because you didn't trust me enough to tell me the truth in the first place." She met his gaze, his fingers gripping her elbows so tightly it hurt. "I told you this before. You can't keep shutting me out, walking away, and then waltzing back in with your highly edited explanations that I'm supposed to just accept."

He winced. "That's . . . harsh."

"I shouldn't *have* to push you into a corner to let me in." Bernie struggled to control the tremor in her voice. "And if you can't trust me as your lover *or* your friend, what's the point? I care about you a lot, Luke, but I can't do this anymore."

"What if I try harder? I can—"

"You can't." She swallowed hard. "And I can't face

the crushing disappointment of never being good enough for you to truly confide in."

He took a step toward her. "You're *way* better than me—"

She held up her hand. "Luke, can you just stop?"

"But I want to fix this. I *have* to fix this."

"So that you look good to yourself—that you sorted out your little Bernie problem and everything else is fine?"

His brow creased. "You know that's not what I meant. I don't want there to be no 'us.'"

"I'm not the solution to your problems, Luke." She went to walk past him, and he half turned and stepped in front of her.

"What's that supposed to mean?"

"Maybe you thought being with me, having sex with me, would . . ." she swallowed hard ". . . I don't know, be a Band-Aid for everything else you don't want to deal with."

He stiffened. "That's a goddamn lie."

"Okay, maybe you thought you were doing me a favor by fulfilling my fantasies while never, ever letting me get close to the new Luke." She bit her lip. "I guess it's a lesson I needed to learn, and I get it now, I really do."

"You know that's bullshit, right?"

"Not to me." She headed for the door feeling like she was walking over the smoldering ashes of all her stupid hopes and dreams. "Maybe we are better off as friends. I'm going to bed. Good night, Luke. You can see yourself out."

She managed to hold it together until she reached her bedroom and heard his truck leave. Even as her tears started to fall, a sense of resolve filled her. Unsurprisingly, her lifetime crush hadn't worked out, but she was still a good person, and Luke . . . was also a good person who deserved to find someone he could love without putting up any barriers—someone who obviously wasn't her.

She lay on her bed and stared up at the ceiling. The thought of never being with Luke, never sharing her body with his or sleeping alongside him hurt so badly she didn't want to deal with it. She'd always loved him, and despite everything that had happened between them, she probably always would. Even as she blew her nose, it occurred to her that Luke had never talked about loving her, which said it all.

She'd get through the hurt. It wasn't as if she didn't have enough to do. The time she'd planned to spend with Luke could now be redirected to building her business empire. She rolled over, groaned into her pillow, and reached for her phone.

She scrolled through to Luke's number and started typing.

> I would appreciate it if we can stay on good terms and get through the next 2 weeks until the auction, but if you want to bail, I totally understand. I just need to know asap. Thanks.

She went to the bathroom to get ready for bed and when she came back, he'd replied.

> I'm still in. Whatever you may think of me, I don't go back on my promises.

He was obviously still upset with her, but at least he was willing to keep up appearances for a while, which was totally on-brand for him. She'd have to face her family and friends over dumping him at some point, and the later that happened the better. She plugged in her phone and got into bed, her mind going over every word Luke had said to her. She also replayed her replies and endlessly corrected them, which wasn't helpful because she'd said her truth, and nothing would change that, but oh, somehow, she wished it could. . . .

CHAPTER EIGHTEEN

"What's up with you?" Noah asked as he heaved a bale of straw into the back of his truck. They'd finished the ranch chores and were heading over to the Murphy place to help set up the seating area for the auction, which was taking place in less than a week.

"Nothing."

"Dude . . ."

Luke faced his friend. "Bernie and I split up."

Noah raised his eyebrows. "I knew that. What else?"

"That's not enough?" Luke asked. "Who told you anyway?"

"Bernie told Jen and Jen told me." Noah picked up another bale. "But even I noticed you've been looking like your favorite horse died all week."

"Why didn't you say anything?"

Noah shrugged. "I guess I was waiting for you to tell *me*. With Max away, I'm the closest thing you have to a best friend if you exclude Bernie, which in this instance is a given."

Luke grimaced at the gentle rebuke. It kind of echoed what Bernie had said about him shutting people out. "I . . . yeah . . . I should have told you."

"It would've been nice not to hear it secondhand," Noah agreed. "But you've always been the kind of guy who kept all his problems to himself."

"Which is why I've ended up in this mess," Luke muttered as he set another bale on the tailgate and shoved it to the back of the bed.

Noah leaned against the side of the truck. "I'm not great at getting information out of you like Max is, but I am here if you need to talk."

"Max just makes me mad enough to spill my secrets, and that's probably not healthy. I don't know what to say about Bernie."

Noah went back to hauling bales. "Do you miss her?"

"Hard to miss someone you see almost every day."

"But does that make things easier or harder?" Noah looked over at him. "I know when I was fighting with Jen that being close to her and not being with her was painful."

"We're still friendly," Luke clarified. "We're both adults."

"Okay."

"What's that supposed to mean?"

"Means you probably screwed up, my friend." Noah nodded. "If you were good about the split, you'd be relieved, not still hurting."

"Who said I was hurting?" Luke demanded.

"Dude, I have to look at your miserable face all day."

"No one likes being dumped."

"True, especially when they know they were the ass." Noah counted the bales. "We're at our weight limit. Let's take these over and come back for the rest."

Luke got into the passenger seat and looked over at

Noah. "I'm starting to remember why I don't confide in you."

"Because you're my boss and you don't want to appear weak?" Noah backed the truck out of the barn and headed out through the forest.

"You suck at this," Luke said.

"If I've got you playing defense, I think I've done good." Noah smiled, which was a rarity unless he was looking at Jen. "Now, all you need to do is work out how to fix it and get her back."

"There isn't a fix. Bernie made that very clear. She wants to go back to just being friends."

"And you're good with that?" Noah gave him the side-eye. "Because, if you don't mind me mentioning it, you don't look like a man who's happy with his freedom."

"Shut it, Noah."

"Sure. I'll leave you to think about it." Noah waited for the top gate to swing open and eased the heavily laden truck through the fence posts. "I'm sure you'll come up with a plan."

Luke spent the rest of the journey looking out the window and mentally preparing himself for yet another interaction with Bernie. Despite his insistence that things were working out just fine between them, seeing her and not being with her was torture. She treated him like an old friend, and he absolutely hated it. He played along because what else could he do? But every friendly smile cut deep and made him aware of just how much he'd screwed up.

She didn't seem as bothered as he was, which made sense because she'd been the one to cut through his shit and hit him with a series of truths he didn't want to deal with. Had he taken her love so much for granted that he'd assumed he could behave however he wanted and she'd still want to be with him?

"Hey, daydreamer." Noah knocked on his half-open window. "You gonna help me with this load?"

Noah's voice cut through Luke's thoughts, and he hurriedly got out of the truck. The area in front of the humane society barn had been leveled, the grass mowed, and the beginnings of a wooden platform started in front of the barn doors so that the animals could be brought out and put back during the actual auction without having to go through the crowds.

Luke put on his work gloves. "Where are we putting the bales?"

"Nowhere, yet. We're just going to stack them here until Bernie decides where she wants them."

"Got it."

Luke lowered the tailgate, grabbed the twine, and hefted the first bale onto the ground. He'd taken a quick look around and saw no sign of Bernie. Having put the café on the back burner in the afternoons while she attended to the million things that needed doing for the auction, she usually turned up at some point.

"Hey, Noah!"

He turned at the sound of her voice to see her coming out of the barn. Her hair was in a single braid down her back, and she wore ancient denim overalls over a shrunken pink T-shirt that left parts of her skin showing. She hadn't seen him, yet, which meant he got to appreciate the full warmth of her smile for his friend.

"Hey." Noah kept working. "We've got a second load to bring over as well."

"That's great!"

Luke straightened and touched his hat to her.

"Bernie."

"Hi, Luke." She immediately turned back to Noah. "When is Bailey arriving?"

"The night before the auction. She and the twins are staying up at the ranch in the snowmobile annex."

Luke remembered the last time he'd been in the annex with Bernie, and they'd gotten so close he'd never wanted to let her go. . . .

"Nice. I can't wait to see her," Bernie said. "The website design has made such a huge difference to our visibility and fund-raising efforts."

"She enjoyed doing it." Noah glanced over at Luke. "Don't let me stop you from helping out here, boss."

"I didn't want to get in your way," Luke said as he walked toward them. "I know how easily you get knocked over."

Noah looked down at him. "You're the one who fell off his horse and broke his arm."

"Only because your horse wasn't doing what it was supposed to do." Luke grabbed another bale and pulled it toward him.

"What is it they say about a bad workman blaming his tools, Bernie?" Noah said to Bernie, who was trying not to look at Luke.

She laughed and turned away. "I'll leave you to it. Come and find me if you need anything. I'll be in the barn."

Noah waited until she was out of earshot before he turned to Luke. "Nice way to engage her interest by not talking to her at all."

"It's all part of my cunning plan to make her come back to me," Luke muttered.

"And how's that working out for you?"

Luke ignored his friend and concentrated on finishing his task. He closed the tailgate and stuck his gloves in the back pocket of his jeans. "Ready for load number two."

Noah got into the truck. "Go and tell Bernie we'll be back, will you?"

"You already told her that," Luke pointed out.

"There's no reason to be rude." Noah raised his eyebrows. "Your mama wouldn't like it."

"Fine," Luke muttered as he stomped into the barn. "Hey, Bernie?"

"Over here!"

Her voice came from her makeshift corner office, and he went in that direction. She was sitting behind her desk, a pile of papers that rivaled the one on his own desk covered the surface, and she was on the phone, leafing through a pile of invoices.

"Yes, that's correct. We'll need you here all day. You can set up before the auction opens in the shade of the oak trees. I think you'll do really well."

She ended the call and turned to Luke, the smile in her eyes fading into wary politeness.

"What's up?"

"Noah wanted me to let you know that we're going back to pick up the second load of bales."

"Okay, thanks."

He paused. "How are you doing?"

"Great!"

He pointed at her desk. "You look busy."

"I am, but it's nothing I can't handle."

"I know that." He tried to think of something else to say—anything that meant he could keep looking at her face. "We still haven't heard from Max."

"That's a real shame." She finally met his gaze. "I hope he's okay."

"Not half as much as I do, seeing as it was my fault he left in the first place." He paused. "I know everyone keeps telling me it's on him, but I still feel responsible."

"That's tough." She nodded, her gaze falling to her phone. "If there's nothing else . . . ?"

"Will you have a drink with me after the auction's done?"

"I'm not really capable of thinking beyond that day right now, so why don't you remind me later?" She picked up her cell. "I'm sorry, I really have to take this call."

"Okay." Luke accepted defeat and turned away. "I'll do that."

He got back in the truck and glared at Noah. "She totally blew me off."

"Hardly a surprise." Noah drove off.

"Then why did you tell me to go and talk to her?"

"Maybe I just like seeing you suffer. You've got to test the waters, boss."

"Well, they're still icy."

"Then you'll need to keep trying. You're a goddamn marine."

Bernie pressed her fingers into her temples and groaned. Every time she saw Luke Nilsen, she ended up with a horrible tension headache. The fact that he'd tossed out an invitation for her to have a drink with him like it was no big deal had almost destroyed her composure. Part of her wanted to rush to agree and watch him smile his approval while the rest of her was cross that the new Bernie was still willing to dance to his tune.

But was "new Bernie" any match for twenty years of Luke love? It was only a week since she'd broken up with him. It would take time and energy to repair her anti-Luke defenses, neither of which she currently had a spare supply of. And she was the one who'd asked him to keep helping with the auction, which meant she was either a masochist or delusional. Until today, he'd kept to his side of the bargain and been pleasant and friendly, and she'd been the same. By asking her out for a drink was he showing his hand—that he still thought he'd be able to reel her back in when it suited him?

"Why are you scowling?" Jen asked as she came in with yet another clipboard and a pile of paper.

"Luke."

"What did he do now?" Jen sat down in front of Bernie's desk.

"Asked me out for a drink after the auction's done."

"I suppose that's progress." Jen looked at her inquiringly. "I mean, we all love a man who won't give up, don't we?"

"It's Luke. He's got all the cards. He's always known how I feel about him, and he's assuming that he can just click his fingers and get me back whenever it suits him."

"He doesn't look like a man who thinks he's winning, Bernie. In fact, when he forgets to pretend everything is totally fine, he looks downright miserable," Jen said.

Bernie folded her arms and fought a sense of guilt. "The only reason he's still annoyed is because I dumped him, and he can't deal with that."

"You're making him sound like some deranged stalker, and we both know that's not really fair." Jen paused. "I'm totally on your side, Bernie, but I seriously think that for once in his life Luke finds himself in a situation where he can't figure a way out, and he's at sea, floundering around. Maybe even going under."

"Good, then he'll know how the rest of us feel."

Bernie scowled at her friend and then sighed. "I don't want him to flounder. I want him to be happy."

"I'm not disagreeing with you," Jen said. "And I don't think you should change your mind about him. He *deserved* to be called out. But if he really cares, he'll have to figure out a way to show you all on his own."

"He never said he loved me."

"Bernie . . ."

"He never said the words." Bernie met Jen's sympathetic gaze. "I suppose that should make it hurt less, but somehow it doesn't."

"Men." Jen shook her head. "What an ass. Any sympathy I had for him has gone right out the window now."

"I bet Noah told you he loved you."

Jen fought a smile. "Not without a family intervention."

Bernie sighed. "Noah and Luke are due back here soon. I'm going to let you deal with them."

Jen cracked her knuckles. "It'll be my pleasure."

After Jen left, Bernie spent half an hour on the phone with Brian going over her revised business plan, which included her decision to let the coffee roasting go and see how things went with her new suppliers and her customers. Brian was very enthusiastic about the changes she'd made and the spreadsheets she'd produced, but Bernie couldn't quite get into it.

"Did Linda tell you I'm coming for the auction weekend?" Brian asked at the end of their conversation.

"Yes, apparently you're staying at Lucy's place."

"We both thought it might be a great opportunity for you to take that trip to Saratoga. You can come back with me when I leave."

"You and Mom are agreeing on something? Has the world ended?"

He chuckled. "We agree about ninety percent of the time about you, although she asked me to ask you about Luke and I declined, so she's probably mad at me again right now."

"What about Luke?"

"She said you'd split up."

"Correct."

"Are you okay about that?" He sighed. "I have no idea what I'm supposed to say in these situations."

"I'm fine about it, and just think about all the hours I'll be able to devote to my business," Bernie said.

"I thought the plan was not to end up with a business empire and no life like me."

"Maybe the money will make up for that."

"It won't," Brian said. "I thought Luke was a good match for you, but that's all I have to say on the matter."

"I wish Mom felt the same. She's being super passive-aggressive about it right now." Bernie sighed. "Okay, I'd better get going. There's a lot to do here, and I have to get back to the café and check in with everyone."

She closed her laptop, put it in her backpack, and went out to her truck. It was annoying how often her thoughts turned to Luke even though she was running around like a headless chicken. He'd always been part of her life, and it was harder to fill the space he'd occupied than she'd imagined. But capitulating and going back wasn't happening. Just because she loved him didn't mean that he got to take that love for granted and give her nothing in return. She wanted all of him, the good *and* the bad. She was more than willing to stand by his side and support him through anything, but she deserved more, and she couldn't force Luke to deal with his PTSD. That was up to him.

She saw Jen chatting with Noah and Luke, who had

just arrived back, and waved, but she didn't stop to talk. She had a café to run and a business meeting with a potential bank to navigate before her day was finished. And Rob had texted her and asked if she had time for a chat. She hoped he wasn't planning on leaving, because he'd been amazing since coming on board.

She parked behind the café, mentally reviewing the plans for the kitchen and prep extension she'd had drawn up by a local architect. She'd need to show them to the loan officer during her online meeting. Once the new kitchen was set up, streamlining her two businesses would be easier, and she had even budgeted for room to expand.

She was greeted in the café by the smell of chocolate and cinnamon and a roomful of contented customers, which always made her feel proud. There had been a noticeable drop off in traffic as the viral video sunk in the ratings, and business levels had returned to slightly above normal.

"Hey!" Kenya waved enthusiastically from the door of the kitchen. "Anton let me make chocolate croissants today, and they turned out great!"

"That's awesome!" Bernie grinned at her. "When you finish your course, will you think about coming to work for me permanently?"

"Definitely." Kenya nodded. "I've learned so much, and I like everyone here. Can I get you a coffee or are you headed out?"

"I've always got time for coffee," Bernie said. "And I need to check in with everyone, so I'll be here for a while."

"Coming up!" Kenya said.

Bernie went into the kitchen where Anton was taking cinnamon rolls out of the oven and Rob was on the phone.

"How's it going?" Bernie asked.

"Good." Anton took off his oven gloves and turned toward her. "I'm just about to head out."

"Anything you need to talk to me about?" Bernie asked.

"Nope. I'm still here, and I've paid my rent for the next three months, so we're good."

"I'm really glad about that." Bernie smiled at him. "And thanks for taking such good care of Kenya."

"She's going to be a great baker," Anton said. "She listens, she doesn't make the same mistake twice, and she's willing to help everyone on the team. I hope you're trying to recruit her when she graduates."

"Already on it," Bernie said, and looked over to where Rob had just finished his phone call. "Hey! Are you free to talk or shall I wait awhile?"

"I'm good."

Bernie thanked Kenya for the coffee and went to the small prep space in the rear of the kitchen while Rob fetched his laptop. All the baking was done for the day, and the whole area was sparkling clean and ready for tomorrow. Bernie sat on a stool, and Rob joined her at the table.

"I wanted to show you the online order numbers." Rob turned his laptop around so she could see the spreadsheet.

"They're still rising," Bernie said.

"Which is good for the business, but if it keeps going like this, we might have an issue with our transportation costs," Rob said.

"Brian said that might happen." Bernie considered the columns. "What's your gut telling you about these numbers? Are they sustainable or is this still the viral-video effect?"

"I think they're accurate because even if that's what

brought people to the service, they're still hanging around and using it."

"Which means you'll probably need more staff, and we'll have to consider running our own delivery trucks."

"Yeah, I'd agree." Rob nodded. "I guess that would be expensive."

"I've already put those cost scenarios in my business plan." It was Bernie's turn to get out her laptop and show Rob. "Can you read through this section and tell me if it would work for you?"

"You're asking me?" Rob looked at her.

"You're the one who'll be managing this side of the business, so of course I am."

He started reading and then sat back. "Looks good. It's more than I expected."

"If you're going to do something, you might as well do it right," Bernie said.

"Go big or go home?" Rob smiled at her. "I kind of like that."

"Of course, a lot of this depends on having someone like you managing the online business." Bernie paused. "You've had your trial month; do you think you'll stick around? I'd appreciate it."

Rob shut his laptop and turned toward her, his expression grave. "You offered me a chance when no one else would. I'll stay and work for you for as long as you want me."

"You've been amazing," Bernie said. "I'm really glad Anton found you."

"I like working here."

"And everyone likes working with you." Bernie smiled. Rob shot to his feet as if all the positivity had started to get to him. "I need to update the replacement-ingredient lists for the wholesaler account before I get going."

"Thanks, Rob."

Bernie let out her breath as he went back into the main kitchen. If Anton, Rob, and Kenya stayed, along with her local staff, she was confident that her businesses would flourish. All she needed now was the money to pay for the kitchen extension, new staff, and potentially a fleet of delivery vehicles. . . .

"Piece of cake!" Bernie said as she stowed her laptop and got to her feet.

Perhaps there was some truth to the idea that when one part of your life crashed and burned, something else went right, because after the Luke debacle, she certainly needed some positive vibes. With a competent staff in place, she didn't have to worry so much about the survival of the café, and that was a great feeling.

She checked the time and went into the café to talk to Casey and Pen, who had just arrived. If she could take all the positivity around her into her meeting with the bank, she was sure she'd secure a loan.

"Kitty!" Sky pointed at something in the paddock.

Luke, who had taken him for a walk around the barn while Jen got on with something, crouched beside him to see what he was looking at.

"That's a cow, bud."

"Big kitty."

"Cow," Luke said patiently. "Moo."

"Moo?" Sky considered the cow and shook his head. "Not moo."

"If you're going to grow up on this ranch, little bud, you'd better work out what earns us the big bucks." Luke hoisted Sky onto his shoulder. "Kitty says meow, cow says moo."

"Bunny rabbit?"

Luke considered that as he walked back to the house. "Carrots?"

"No." Sky was very definite about that.

"I'll have to ask your mom." Luke gently set Sky down on his feet in the mudroom. "Let me help you with your boots."

"I do it." Sky bent down and immediately fell on his behind.

"Fine." Luke watched him wrestle with the boots until he got them off. "Good job. Now, let's do your coat."

He walked through to the kitchen holding Sky's hand to find Jen just putting something in the oven. She still wore her scrubs, since she'd just got back from her shift at the local clinic where Luke's mom also practiced.

"Thanks for looking after him." Jen bent to kiss Sky's head. "Were you good for Uncle Luke?"

Sky nodded. "Big kitty said moo."

Jen looked at Luke. "That's what he calls the cows."

"So he told me." Luke helped himself to some coffee as Jen washed Sky's hands and put him in his high chair for a snack. "What we both want to know is what bunny rabbits say."

"Oh!" Jen grinned. "That's a sneaky one." She turned to Sky. "Bunny rabbits say sniff." She blew air out of her nose to demonstrate, and Sky copied her.

"Do they?" Luke raised his eyebrows as Jen lowered her voice.

"They do in this house. It's a great way to get him to blow his nose properly."

"That's brilliant," Luke said. "I'll have to remember

that if I ever have kids." He paused. "Not that it's likely any time soon."

Jen gave Sky some carrot sticks and avoided Luke's gaze.

"Nice try but I'm not getting drawn into discussing your relationship problems."

"Why not? We all discussed yours and Noah's."

"Because Bernie's my friend."

"Noah's my friend." Luke shrugged. "It didn't stop me trying to help him correct the worst mistake of his life."

Jen finally looked at him. "You admit you made a mistake?"

"Hell, Jen, of course I did. That's who I am." He waited to see if she'd respond, but she was being remarkably discreet. "I screwed up. I admitted it to Bernie, and she still doesn't want to get back with me."

"I'm not the person you should be talking to." Jen gave Sky some ranch sauce to dip his carrots in.

"I asked Bernie if she'd have a drink with me after the auction and she wasn't interested."

"I wonder why."

"I'm beginning to see why you and Noah make such a great couple." Luke frowned. "If I don't know what I've done wrong, how am I going to fix things?" Jen was staring at him and shaking her head. "What?"

"Okay, against my better judgment I'm going to ask you something." Jen sat opposite him. "What's the most important thing in a successful relationship?"

Luke swirled his coffee around in his mug. "Compatibility? Mutual respect? Having the same values?"

"All those things are important, but what else?"

"Knowing the other person has your back?"

Jen lowered her head into her hands and groaned,

which made Sky laugh. "I knew I shouldn't have started this."

"What am I missing? I mean there's the physical element, but that's been great with Bernie, and—"

"Okay, Captain Oblivious. I now understand why Bernie wants to murder you." Jen shot to her feet. "I have to start on dinner. Can you keep an eye on Sky until he finishes his snack, and then take him to the family room? He can watch that show he loves with the green and yellow bug people. It's all set up, ready to go."

"Sure." Luke stayed with Sky as Jen started on dinner prep. "You know it's only three o'clock?"

"It'll give the lamb plenty of time to marinate," she said without turning around as she furiously chopped herbs.

The smell of rosemary and mint drifted toward him. He had a sense that her desire to cook was closely related to her desire to get away from him. This was why he needed someone like Max or Bernie around to hit him over the head with the truth because sometimes he got so caught up in all the options that he missed what was right in front of him.

"All done." Sky belched loudly and laughed.

"Good job, dude." Luke cleaned Sky's face and the tray and took him out of the high chair. "Let's go and watch some TV."

CHAPTER NINETEEN

"I think we're going to need more chairs," Anton said as he went past Bernie with a stack of them.

She'd shut the café down, but her staff had volunteered their time to help with the mobile coffee shop and anything else that needed doing to make the auction a success. It was a beautiful, sunny day, and the forecast didn't predict rain until the evening. She'd barely had time to gulp down a cup of coffee while managing the hundreds of last-minute tasks to make sure the event was successful, but at least she didn't have time to think about anything else.

"I can call around and see if any of the local ranchers have hay bales they could lend us," Bernie said to his retreating back. "Because we definitely don't have any more chairs."

She consulted her spreadsheet and her cell contacts and tried Noah—except her thumb slipped and she somehow got Luke.

"Hey!" She forced some brightness into her voice. "I'm sorry I pushed the wrong key. Is Noah there?"

There was a short silence. "You *can* talk to me, you know."

Oh, how she wished that were true, but he didn't seem to hear her. . . .

"Okay, I was wondering if you guys had any more bales we could use for seating. The crowd is already getting large, and we're an hour from kicking off."

"I'm sure we can bring some over. We were just about to leave."

"Thanks! I'd appreciate that."

"You're welcome. See you soon."

He ended the call, leaving her staring at her phone. Would she ever feel comfortable with him again? Seeing him and not being with him was like endlessly hitting her head against a wall and wondering why nothing got better. He had a family ranch to run, and he wasn't going anywhere, but maybe she could? The thought of leaving the only home she'd ever had was daunting, but how would she feel seeing future Luke with his wife and kids coming into her café, expecting her to be fine with it?

She'd never be fine with it. She loved him, and the only way to live with that was by not having him anywhere near her.

"Bernie?"

She looked up to see Brian and her mom waving at her.

"Hey! You made it." She went over to give them both a hug. "Where's Dad?"

"He's explaining to the twins how to act as parking attendants because it's getting crazy out there and he doesn't want anyone getting into the wrong fields," her mom said.

"I'll pay them for their efforts." Bernie grimaced. "I didn't realize it would be this busy."

"It's for a good cause." Her mom patted her shoulder. "Mike knows that."

Brian smiled at her. "It's looking great. You're an excellent organizer."

"Thank you."

She hadn't had a chance to sit down with him since he'd arrived late the previous night and gone straight to bed, and she'd been up since four.

Brian moved her slightly away from her mom, who was chatting to Kenya.

"Have you thought more about coming back with me after the auction? Linda assures me that she and your siblings will set things to rights here and start processing applications and payments for the puppies."

Linda had said the same thing to Bernie at dinner the previous night. She hadn't really given her mom a straight answer.

"I think I will." She looked up at Brian. "I warn you that I might just sleep for forty-eight hours straight."

"Fine by me." He smiled. "I'm just thrilled you're willing to come."

"I have a lot to think about," Bernie confessed. "And maybe being away from here will help with that."

He nodded. "If you're willing, I can set up a couple of meetings with potential business partners while you're staying with me."

"Partners for what exactly?" Bernie asked.

"I think your online bakery business has the potential to go nationwide, and you might need some financial partners of a higher caliber to invest in you."

Bernie blinked at him. "*What*?"

"In fact, I might be willing to invest in you myself."

"That's . . . nuts."

"There's no rush. We can talk about it when we get to Saratoga, but think about what it might mean to you and your business." He met her gaze. "You've got what it takes to be very successful, Bernie, and I'd like to help you reach your full potential."

He walked off to find her mom, leaving Bernie staring into space, her mind racing off in a hundred different directions.

"What's up?" She jumped as Pen poked her in the side. Her cousin's hair was in two high pigtails, and she wore a short, flowery dress, pink boots, and carried a tartan purse. Nothing matched, but she somehow managed to carry it off.

"Nothing! I was just . . ." Bernie made a vague gesture in the direction of the barn. "About to go in there and do something."

"Probably with the puppies," Pen said helpfully. "What was that man talking to you about?"

Bernie eyed Pen. "You know it's rude to listen in to other people's conversations, right?"

"Well, sure. But sometimes it's just really interesting and I can't help myself." Pen opened her eyes wide. "Is that your birth dad? Mom said he was going to be here today and that he was staying at the ranch."

"Yup, that's Brian. I'm going to Saratoga with him after the auction."

"Where's that? Spain?"

"The peninsula," Bernie said patiently. "Near San Francisco."

"Okay." Pen nodded. "Have you seen Rob? He keeps disappearing on me."

"He's probably terrified." Bernie grinned at Pen. "He's shy."

"I know. But that's why he needs to talk more." She waved at Bernie. "See you later. I'm all set up to help backstage with the puppies!"

"Great," Bernie muttered as her cousin skipped away. "I do hope someone is supervising you."

She went into the barn and spent a quarter of an hour going over the schedule with her volunteers, explaining how the bidding process worked, and most importantly, how to show the puppies and dogs off to advantage without scaring the bejesus out of them. Most of the people helping had done it before, but there were always newbies, and Bernie was determined that everything would go as planned.

Just as she finished, MJ came up behind her and whistled right in her ear, making her wince.

"Sorry, sis, I thought you were farther away." He took off his hat and scratched his head. "Is Pandora on your list, because I'm wondering how much you think she might go for and whether I have enough in my savings account to bid on her."

"She's not in the auction." Bernie paused. "I thought she should stay with you."

"Like, for real?" The delight and relief on MJ's face was unmistakable. "That's so cool!"

"You've formed a real bond with her. She'll be sad when her puppies leave, and I expect you to give her all the love she deserves for being such a great mom."

MJ hugged her so hard, he almost took her breath away.

"Thanks, sis. You're the best. Can I take her out with me to help park the cars?"

"Absolutely not," Bernie said firmly. "She's much safer where she is."

She was still smiling when she emerged from the barn and ran right into Luke and Bailey.

"Bernie! This is awesome!" Bailey hugged her and then turned to include the others. "This is Cameron, and this is Mya."

"It's great to meet you," Bernie said as they exchanged

hellos. Noah and Bailey sure came from a good-looking family.

"You, too," one of them said; Bernie wasn't sure which because they were identical. "We've come to look at the kitties—is that okay?"

"Sure! Go ahead and check in with Jen. You can tell which ones are up for adoption from the information sheet on the door of each cage," Bernie called out as they were already on the move. "Wow, they really must like cats."

"Yeah." Luke hadn't gone with them. It was hard to see his expression because the sun was behind him, and his Stetson shielded his face. She wished her heart didn't jump for joy whenever he came near her. "Where do you want the bales?"

"Wherever you can see a place to fit them," Bernie said. "And thanks so much for bringing them."

"You're welcome." He touched his hat and walked away.

She stared after him. Was that where they were now? Barely speaking—and was that better than arguing? She couldn't do this for the rest of her life. All she wanted was for Luke to be happy.

A few minutes later, she saw him and Noah carrying the bales through the crowds and placing them near the chairs and stage. They were getting more than a few appreciative glances from the female part of the crowd as they effortlessly moved the heavy bales around. Personally, she would be quite happy to stare at Luke in motion forever.

"Bernie?" Anton called out to her. "I'll shut the refreshment station down while you're doing the auction thing, okay?"

"Best to keep one server there," Bernie advised. "Not everyone is into adopting cats and dogs."

Anton raised an eyebrow. "Then why are they here?"

"Supporting their loved ones who do, I guess." She smiled at him. "Have you taken a look at the cats yet?"

"You just want me to make a long-term commitment to stick around."

"But with a cat." She winked at him. "Think about it."

He laughed and wandered off. Bernie went up onto the stage and turned the microphone on.

"We will be starting the auction in ten minutes. Please take your seats and make sure you have your numbered cards on hand so we can record your bids."

There was gentle movement toward the seating, but Bernie knew from experience that it would take at least two more announcements before everyone finally got the message. She reckoned the turnout was twice as high as last year, which had to be due to Bailey's crazy PR campaign.

"Will all the humane society volunteers please join me in the barn for our final prep meeting. Thank you."

She stepped into the barn and was soon surrounded by the familiar faces of her family and friends who had worked long hours to help pull the auction off. Luke stayed at the back, his blue eyes steady as she went through her last-minute instructions. He made no effort to come near her. He was helping wrangle the puppies in and out of their crates for their appearances on the stage. He was always a calming influence on proceedings and had often talked her off a ledge. But those days were gone, and she would have to manage for herself.

As Casey gave the five-minute warning, Bernie walked to the back and peered in at Pandora and her puppies, who were all sleeping peacefully. She leaned her forehead against the door and took a couple of deep, steadying, breaths. Everything was changing, and she wasn't sure if she'd ever be the same person again.

"Hey."

She didn't need to turn around to know who was behind her.

"You've got this." Luke briefly squeezed her shoulder. "You know you always panic just before it starts."

She slowly turned around to face him. "Thank you."

He shrugged. "You're welcome."

"No, really." She held his gaze. "You didn't need to do this, and yet despite everything, you took the time to find me and calm me down."

His smile was so sweet it took her breath away. "I still know you better than anyone else, Ber."

She couldn't look away even as her throat tightened with the effort of not bawling and throwing herself in his arms.

"Don't cry." He reached out a hand to her and then swiftly withdrew it. "You've got to find all those puppies good homes."

She nodded, almost too overcome to speak, and blurted out. "I miss you, Luke."

"Yeah?"

"I wish I wasn't leaving—"

Linda came around the corner, clapping her hands. "Come on you two—it's showtime!"

Bernie wasn't sure what she'd been about to say and was glad to be interrupted, but Luke looked frustrated. He caught her hand as she went past him.

"Look, can we talk after the auction?"

"Sure." She kept moving. "Now, I really have to go. There are dogs who need loving owners and new homes."

"That's my girl."

* * *

Even though the crowd was large, and the amounts raised for the pets was well above the previous year, Luke barely noticed how the auction was going because Bernie had finally looked at him and was willing to talk. He'd been thinking a lot about what Jen had asked him and had concluded that the only person who could truly answer the question was Bernie herself. If he asked her what she needed from him in good faith, would she tell him?

"Hey." Noah nudged him. "I'm off to help Jen. Apparently a lot of people are adopting cats. Can you keep an eye out for your mom? She's got Sky."

"Sure," Luke said. "I was just going to get a cup of coffee."

"Ask her to meet us in the barn near the cattery, okay?"

"Will do."

Luke pushed his way through the crowd of attendees, who were having a great time, to the corner of the field where Bernie had organized a beverage stall, an ice cream truck, and a taco truck, which seemed to cover all the bases. There was also a face-painting stall for the kids, and a water station for the pets. Luke wasn't sure how he'd feel having all these people tramping over one of his fields, but Mike was obviously okay with it, and from what Luke could see, everyone was being respectful of the space.

"Hey, Luke."

He'd reached the end of the line for the coffee and found Brian in front of him.

"Hey."

"The auction went well, I think," Brian observed. "Bernie must be pleased."

"We certainly made more money than the last few years," Luke agreed.

"She is an excellent multitasker. Much better than I could ever be."

"That's just Bernie. She's good at everything she sets her mind to."

"Did she mention that I think her online business has great potential?" Brian asked.

"To be honest, I haven't seen much of her in the past couple of weeks. She's been too busy with the auction stuff," Luke admitted.

"And you split up. I'm sorry, I forgot about that." Brian nodded. "She seemed very happy with you."

"I thought so, too, until she dumped me."

Brian looked at him. "One has to wonder if having a parent walk out on you when you are a child has long-reaching effects on that person's ability to believe someone will stick with them. Perhaps the determination to be the person doing the leaving, rather than the one being left, becomes instinctive or imperative."

While Luke tried to decipher that, Brian gave him a friendly smile. "I'm next in line. Have a great rest of your day, Luke."

"Same to you," Luke replied automatically, his thoughts still on what Brian had said.

Was that what Jen had been getting at? That Bernie didn't believe anyone would choose to stay with her and put her first? She was often self-deprecating about her skill set and—Luke suddenly remembered her confessing her worry about ever really being part of the Murphy family.

And he'd missed it. He'd taken that hesitancy as so much a part of her that he'd forgotten to apply it to himself and their relationship. He forgot all about getting coffee and spun around, trying to see where Bernie had gotten to. She'd agreed to see him after the auction, but he needed to talk to her right that minute.

"Hold up there, boss."

He backed into someone, turned to apologize, and went still.

"What the hell are you doing here?" Luke said.

Max raised his eyebrows. "You texted me. I came to tell you you're an ass in person."

Luke opened his mouth, and no words came out. Max took him by the arm and led him over to a quieter spot. Luke shook off his friend's hand and stepped back from him.

"Why did you come back?"

"I just told you."

"Bullshit."

Max shrugged. "Okay, well it was part of my decision, and you definitely asked me for help."

"I don't need your advice about anything."

"Yeah, you do. How you could screw up your relationship with Bernie—a woman who has loved you forever? What did you do? Seduce her mom?"

Luke glared at him. "I asked you a question, and you still haven't answered it. Why are you here?"

"Because I need my job back? You said I was welcome anytime." Max paused. "Or maybe you didn't mean it."

"I assumed that if you did come back, you'd have a reasonable explanation and maybe you'd start with an apology."

Max winced. "Yeah, okay about that. I suck, and I shouldn't have left without explaining what was up, so I apologize. Now, can we get back to the most important thing, which is sorting out your love life?"

"Hi!" Luke half turned to find Bernie's cousin Pen waving at him. "I hope you don't mind me interrupting, but if you do want to get back with Bernie, Luke, you'll need to act fast, because she's leaving with her birth father right after the auction. For Spain, I think she said."

"What?"

Pen grimaced. "Sorry, I'm a terrible eavesdropper and I knew that you and Bernie had a thing going, and I'd hate to see her lose the love of her life." She blew Luke a kiss and winked at Max. "You are so pretty!"

"Thanks." Max stared after her as she skipped away. "Was that Bernie's cousin, Pen?"

"Yeah." It was Luke's turn to frown. "Bernie didn't say anything about that to me."

"She's always a little spacy," Max said. "She probably got it wrong."

"But Bernie said . . ." Luke tried to recall their last conversation. "That she'd meet me after the auction to talk."

"Maybe she was just trying to get rid of you?" Max suggested.

Luke shot him a look. "Not helping."

"Not trying to. Did Bernie say *when* that would be by any chance? Like a week after the auction? A year?"

"She said she missed me and that she wished she wasn't leaving—" He frowned. "Crap. She meant she'd miss me future tense, when she was no longer around."

"Okay, but why would she go?" Max asked. "This is her home."

"Because Brian thinks she's onto something with her new business. Maybe she intends to base herself in Silicon Valley with him." Luke felt like someone had punched him in the chest.

"It's possible." Max considered him. "Especially if she

thinks she's going to have to see you around town for the rest of her life when you dumped her."

"I didn't dump her."

Max whistled. "Good for Bernie. What *did* you do?"

"I guess I didn't give her what she wanted from me," Luke said, his gaze returning to scan the crowd. "Maybe I can fix that before she gets on that plane and leaves."

Max placed his hand on Luke's chest. "Before you race off trying to find her, how about I do that, and tell her to meet you in the barn?"

Luke stared at his friend. "Promise you won't say anything to her."

"Me?" Max looked pained. "I'll keep everything zipped, I pinky swear." He stepped back. "Now go and wait in the barn and I'll bring her to you."

Luke started walking. "We can meet in her office."

"Got it, boss."

Bernie's face hurt from smiling so much, but she didn't care. The auction had been a huge success, Pandora's puppies and all the other adorable dogs had found new loving homes, and for the first time ever there would be enough money to fund a yearly paid position for the animal shelter, which would free up Bernie's time.

"Hey!" Max appeared out of nowhere and took hold of her elbow. "Come with me, okay?"

Bernie dug her heels in. "One, what are you doing here, and two, why would I go anywhere with you?"

He grinned. "Can I take a raincheck on the first item and focus on getting you to the barn to talk to Luke?"

"Why would I want to see Luke?"

"It's important."

"Did he ask you to find me?" Bernie asked.

"Trust me on this—he needs all the help he can get not to screw up his love life, so I'm lending him a hand." He considered her. "Luke's hurting, Bernie, and I want to help him."

"What about my feelings?"

"You love him," Max said simply.

Bernie stared at him and started walking, Max at her side. She'd been planning on talking to Luke when she got back from Saratoga, but maybe getting closure now would be healthier for both of them, even if it hurt.

"Fine, let's rip off the Band-Aid," she muttered.

"Or fix the break," Max suggested as they entered the cool interior of the barn, which was still thronged with people checking out the cats and their newly acquired puppies under the watchful eyes of the volunteers. "He said he'd wait in your office."

Bernie headed for the back corner of the barn. She saw Luke through the open door. He was leaning back against her desk, head down as he contemplated his boots. She didn't trust herself to close the door and be alone with him. And there was always the possibility that an emergency might arise and someone needed to get to her immediately.

"Hey. Max said you wanted to talk to me."

Luke looked up. "Is it true that you're leaving with Brian tonight?"

"Who told you that?"

"Pen."

Bernie sighed. "She's terrible."

"True, but it did make me wonder why you said you'd talk to me after the auction, and yet you were planning on leaving."

"I didn't specify a time," Bernie said.

"I get that now." He took a deep breath. "I don't want you to leave."

"I wasn't aware that you had any say in my decision-making."

"I don't." He held up his hand. "And I know that's my fault, but I wanted to say something important."

"Okay."

He got to his feet. "I've been thinking about what's happened between us. I realized there was something I'd missed that needed to be said."

Despite everything, a faint flare of hope ignited in Bernie's heart. And she nodded for him to go on.

"I guess you needed to hear me say that I'll always put you first and that I'll always have your back."

"I think I already knew that," Bernie said slowly.

"But I didn't *say* it to you." He met her gaze. "You haven't always had that in your life, and I should've remembered that and spelled it out."

He looked at her so expectantly that she almost took a step back. Okay, so maybe this was his attempt to make sure that despite everything, they could go back to being friends.

"Well, thanks for sharing. It's always good to know your best friend supports you. Anything else? I have a lot of packing to do."

Luke blinked at her. "That's not—"

"Oh, for god's sake." Max blew into the room like a mini hurricane. "You two need your heads knocked together."

"Get out." Luke pointed at the door.

"Not happening." Max scowled at Luke. "That wasn't what Bernie needed to hear from you, doofus!"

"Like you know what she needs better than I do?"

"Everyone does, you complete blockhead!"

"Excuse me . . ." Bernie said as the two men squared up to each other. "I am not—"

"She goddamn loves you!" Max pointed at Bernie. "And that's all you've got for her—that you have her back?"

"I do have her back!" Luke raised his voice. "She's my best friend!"

"And what else is she, Luke?" Max wasn't backing down.

"Not that it's got anything to do with you, but she's my *everything*!"

"Excuse me?" Bernie pushed past Max to stand in front of Luke. "I'm your *what*?"

"My everything. You're my rock, my best friend, my love, and I don't want to be without you." His voice cracked. "How can you not know that?"

"Your love?" Bernie asked. "You *love* me?"

There was a long pause.

"Hell." His brow creased. "That's it, isn't it? I never said those three words to you. That's what Jen and Max have been banging on about."

"Congratulations, boss," Max said as he left the room. "You finally got it." He closed the door behind him.

Bernie cupped Luke's chin. "Do you really mean it?"

"Absolutely, one hundred percent." He kissed her gently on the lips. "And I promise that if you give me the chance, I'll make sure to tell you I love you every single day for the rest of our lives."

"That's the nicest thing you've ever said to me," Bernie whispered. "I'm just not sure I have enough hope left to believe it."

"I can't stop you doubting me, but I will do everything I can to show you I mean what I say. I know I have issues and that I need to be honest with you about them. I want to let you in, but it's scary for me because I'm used to being the one in control." Luke held her gaze. "I love you, Bernie. Can you at least trust me as a friend on that while I work on the rest of it?"

She considered him. "I guess I'll have to, because if you can try, I have to believe we can succeed together."

He kissed her again. "I won't let you down."

"I'm still going to Saratoga."

"And one day I hope I'll be able to come with you. I'm working on that with my new therapist." His smile deepened. "At least I've got the puppy video to watch when I miss you." He paused. "I think that was the moment I realized I was in love with you. Shame I didn't tell you about it."

"Pandora and her puppies are magical."

"At one point I had a crazy plan to bid on all of them for you, so you'd see how much you meant to me," Luke said. "But I thought you'd rather they went to good homes."

"That *was* a very romantic thought." Bernie kissed his nose.

"Yeah."

"I might be even busier this coming year." Bernie was determined to get it all out so that he knew what he was getting himself into. "Brian thinks my online business could get much bigger."

"He mentioned something about that to me," Luke said. "I don't mind being married to a millionaire, as long as she still loves me more than her money."

Bernie stroked his bearded cheek. "I loved you first, and that won't change."

His expression softened. "I don't deserve you."

"True, but you've got me anyway."

He laughed and hugged her hard. "I guess we'll have to talk more when you get back from Saratoga." He hesitated. "The one in California, right? Pen wasn't sure."

"I'll be back in a week." Bernie reluctantly eased out of Luke's arms. "We can definitely talk then." She took a deep breath. "I need to wrap up this auction and get ready to leave with Brian."

He caught hold of her hand. "I'll be right there with you."

"Thank you."

His smile was a sensual combination of sweet and hot promise as he opened the door to reveal Max leaning against the opposite wall.

"You two worked it out yet?"

"We have." Luke walked over and punched his friend hard in the arm. "No thanks to you."

"Hell, I made it happen, dude!" Max grinned at Bernie. "Tell him."

"Max did help," Bernie agreed. "Which is why you should be extra nice to him and give him his job back."

"She's right." Max looked at Luke.

"I never fired him in the first place," Luke said loftily. "Let's just consider your absence as unpaid vacation."

"Good man," Max said. "And I do have an explanation about why I had to leave, but it'll keep for another day."

"Or you can spill at dinner tonight. Has Noah seen you yet?" Luke asked.

Max touched his chin. "Seeing as I'm still vertical, the answer is no." Luke grinned, and Max went still. "He's right behind me, isn't he?"

"I sure am." Noah's deep voice echoed around the space. "And I can't wait to catch up."

Bernie grabbed Luke's hand and hurried him toward the cattery. "I think we should leave them to get reacquainted, don't you?"

"Great thinking." Luke smoothed some loose hair behind Bernie's ear. "I love you, Bernie."

"And I love you, too."

He smiled at her. "Let's go and find Brian and your folks and let them know we're back together and that this time it's for good."

Bernie smiled back. Her best friend, her lover, and the man she wanted to spend the rest of her life with had considered buying all the puppies just for her. What more could a woman want? Perhaps, in time even Cleopatra her cat would come to appreciate Luke's finer qualities. . . . She took hold of his hand and walked toward the entrance of the barn, where her family and friends awaited her. There was so much to look forward to, and with Luke at her side, there was nothing to fear.

Visit our website at
KensingtonBooks.com
to sign up for our newsletters, read
more from your favorite authors, see
books by series, view reading group
guides, and more!

Become a Part of Our
Between the Chapters Book Club
Community and Join the Conversation

Betweenthechapters.net

Submit your book review for a chance to win exclusive
Between the Chapters swag you can't get anywhere else!
https://www.kensingtonbooks.com/pages/review/